MW01267703

Coming to My Senses

This novel is dedicated to my husband and friend, Brad Rice, who understands how dreams are gently woven into stories and songs through the magic of words and music.

Coming to My Senses

Pam Rice

Five Star • Waterville, Maine

Five Star First Edition Women's Fiction Series.

Published in 2002 in conjunction with
Pam Rice.

Cover art by Mildred Walker.

Set in 11 pt. Plantin by Myrna S. Raven.

Printed in the United States on permanent paper.

Library of Congress Cataloging-in-Publication Data

Rice, Pam, 1950–
    Coming to my senses / Pam Rice.
       p. cm.—(Five Star first edition Women's Fiction series)
    ISBN 0-7862-3034-7 (hc : alk. paper)
    1. Aged women—Fiction.   2. Visually handicapped—
Fiction.   3. Self-helf groups—Fiction.   4. Mountain life
—Fiction.   5. Colorado—Fiction.   6. Widows—Fiction.
I. Title. II. Series
PS3568.I292 C66 2002
  813'.6—dc21   00-052836

Chapter 1

For Addie Brummel the early summer days on Race Avenue in the late 1930s were timeless and endless. At sixteen, she was too old to romp and play about like a child, and unfortunately, too young to romp and play about like a grown up. There was nothing very interesting or exciting about Addie outside the borders of her imagination, where she was indeed, at times, something very near wonderful. In fact, she lived comfortably in a two-story brick home on a tree-lined street in Denver with her uncle and a spectacular sister, Sarah. And it was Sarah, who bustled about the home on this early afternoon, one eye on the clock, the other on the mirror.

"You've got to help me, Addie. Now, listen," Sarah commanded holding up first one dress, then another. "Oh, which one?" she drawled. "Addie, are you listening?"

Addie perched on the edge of the bed and studied Sarah intently. "I don't know what to say to him, Sarah. He'll know it's not true."

"No, Addie, he won't know!" Sarah turned toward her sister, her eyes pleading. "You can do it, Addie. You just tell him that something came up, okay? And you tell him it was real important." She held a red, low-cut, floral sundress against herself and swung back to the mirror. "This one, this is the one!" she beamed. "Real important, Addie. Can you do that for me?"

"I'll try," the younger girl answered meekly.

"And don't you turn all red. Don't you do that or he'll know!"

"Sarah, I can't keep from turning red. I can tell him you're away. I can tell him you're real sorry. But I cannot not turn red!"

"Oh, Addie, try! Just try real hard, hon."

Now Sarah was lost in her thoughts, her clothes, the afternoon before her. She ran a brush through her long, silky blond hair and began to apply rouge and lipstick to an already perfect face. She forgot Addie. She forgot everything but the picture in the mirror before her, and that she relished with satisfaction. She was twenty-two years old. In Sarah's mind, that made her a woman. She was a woman who had beauty, softness and wit. She could turn a man's head without trying and had never had an absence of suitors. She had everything but what she wanted—a husband. And it couldn't be just anyone. Oh, she'd had plenty of offers, plenty of broken hearts when she turned down one proposal after another. No, it had to be right. She made no excuses for herself. Sarah Brummel would marry a rich, fine-looking man who could give her everything and more. Until she found him, until the right one came, she would plunder through men like a tank on a mission.

When she was finally ready, Sarah once again sought out Addie as the only source of approval or disapproval in the home. Addie studied her sister, head to toe, without comment. "Well, what do you think?" Sarah broke the uneasy silence.

"You look great. You always look great."

"You sweetie!" Sarah hugged her sister playfully. "Do you think he'll like it, I mean, like me?"

"Which he?"

"Addie! Daniel—that's which he. Wait till you see him. You'll understand."

"But that's what you said about the first guy, the one

I'm lying to for you," said Addie.

"You're not lying, Addie. I'd never ever ask you to lie!" Sarah objected. "Something important has come up. It's called Daniel." She tossed her hair over her shoulders and hurried downstairs. Addie followed behind.

"So I tell him that something important called Daniel came up and you had to leave?"

"Addie, you can be so exasperating!" moaned Sarah.

"I'm teasing."

"I know that, sweetie. You're so good. You'll do fine. Oh, look! He's here!" Sarah pulled back the curtain and Addie squirmed in behind her in time to see a cherry-red roadster pull up to the curb. Its driver wore a sporty cap and may have had a pipe in his mouth but before Addie could be sure, Sarah ran out the door, down the steps and the car vanished in a cloud of blue smoke.

They could not have been gone fifteen minutes when the bell summoned Addie back to the front door. She paused in the hallway to catch her own reflection in the old oak mirror on the wall and gave a start at what she saw. Her strawberry blond hair was standing on end from the combination of summer heat and thick natural curls. Her forehead was smudged, her blouse had a spot on it, and yes, her cheeks were bright red. She quickly made whatever small correction she could without the help of a brush or washcloth as the bell rang a second time.

"I'm coming!" she muttered under her breath. She was not prepared. She was not prepared for the blast of hot summer air that took her breath as the door opened for a second time. She had not arranged the story of her sister's absence quite right in her mind. And most of all, she was not prepared for Jacob McNeil, who looked amazingly cool in defiance of the heat, unaware of the disappointment that lay in store for him.

Jacob was, to Addie, the definition of a handsome stranger as he stood before her in the uniform of a soldier. He was tall and commanding with dark hair and eyes. An early shadow on his face made him appear to her as mature and strong as her austere uncle, a renowned local judge by the name of William Baxter, who was rarely at home. This newcomer was not a man who would easily accept a last minute excuse, even from a young beauty like Sarah. He had come with an expectation and an assurance that his plan would be fulfilled. Jacob was a serious man, yet a sparkle danced mischievously in his eyes as he faced the younger sister of his presumed lady.

"Good afternoon, miss," he said, almost as a question, at seeing her surprise. Although his lips were straight and courteous, his eyes danced even more as Addie stood before him, mouth dropped, eyes wide, and face ever so red. "Good afternoon," he repeated, and after another pause, "Are you okay?"

"Okay? Why yes, of course," she stammered. "Won't you come in?" She swung the door open and he strode past her into the darkened entryway. Without a word she directed him into the living room and pointed again to a nearby chair. He sat upright, hat in hands, and studied her up and down.

"She's not here," Addie blurted after a long silence. "My sister Sarah regrets, or rather she regretted, that something very important came up and she had to leave quite unexpected and suddenly. She's not here and I . . ." A new wave of redness drowned her and Addie could not go on.

"That's unfortunate." Jacob paused thoughtfully, then continued. "You see, I have tickets for the movie. It's too late for a refund." He paused again, this time joined by

Addie whose mind was filled with wonder that Sarah would break a date with this man. His very presence in the room made her feel light-headed. What possible advantage could a red sports car give Daniel to make Sarah choose him instead of this serious, young gentleman before her?

"Listen," he jumped into her thoughts, "why don't you go with me instead? I'd hate not to use the tickets. Will you go?"

"Me?" Addie asked incredulously. The only place she had ever gone with a boy was to Hartman Drug for a soda, and that had been a less than memorable experience. The young man had been using her to make another girl jealous. The ploy had worked and Addie had lost her stool at the soda fountain the following weekend. "Me? Go with you?"

"Why not?" his somber face broke into a full grin and with eyes still twinkling, he teased, "You're old enough to date, aren't you?"

"Of course I am!" she retorted, unconsciously taking a step backward, which caused her to trip and grab for the arm of a nearby chair.

Jacob automatically reached for her. "Are you okay?"

"Why must you keep asking if I'm okay?"

"Never mind that. Tell me your name," he said. "I'm Jacob. Sarah probably told you that. I can't properly escort you to the movie unless I know your name."

"I'm Addie, uh, Adeline," she stammered.

"Adeline," he repeated. "A lovely name. And how old are you, Adeline?"

"I'm . . ." she drew a deep breath. "I'm nineteen, Jacob. Nearly twenty." She faced him squarely, shoulders back, daring him to question this new bit of information.

"That settles it, then. Almost twenty is old enough to date. If we hurry we can catch the streetcar and be there on time."

11

"But I can't go like this!" She gestured to her clothing. "And it's Sarah you came for."

"Perhaps you also have other plans?" He asked.

"Oh, no, it's not that. I mean, I'd love to go. I really would. It's just that—"

"Go on then," he chided her gently. "If you hurry there's time for you to change if you'd like. You look fine, but if you'd like, I'll wait." Now a kindness, a sort of understanding, hovered about him and Addie believed that it would be fine to venture into the Denver afternoon with this young soldier and see a movie. It would be a kindness after Sarah's obvious indiscretion. It was the least she could do. Her heart pounded.

The rest was a blur: the soft blue dress with the wide peter pan collar—a castaway from Sarah when she adopted her more sophisticated look; the streetcar ride as they chattered aimlessly about the afternoon sights and sounds of the city; the movie—a love story—a man going off to war. Addie was overcome by tears at the end and a strong hand passed a soft handkerchief to her when she tried to wipe her eyes without being noticed. The same hand was once again at her elbow as they crossed a busy street to the coffeehouse for more conversation, laughter, and the bittersweet smell as the cups were refilled again and again. Dusk fell as they boarded the streetcar to return to Race Avenue, then slowly walked back, retracing their previously hurried footsteps. The home was still quiet as they climbed the steps to the porch, in the early evening sunset.

"Thank you for taking me, Jacob," Addie's eyes glistened as she spoke. At that moment she felt very grown up. She was standing where Sarah must have stood many times before, looking up into the eyes of a handsome suitor, bidding him farewell. "It was a wonderful movie and such a good time." This must surely be what a woman would say at this moment. Did Sarah's heart pound so loudly at these times?

"It was fun for me, too. It worked out okay, didn't it? I mean with you going in Sarah's place."

"Yes," Addie agreed. "It worked out well."

"You'll let her know then, not to be troubled because she had to cancel?"

"Oh, yes, of course," Addie responded. Then remembering she was only a stand-in for Jacob's original choice, she asked, "Is there anything else you want me to tell Sarah? A message or something?"

"No, nothing else. Thanks again for going with me." He extended his hand and caught her smaller hand with a gentle squeeze. "You've been a good sport." Then he turned to leave and she watched him, unable to move herself toward the door. When he reached the end of the walk he stopped abruptly and turned back as though he had forgotten something important. "Oh, *Addie*," he emphasized the syllables of her name. "It is Addie, isn't it?"

"Well," she stammered her cheeks flowing with red once again. "It's Addie, Adeline, whatever. I mean . . ."

"And it's what?" he grinned. "Sixteen, almost seventeen maybe?"

She felt the redness engulf her from head to toe. Then he was gone.

"Mom! Mom, wake up! You're going to burn the whole house down!"

"I'm awake! Joe, is that you? I didn't hear you drive up." Addie leaned forward in the old rocking chair on her porch and saw the slender, dark form approaching. A soft breeze whispered through the pine trees in the sloped yard before her. It was a constant sound in the mountains, one that never disappeared. With it came the sweet smell of the pines, musty and wooden.

"Do you know if I'd been a few minutes later, or worse yet hadn't come at all, you'd be on fire? You and your whole house, Mom!"

Awkwardly she turned in her chair, half rising as she did so. Was there a fire? She hadn't been sleeping, had she? She sat back nervously then, like a child caught in a forbidden act. "What is it, Joe? What did I do? I wasn't, I mean I don't think I was sleeping. I was just sitting here on the porch. I don't think, I don't remember . . ."

"You don't know, do you?" he demanded. "Mom, we can't keep doing this. I'm sorry for you, truly sorry. But I can't just let you stay up here and kill yourself. And possibly take half of Pinecliffe with you! You understand that, don't you?"

The woman did not respond. Her son, too, stood silently before her, the roar of the trees the only sound between them. Finally, he drew closer to her chair and knelt down beside her. "Look, Mom, I'm not here to cause trouble. I don't know what to do any more than you do. I drove up here to surprise you, and I walked into a kitchen full of smoke. I didn't know where you were. Mom, do you know you left something burning on the stove? Do you even remember putting something on the stove at all?"

"Of course I know. I'm not senile! I have a stew simmering for dinner. I don't know how that could have caused a fire."

"You left it boiling and decided to take a nap, that's how!"

"I left it simmering, Joe," Addie responded. "It

shouldn't have been a problem. I always let my food simmer like that."

"The burner is on high, Mom. You know, as in bright orange and very hot. Hot enough to burn your house down after the stew dried up to nothing! There's no stew in there. There's hardly a pan left. Ten more minutes of that and who knows?" Exasperated, he stood and walked to the rail of the porch where he took a deep breath and sighed heavily.

Confused, his mother murmured, "I thought I had the burner on low. I can't imagine how . . ." As she rose all the way up from the chair this time, it rocked back and scraped the wall where a permanent indentation awaited it. "Let me check."

Joe gently grabbed her arm and stopped her. "I turned it off, Mom, and opened a window to let the kitchen air out. There's nothing you can do." He paused. "But you and I need to have a talk." Reluctantly, she went back to her chair and slowly lowered herself between its outstretched arms.

"The problem is," he began softly, "you thought you had the stove dial set right, but you didn't really know. You didn't know because you can't see it. On top of that, you've had trouble with your heart. Mom, I can't be here to help you, to look after you."

"I haven't asked you to be here, Joe. That's not your obligation."

"It's my responsibility. I'm your son. And I love you, Mom. I don't want anything bad to happen to you."

Addie started to speak then stopped as tears filled her eyes. She turned her head away so he wouldn't see. Pacing back to the porch rail, he stared off into the trees, wanting not to see her face just as desperately as she wished to hide it.

"Look, Mom," Joe began again. "If you lived near us in Richmond it would be different. I'd be a phone call away. I could check on you every day. Judy could come by and help you after school. But with you living out here in the mountains all by yourself, we can't be here for you. If you need me, I'm forty-five miles away. If I hadn't pretty much by chance driven out here today, God knows what . . ." he trailed off.

"But I'm not out here all alone," she protested. "I feel like I've lived here forever. I have many wonderful friends. You know they look in on me."

Disgusted, he retorted, "Your nearest neighbor is five miles away in Pinecliffe when the summer people aren't at the lake, which is most of the time. They all have other things to do besides look after you. Most of them don't even know you have problems. You're too darn proud to ask for help, to tell anyone the truth."

"Oh, Joe," she remonstrated.

"No, let me finish!" he said, holding up his hand. "It isn't safe for you to live here anymore. You can't take care of yourself on your own. You've got a bad heart; you're practically blind. You can't drive into Pinecliffe anymore." He paused, then slowly continued. "Mom, you're not still driving, are you?"

"No," she whispered. "I mean, if there were a real emergency I could follow the edge of the road and get into the village okay."

"For God's sake, Mom!" He nearly screamed at her. "It's not enough that you're trying to burn the house down! You want to kill yourself or some poor little kid out on the road, too?"

"Joe, you know I wouldn't do that. Don't talk to me like that!"

He took another deep breath and pulled a second wooden rocker across the porch next to her, then sat down. "All right, Mom. I don't want to lecture you, but you've got to understand a few things. I'm forty-eight years old and trying to keep my accounting firm going, which takes all of my time. I have a wife who is equally busy, and I'd like to somehow keep this marriage intact. I have a twenty-one-year-old son who acts half his age and therefore also manages to demand a lot of my attention. I can't remember the last time I went fishing or played golf. What I'm saying is, I don't need this!"

The tears welled up again and Addie tried to push them away without her son noticing. She dabbed at her face then wiped her wet fingertips on her apron.

"You should have had a daughter, Mom," he teased her. "Guys don't know how to do these things." She laughed softly but didn't speak. After a few moments he sighed. "I do love you, Mom. You're the best!" He took her hand in his and squeezed it gently. "I know how you love it here. This is your home. I love it, too. I remember when you and Dad bought this place, and later when you retired here. I know every inch of Bear Lake." He nodded toward the glistening water that peeked through the trees at the bottom of the slope. "Remember, you and Dad rented a hotel room the night Judy and I were married so we could spend our wedding night here? You stayed at a hotel instead of us!"

"I remember."

"I know what it means to you to be here," he repeated.

You don't, she thought, but said nothing.

"I'm not asking you to get rid of the place, Mom. I'd never ask that of you. Dad's buried in the cemetery over the hill, and I respect the fact that your friends are all here. But you can't stay here anymore. You've got to realize that you

17

belong in the city. It'll be better that way. We can help you more, do more for you. Even Michael could run errands for you between his classes at the college. We can still spend a weekend or two here in the summer." She didn't respond. "Mom, are you listening to me?"

"I'm listening. But I'm okay, Joe. What happened today was an accident. I'm safe here, son. You're making too much of this."

"I'm not," he said soberly. "It's dangerous, Mom. Something terrible is going to happen to you if you stay here, and I can't sit back and allow that. Anyway, listen," he clutched her hand to his face and kissed it softly. "There's a new assisted-living complex that recently opened in Richmond. It's six blocks from my office and close to Judy's school, too. It's called Gateway and I've heard it's really nice. You can have your own room there, you know, your own bed and things that you're familiar with. But at the same time there will be people looking after you. They have staff who will fix your meals and clean for you and do your laundry. And if you're ill, a nurse checks on you. There are activities going on all the time and even a bus to take you shopping. It would be perfect for you, Mom."

"You sound like a commercial," she responded.

"Ah, Mom, give it a chance," said Joe.

"When I'm old, I will!" quipped Addie. "I've got a lot of living left to do, and I plan to do it right here." Joe sighed heavily. Addie patted his knee and continued lightly. "Those retirement homes are good places, Joe. For the right person, they're wonderful. But not for me, not now. I can manage fine right here. Come on, now, let's see if we can fight our way through all that smoke and find something to eat."

She stood to go inside, but her son didn't follow her.

18

"I'm not going to drop this with you, Mom. I don't want to force you do something, but I will if it's for the best."

"I told you I'm all right. You're making too much of this."

"No, Mom, I'm not. I'm going to pick you up one of these days when I can find the time, and I'm going to take you to town to tour Gateway. Hopefully, you'll see what a great opportunity it is for you and you'll know I'm right." She shook her head and turned away from him.

"Have you got anything else to fix to eat? How have you been getting to town to buy groceries?" he asked.

"Fran Wallace takes me whenever I need something," she responded.

"Sure," said Joe. "Correct me if I'm wrong, but aren't Fran and old Wally in Florida?"

"Well, I . . ." she stuttered. "You certainly seem to know my business!"

"That's my job!" he teased her.

"Now you're stealing my line, Joe. Whenever I scolded you as a child you asked me why and I told you it was my job, remember?" she said laughing and trying to change the subject.

"I think our jobs have reversed, Mother," he replied seriously. "And I'll tell you how I know that Fran's away. I saw old Doc Siegfried the last time I was here. Remember? You were worried about your bills. That's not like you! So I stopped by to see what he thought."

"And?" she asked warily.

"Doc said, 'We're all getting old.' You know how he is. But he agrees with me that your eyesight is failing, and you did have that scare with your heart. He as much as said it probably wasn't safe for you to be out here alone."

"John Siegfried said that?" she demanded. She had

19

known her physician as long as she had known the mountainside and its little shining lake. Like the gentle nature of the area, Dr. Siegfried was a reliable and trusted friend.

"Yes, in so many words he said that," replied Joe. "Let's drop this for now, Mom. I told you I don't want to argue. Let's you and me drive into the village and pick up a few groceries and a hamburger at Scottie's, okay?" He guided her toward the door as a parent would a child. "Where's your jacket? It's starting to cool off. I want you to think about what I've said today. Really think about it. And quit being so stubborn!"

Hours later, she again rocked back and forth in her spot on the porch overlooking the forest and the water. The sun had fallen behind the trees. The sound of Joe's car winding down the dirt road to the highway that would carry him away from Pinecliffe and back to the city, had faded away. Wearily, she leaned her head back and took a deep, quivering breath. She could see him then, standing on the hill near the fort of rocks just beyond her property line. The area where so many children had fought make-believe summer wars held only the silhouette of this single soldier now, his hat in his hands.

Addie, he called softly to her.

Jacob? She replied.

Dear Addie, he whispered. *Don't let them send you away, my love. Hold on. Do you hear me, Addie? Hold on.*

Chapter 2

"Well, if it isn't Addie Marsh. What brings you here today?" John Siegfried patted Addie's arm as he moved to the front of the examining table.

A tall man with solid gray hair and soft blue eyes, he was as permanent a fixture in Pinecliffe as the post office and the general store. He was loved and respected by the permanent residents. He also treated most of the tourists who flocked to the tiny mountain town during the summer months.

Many were the times that Dr. Siegfried had tied his rowboat to the narrow dock on Bear Lake below the Marsh cabin and climbed the hill for a cup of coffee in exchange for a report on fishing conditions.

That morning Addie had called the physician's office. After teasing that the doctor should resume making house calls, as he had many years before, Hazel Siegfried offered transportation and Addie was saved from the awkwardness of imposing upon her friend for a ride.

And so it was this day that Addie was seeking not the expertise of the gentleman before her, but friendship. "I'm getting old, John. Do you have a cure up your sleeve for that?"

"Wish I did," he chuckled. "I'd be a wealthy man!"

"Actually, I'm here because I heard a rumor," she ignored his comment. "Joe was out to see me and gave me a tongue lashing. He wants me to move to the city, to be closer . . ."

"He's worried about you."

"Yes," Addie said. "He thinks I'm going to kill myself if I stay up at the lake. He says I'm not safe anymore. And the rumor is that he said my doctor feels the same way! Is that so, John?"

Dr. Siegfried laid his stethoscope on the counter and leaned against the table where Addie was sitting. Glancing at her sideways, he said, "I don't know what Joe told you. He stopped by here a couple of weeks ago, and he had a lot of questions. I may have said that living at the lake wasn't the best possible situation for you. You had a bout with your heart and your sight is failing. You're alone out there except for the summer months. If something happened, if you needed immediate help, no one would be there."

"But if it's my time to go, out by that lake is where I want to be. You know how I feel about that place. It's home."

"How well I know," he sighed. "My wife and I aren't that far behind you, Addie. The very thought of moving to the city scares me. Still, I've got Hazel. If I were all alone like you, I really don't know what I'd do. I know my kids would eventually want me to do the same thing."

"They don't understand what they're asking," she said.

"It's a different world now. Young people don't take care of their parents like they used to. Families are scattered all across the country and everyone works. Their time is precious to them. If they find themselves faced with caring for an aging parent, they want it to be on their turf and at their convenience. That's the way society is these days."

"I understand that. But I'm not asking to be taken care of. I'm fine living on my own. I think Joe is overreacting!"

"For all the right reasons." The doctor smiled. "I'm sure he's as confused as you are. I can't tell either of you what to do. You could manage for the next several years without another problem. Or, you could end up stranded out there when you really need help and can't get it."

"I guess that's a chance I have to take."

"Maybe," he answered, "or maybe you need to do a little more homework."

"What do you mean?"

"I mean, what does he propose? Where would you live *if* you moved into the city? On the other hand, *if* you want to stay here, what can you do to put his mind at ease? What's changed all of a sudden that he's so concerned?"

"I wouldn't live with them," she answered thoughtfully. "He didn't ask me to, and I wouldn't want to. I guess we both need our space. He wants me to look into a new retirement home called Gateway. Have you heard of it?"

"I have," John nodded. "It's what's called assisted living. It's not apartments, but not a nursing home, either. I've been there. Maude Ellis from Twin Spruce lives there now. She seems to like it, and it's a beautiful place. State-of-the-art really. I still call on Maude when I can get there. She's been my patient since I was wet behind the ears."

Addie laughed, then continued, "It's not Gateway that bothers me. As I told Joe, it's good that there are places like that. It's just that I don't think I'm that bad off. Not yet."

"Maybe if you went to see it, Addie," he suggested. "You know, just look it over for future consideration. You can't make a decision if you don't have all the facts."

"Oh, Joe will see to that," said Addie. "His parting words were that he'd be back out to get me to take me to see my soon-to-be new home!"

"What is it that has him up in arms thinking you need to move?"

"Oh, he came in when I guess I'd dozed off. I had a pot of stew on the stove, and he said it was burning," she explained. "I wasn't really asleep."

"Then how did it burn?"

"He said I had the burner on high. He thinks I can't see what I'm doing. And then he's waiting for me to have a heart attack every time I turn around."

"Your heart has actually been stable since your little scare. I'm not too worried about that as long as you stay on your medication. Has your eyesight worsened?" he asked.

"It's gradually getting worse. I can see, though, just not well," she said.

"Then here's more homework, Addie," he patted her arm. "There's a support group that recently started. They meet one afternoon a month at the library. Laura Benning, a Rehabilitation Teacher from Richmond, comes out and teaches people who are visually impaired or legally blind how to manage on their own. She leads the group and some of my other patients who attend seem to benefit. As I understand it, folks are involved from several small towns in the county. The new van that was purchased for senior citizens picks people up for the meetings."

"Are there that many blind people in the area?" she asked in surprise.

"You bet there are. The incidence of legal blindness increases with age. This county is full of old folks with their heels planted firmly in the soil—determined not to leave no matter what! Sound familiar?" The doctor nudged her gently and she knew he was grinning.

"I don't know, John," Addie shook her head. "I'm not blind yet and I can still do most things pretty well. It's not that bad. Maybe if I tried laser surgery or got new glasses."

"I've got a report here from your ophthalmologist," said the doctor as he shuffled through papers in a folder. "She says you're not a candidate for laser. Actually, Addie, only a small percentage of people with your eye condition are, even though a number of treatments are being studied. What did she tell you about glasses?" he asked.

"She said they wouldn't help. She said I'd just be wasting my money, that there's nothing anyone can do for me. Maybe I need a new eye doctor."

"Kill the messenger, huh?" John laughed. "Look, Addie," he continued. "It wouldn't hurt to check on that new program. Try it the next time they meet and see what you think. At least that way you could show Joe that you're listening to him, that you're going to get some help. He might even quiet down about Gateway then."

"Ridiculous!" responded Addie.

"Yes, dear," he hugged her. "Now, let me listen to that worn-out ticker of yours, then I'll find some information about the support group for you." He went on despite her objections. "C'mon. They probably even serve refreshments. It can't be all bad."

They married in the summer of 1940, nearly a year to the day from their first meeting. By that time Sarah had already married Daniel Gerlock in a lavish church wedding some months before and was comfortably settled in a three-story, redbrick mansion on an estate that took up an entire city block. It seems that Daniel was the heir of a third-generation banking family in Denver. In addition to the red roadster, he possessed numerous other qualifications for the position of Sarah Brummel's husband and he quickly succumbed to her charms. Their rush to the altar left the little car in its own haze of smoke.

Addie's wedding was different. It was held in the tiny church in southeastern Colorado where the groom had spent his Sunday mornings while growing up the son of a farmer. The youngest of four children, Jacob was surrounded by family and friends. Neighbors arrived laden with handmade quilts, cookware, and other practicalities for the young couple. In addition, baskets of food and desserts sat on outdoor tables awaiting the impending celebration after the vows were spoken.

Sarah, who was suffering with morning sickness, did not attend. To the older sister's chagrin, her over-protective in-laws would not consider letting the mother of their first grandchild make the long drive. Daniel had dutifully agreed. Not wanting to upset the family who had subtly conveyed their disappointment that Daniel had not married a more prominent socialite, Sarah atoned for the slight by sending an oversized bouquet of roses that dwarfed the tiny wooden altar of the little country church.

Addie's Uncle William traveled from Denver with apologies that he must return immediately following the service to continue presiding over an important trial. Later, Addie thought that this had been a blessed stroke of fate. She could not envision the stately gentleman taking part in the informal outdoor reception that followed. The country band made up of Jacob's old high school buddies played nothing comparable to the classical music the judge preferred. The warm summer breeze, lifting particles of dust from the dry soil, was already playing havoc with his chronic hay fever.

It was only important to Addie that her uncle came to see the child who, at the age of three, had been thrust upon him by the accident which took the lives of his sister and her husband. Their two orphaned daughters were placed under his guardianship and, with the assistance of various nursemaids, he had done what was expected of him, in spite of his own desire never to marry or have children. He raised the girls without question or complaint and for that Addie loved him.

As the church bell tolled its invitation across the countryside, Addie stood near a side door. Her hand rested on her uncle's arm as they waited for the signal to enter the front door and begin the procession down the aisle. Surrounding them were miles of corn and wheat fields sprinkled with farmhouses and out-buildings. The McNeil farm was southwest of the tiny town that consisted of a church, a post office, a feed store, and a schoolhouse. At this distance the farm was recognizable only by a clump of trees that offered shelter from the hot summer days and winter blizzards which were native to the area.

Addie felt dizzy and clung tighter to her uncle's arm, afraid for a moment that she might faint. It was like a dream; this place where no mountains hovered on the skyline and the only tall buildings were silos scattered across the interminable prairie. They had arrived just the day before, and Addie had marveled as the foothills and the cities disappeared behind them, replaced by a maze of farms and ranches. Jacob laughed as he reminded her that his hometown was very much a part of the wonderful diversity of Colorado, though it was only miles from the Kansas border and the Oklahoma panhandle.

Addie had spent the previous night at the home of a McNeil cousin who lived nearest to the church. Jacob had decided they would settle here where his family would look after Addie if he was called away to the war that loomed on the horizon. To Addie, that was all part of the dream. The war was as invisible to her on her wedding day as the Continental Divide. Both were distant and far away, nonexistent.

Soon they were gliding down the aisle, the judge sober-faced and staring straight ahead. Addie beamed, her eyes damp, her cheeks deepening with color. Jacob stood before her in his uniform as he had the day they met. Again the dream swallowed Addie. This man, this good, tall, strong man, was soon to be her husband. This man loved her as no one else ever had. For the first time in her young life, there was someone who belonged just to Addie. There was someone to whom she was the most important person in the whole world, and this day he would vow before God and everyone present to be hers forever. Her heart pounded with excitement as she and her uncle stopped before him. The wedding march faded on the small church organ and Jacob's mother stifled a soft sob, then sniffled.

The dream continued with the minister's gentle voice. The little congregation was attentive—no one objected, everyone held their peace. The vows were spoken with love and pride. The newlyweds triumphantly emerged from the candlelit alcove into the late afternoon sunlight. Then there was laughter, music, and dancing, their eyes meeting even when groups of well-wishers separated them.

The dream, oh yes, the dream. The same pony cart that had taken the senior McNeils to the little farmhouse long ago on their wedding night now carried Jacob and Addie. They traveled down the well-worn dirt road beyond the same farm to the hired-hand's cottage that would be their new home. Jacob's grandmother, mother, and sister had spent days before scrubbing, decorating the walls, and making up the bed. At the last minute a vase of fresh flowers was placed on the table in the center of the room.

As the moon began to rise in the pink evening sky, they arrived before the little house. Gently, as though she might break, Jacob carried his bride through the door. They were home, and the dream continued.

★ ★ ★ ★ ★

In the days that followed, Jacob resumed his work about the farm. For now, he was excused from duty to help his family, but he could be called to serve at any time if war was declared. He was a soldier in overalls with a pitchfork in his hand, a farmer in uniform with a rifle in his arms. Most of all he was Addie's husband, partner, and friend. As he worked in the fields during the day, Addie cared for their tiny home and carefully prepared meals that she thought would please him. And she waited.

Sometimes the hours went by so slowly. She would stand and watch the distant fields, hoping for a glimpse of Jacob. After a time, she could recognize him . . . no matter how far away. When finally he came home, she was as giddy and playful as the old collie that bounded from his shelter beneath a tree to meet Jacob before Addie.

In the evenings, hand in hand they would walk across the fields and talk endlessly. Sometimes they wandered so far that night had fallen before they returned. Moonlight flooded the path and even in the darkness, they found the way back to the hired-hand's house.

Later as they lay, quiet and renewed, Jacob would whisper, "Addie, are you awake?"

"Sort of."

"Will it always be this way, Addie? Just you and me here on the farm, happy like we are now?"

"Yes, Jacob," she would whisper through her sleep. "It will always be this way."

"I'm Cecil and I have macular degeneration. I don't see too good, either." A ripple of laughter crossed the room as Cecil added, "This is my driver."

"I'm Maggie Parks, and yes, I am Cecil's driver," the

small woman sitting next to the bear-sized man responded. "I'm also his wife, as most of you know." Another ripple of laughter. "My eyes are not impaired, but I'm here because of Cecil's problem."

"We're always glad to have friends, spouses, family members or anyone who's interested. That's what support is all about." Laura Benning, the young woman running the group, spoke up. "For those of you who are new today, this is how we start our meetings. Even though most of us know each other fairly well, we do introductions so we all know who is here. Our tables are lined together to form a square and this exercise also helps identify where everyone is sitting."

"Like everybody doesn't sit in the same place every time!" A young man's voice came from the side of the square of tables. "It's like church. Don't sit in my pew, man!"

"Anyone can sit anywhere, Leo," Laura responded. "It's just human nature, I guess, that people usually choose the same spot."

"Well, I'm Alice Mumford." The introductions continued. "I'm from Melville and I've got macular, too. I always sit by Cecil so I can keep him in line. Maggie is much too easy on him!"

"Hey, watch it, watch it!" Cecil laughed.

"That's why I'm here, Cecil. Because I can't watch it anymore!" Alice let forth a robust burst of laughter, her heavy frame shaking.

"Looks like we've got a few comedians today," Laura said. "Marie, you're next."

Anonymous prompting followed silence across the table. "Marie, it's your turn."

"What?"

"Tell them who you are," a voice encouraged.

"Who what?"

"Introduce yourself, Marie!" Cecil boomed.

"I'm Marie Reinholdt," she finally said in a voice just above a whisper. A steady, high-pitched ringing commenced. "Wait a minute," she said nervously, "I've got to adjust my hearing aid. There."

"Are you okay, Marie?" Laura asked.

Silence. "Marie," the other prompter resumed, "Are you okay?"

"Well, I had a little cold but it's better."

"That's good. Now, tell us about yourself, honey."

"Oh, well," she faltered. "I can't hear as well since the cold. And my eyes, you know about my eyes." Silence. A more serious silence hung above the table.

"I'm May Evans," the prompter then identified herself as she patted Marie's hand. "I live here in Pinecliffe, and I have glaucoma. I can still see pretty well, but I want to learn in case . . ." Her voice was strong and self-assured. "I live down the street. Lucky for me I can walk to the meetings. And I can still drive in daylight."

"Let me know when you're driving, May, so I can stay inside that day!"

"Now, Leo," she insisted. "I only drive in areas I know well. I wouldn't hit you, dear. Go ahead, Susanna, you're next."

"I'm Susanna, from Twin Spruce. I have diabetic retinopathy and I'm totally blind," a gentle, quiet voice reported. "Most of you know my mother, Jean."

"Hi folks, I'm Jean. Mother and driver, and I'm glad to be here."

"I'm Leopold, the troublemaker. My optic nerve got in front of a self-inflicted bullet and that's why I'm here. Nobody else wanted to take care of a suicidal blind guy so I was moved out to Pinecliffe with my Grandma. That was what? Over a year ago now? Man!"

"Now you're learning to take care of yourself, right, Leo?" Laura asked confidently.

"Heck, yes! I can do everything but drive a car. I'm leaving that up to May."

"Leo . . ." May began.

"No big deal." Leo drummed his fingers on the table. "C'mon, who's next?"

The introductions continued. Addie found herself clinging to the sides of her folding metal chair as though it was a lifeboat in a storm. She felt hot and knew that her face was burning. A knot formed in her stomach. *What am I doing here? I don't belong here.* She thought of caustic Leopold and gentle Susanna and the little woman who couldn't hear well *or* see. It felt as though a horrible nightmare was unfolding. She couldn't bear it. She longed for her porch, her rocker, and a cool autumn breeze on her face. The conversation continued, but it was muffled and distant. She clung harder to the chair until her fingertips were numb and her hands began to tingle.

". . . And this is my first time here," the man next to her was saying. "I'm not sure what I can do for this group, but Laura wanted me to come. I've been blind all my life. I don't really even think about it. It's just a part of who I am."

"That's what you can do for this group, Walter," Laura said. "You can help the others put their vision loss into perspective. It's one characteristic of who they are; one of many. And yes, it's a nuisance at times. But it's not the end of the world. And it shouldn't separate anyone from the rest of the world!"

"That's right!" Walter agreed. "I'll do what I can to help."

"Good!"

The room became quiet as Addie slowly realized that it was her turn to speak. "You're a newcomer, too?" asked Walter. Still clinging to the chair she said, "Yes, yes. I'm Addie Marsh. I'm from here. I mean, I live outside of Pinecliffe, on Bear Lake."

"Addie Marsh? Bear Lake?" a familiar voice called out. "Addie, it's Harriet Stevens. Remember?"

"Harriet?" Addie's fingers slowly released their grip as she recalled a tall, thin red-headed woman with freckled cheeks and deep dimples in her perpetually smiling face. "Are you blind? I mean, oh dear." The tingling sensation ran up both arms as she fought to stay composed.

"It's okay, Addie," Harriet laughed. "We all have some degree of blindness or vision impairment or low vision if you want. It's okay to use the *B* word, right, gang?" Laughter and comments once again flowed around the table.

"The *B* word, but not the . . ."

"Leo!"

"Anyway," Harriet continued. "Addie and I go way back. Our kids used to play together in the summers. Our husbands fished. Those were the days, right Addie?"

"Those were the days, all right." She fidgeted, rubbing both arms as the tingling continued relentlessly.

"It's a shame how easily we lose touch after the kids are grown or our spouses pass away," Harriet reflected. "Let's catch up after the meeting."

"There you go, Addie," Laura said. "You already know someone here. Do you feel like telling us a little about yourself, about your eye condition? That is, if you're comfortable."

I am not comfortable! Addie screamed inside herself. Then, beginning slowly, she said, "Well, I can still see, but not well. I can't see what I look at directly, but I can see to get around out of the corner of my eyes. I can see people but not their faces." Knowing murmurs concurred from around the table. "I can't read unless the print is very large and dark, like a headline. I think the doctor called it . . ."

"Degeneration," said Cecil. "Macular degeneration. It's the same condition a lot of us have. It occurs when you get older and you're just starting to relax and enjoy life. No more reading, driving or watching television."

"Do you drive, Addie?" asked Leopold. "Maybe you and May can have a drag race."

"Oh, no," Addie shook her head. "My son saw to that a couple of weeks ago. My grandson needed a car for college, and my son needed to get my car away from me. So I no longer have a car!"

"Leo," May interrupted the understanding laughter in the room. "I don't think you should comment on my driving. You don't know what I can and can't see, and my doctor said it's okay in certain conditions."

"Whoa," Laura interrupted. "Let's finish our introductions and we'll return to that. Welcome, Addie. David, you're next."

The person on Addie's left side had been quiet from the moment she had sat down. Addie hadn't been able to tell by the stark frame if it was a man or a woman until she smelled soap and a hint of English Leather cologne, the same cologne Joe had worn when he was a teenager.

"I'm David." A surprisingly deep voice filled the room. "We have a farm in Fremont. I lost my sight in an accident two years ago. There's nothing more to say."

The introductions moved on, twenty in all, until finally

34

the leader said, "I'm Laura Benning. I think most of you know me. I'm a teacher with the Department of Rehabilitation, Blind Services. I travel to your area two or three times a month, to work with people in their homes and conduct this monthly meeting. What a great turnout we have today!"

Laura opened the meeting by reading an article describing current research on retinitis pigmentosa and its possible impact on related eye conditions. Then she presented a shorter article on the impact of nutrition in preventing further vision loss with some diagnoses.

Did she say to eat carrots, or am I losing my mind? Addie wondered. A sense of awareness engulfed her as she sat listening, trying to comprehend. The awareness was not of the speaker, however, but of the faceless forms surrounding her, the bright sunny meeting room, a clock ticking in the corner, and coffee brewing in the kitchenette. She had been in this same room many times for potluck luncheons, wedding receptions, summer arts council meetings, Pinecliffe community development dinners, and Bear Lake Water Board District meetings when she was treasurer. She knew the room; a common gathering place attached to the back of the Pinecliffe Library and bordering the community chapel. She knew the room, but not this purpose, these players.

"Any questions?"

Many, thought Addie. *Many.* She did not speak.

"All right, then," Laura sighed. "Let's open a can of worms. Driving."

"I'm not saying everyone here should be driving," May was immediately on the defensive. "I am saying it's an individual decision made by a person and her physician based upon medical evidence of the eye condition. And other conditions, too, I suppose. I know what I can and can't do. I'm very safe. And I think it's my business and mine alone."

"You couldn't pay me enough to get behind the wheel of a car," said Alice.

"But that's what's right for you," said May. "You made your decision and I'll make mine."

"I think most of us know when it's time to quit," said Harriet. "My license is still valid until my next birthday, but I can tell you the exact moment when I decided to stop driving. I was on my way back from the city, before Christmas a year ago. The trees all looked crooked to me and the center line was wavy and parts of the road seemed to disappear. I remember clinging to the wheel and crying and praying, 'Lord, get me home safe and I promise I'll never drive again.' When I got into Pinecliffe, that spot where you pass the school, all I could think of was what if a child ran out and I didn't see him? I never want to have that feeling again."

"I think giving up driving was the hardest part of this for me," Susanna said. "We live just far enough out that I couldn't get to Pinecliffe to be a part of the kids' school programs. My husband commutes to Richmond to work and if it hadn't been for Mom, I don't know what I'd have done."

"I guess I'm lucky," said Walter. "I never could see well enough to drive. Well, that's not entirely true. My brothers used to take me out on the old dirt roads when we farmed in Oklahoma, and they'd take bets on how far I could drive before I went off the road. That was in the old model A days," he laughed. "I'm as old as the hills! But seriously, you don't know what you've missed if you haven't done it all your life. My brothers are all gone now, and I'm still here. I guess I'm just lucky . . ."

"Well, it's hard for me, too," Maggie Parks said tentatively. "Isn't it, Cecil?"

36

"I don't know, darlin', you can see. You still have the privilege of driving."

"You know what I mean."

"You mean having me for a passenger?"

"Yes, a passenger and back seat driver!" But her voice was loving as she continued, "You've almost worn a hole through the floor on your side of the car."

"Applying my imaginary brakes! You know you drive too fast, mother."

"I do not!" cried Maggie.

"I'll drive for you, Cecil," offered Leo. "Let's go fishing, man."

"What's our new lady's name again?" asked Cecil.

"Addie. Addie Marsh."

"Okay, Addie," Cecil said mischievously, "when you hear a big splash out there at Bear Lake you'll know that's me and Leo out for a drive! Run down and throw us a line, will you?"

"Of course." Addie imagined herself dragging two wet men to the shore as their car slowly sank beneath the glassy surface of the lake.

Laughter subsided as the discussion continued. The group discussed driving and other losses. Someone emphasized the word *alternatives* and Laura praised this insight. May continued valiantly to defend herself. Next to Addie, David remained silent and rigid. He never spoke or laughed with the others. She could feel him breathing, hurting, filled with anger. His pain became her pain. They were drowning together in a sea of English Leather.

Dr. John was right—there were refreshments at the conclusion of the meeting. A plate of homemade cookies and a bowl of fruit, compliments of Alice, were passed around the table as another group member poured coffee. The room filled with the happy buzz of conversation. Laura walked around the table and thanked Walter for coming. He promised to stay involved in the group and offered to give a talk sometime on using a dog guide. It was not until that moment that Addie became aware of the dog lying beneath the table only a few feet away from her.

"I didn't know you had a dog!" Leaning toward David in surprise, she asked, "Did you know there's a dog right here by us?"

"No."

"He's so good, isn't he?" In spite of her amazement, Addie cringed at David's cold, shallow response.

"He's my driver!" Walter reached beneath the table. "Come here, old boy. Come meet Addie!"

Before she realized that the dog had stood, a paw landed on her knee as a cold, wet nose pushed against her hand. "Well, hello there!" she laughed.

"Addie, meet Gordon," said Walter.

"Gordon? That's your dog's name? Gordon?"

"That's not my fault," explained Walter. "You see, when a litter of potential dog guide puppies are born, it's given a letter. Gordon's litter was identified with the letter *G* and every puppy in that litter was given a name starting with *G*. There were Goldie and Gus and even Goosebump. I got Gordon, and actually, the name suits him."

A small group formed around them. Apparently Gordon had escaped detection by most of them. "Is it okay to pet him?" someone asked.

"When he's not working, it's okay," said Walter. "But you should always ask the handler first. If a dog's working as a guide, you should never do anything that might distract it. I don't want to end up in Bear Lake with those other two fellows!"

Addie almost tried once again to bring David into the conversation, then reconsidered. He seemed so far removed from all the commotion around him. Turning back to Walter she asked, "He likes the attention, doesn't he?"

"Does he! After having to put up with me day in and day out, this is a real treat for him!"

"The Old Mobile is here!" someone called out. The van had been fondly nicknamed by several of its regular, senior riders. "If you came on the van, better get going!"

Addie rose, telling Walter good-bye and giving Gordon a final pat on the head. She turned to speak to David before leaving but found his chair empty. She had not known when he'd left, and sadness crept over her again.

"Oh, Addie," Laura hurried toward her. "I wanted to talk to you before you leave. I get so busy at these meetings, there never seems to be enough time." She held a notebook and pen and periodically jotted something down while she spoke. "Did you enjoy the meeting?"

"Oh, yes. It was very nice," said Addie, thinking how warm the room suddenly felt and how she longed to be out in the fresh air. She dreaded boarding the van, like a child on a school bus. She wished it had been just a very nice tea party and not a support group.

"Good!" Laura could not read these thoughts and was encouraged by Addie's remark. "I'd like to schedule a time to visit with you in your home when I'm next here, Addie. There might be some other ways we can help."

"Thank you, but I'm really doing well," said Addie carefully. "I'm sure there are others here who need your time more than I do. I don't want to miss my ride. Thank you for the meeting."

Because she lived the farthest away, Addie was the last

one to be taken home. Carol Wilmont drove expertly up and down the familiar lanes and dead-end roads delivering each person safely home. She talked endlessly of her three teenagers and her husband, Herb, and the Pinecliffe Bears High School football team. They were headed for the play-offs and had a good chance to win the state championship. The team mothers were having a bake sale, and if the girls would just quit calling the boys, what a better world it would be. Beneath Carol's chatter, Harriet Stevens updated Addie on all that had happened since they'd last seen each other. When they reached her blue mailbox she told Addie, "It has a little white bird painted on its side. I did that when I could still see; now it's just a blob to me. But I still paint. I'm not a quitter. Call it modern art. . ." She was still talking as the van pulled away.

Addie dozed, then started as Carol swerved, probably to avoid a rut in the dirt road. "You're my last rider for the day," she called back to Addie. "You've never been on before, have you, Mrs. Marsh?"

"No, this is my first time."

"You know we can pick you up any time. You just call ahead if you have a doctor's appointment or need to go shopping."

"Thank you."

"We even go to the city every other week. Do you have the number?" Carol asked.

"Why, no, I guess I . . ." Addie fumbled in her purse for a pen. "Friends usually take me where I need to go and I really . . ."

"Would you like me to write it down for you when we stop?" the driver offered. "I'll write it big."

"Please."

Carol's conversation persisted as she drove, "I didn't realize you had problems with your vision, Mrs. Marsh." When Addie didn't respond she continued, "I'm the same age as your son, Joe. Do you remember me? The girls from Pinecliffe always went out to the lake because the city boys who came up for the summer were so much cuter than our guys. Your Joe was a looker. All the girls were crazy about him when we were in high school! And you had an older son," she rambled. "I don't remember him as much. But Joe . . . and then I married Herb Wilmont. I thought I'd leave Pinecliffe, but here I am. It's not so bad, though. It's a good place to raise kids."

Finally the Old Mobile made its way up Addie's drive. "Here we are. Do you need some help?"

"Heavens, no!" Addie reached for the sliding side door. "I can do just fine."

"Here's the number," Carol placed a piece of paper in Addie's hand. "You call, okay?"

"Thank you, Carol. You're a good driver." She could hear the van pull away as she fumbled to fit her key into the keyhole.

The little cabin always had a welcoming, musky smell when she first arrived through the entryway into the kitchen. It was a combination of smoke from the fireplace and the old cedar logs from which the structure had been built. This and the odor of food, household cleansers, and just every day living felt right to Addie. Her old yellow tomcat welcomed her with a stretch and a yawn from his resting spot on the ledge under the picture window at the rear of the house that looked down on the lake.

"Hello, Rufus!" She scooped him into her arms as he purred gently and nuzzled her chin with his nose. Stroking his fur, she carried him out to the comfort of the wooden rocker on the back porch. Rufus curled up in a ball in her lap. A blue jay darting from tree to tree broke the silence momentarily, causing the cat to raise his head. Then all was peaceful once again. Pulling her sweater about her shoulders, Addie took a deep breath.

I'm home, Jacob. Thank God, I'm home.

Chapter 3

The first snow of the season fell in late October giving Pinecliffe and nearby Bear Lake a Christmas card appearance. It was a scene etched in Addie's memory that even diminished eyesight couldn't take away. This was a wet snow, which quenched the drying earth and caused the final leaves of autumn to fall to the ground. A peacefulness accompanied the first winter storm at the lake. Since moving to the area years before, Addie had carried on a debate within herself as to which of the seasons was her favorite. Always, she was sure that the present time was the best, until a new season dawned sudden and unexpected. Then she remembered why *this* was her favorite and not the previous one. Today's change was no different. It was quiet and cleansing. Addie began her annual ritual of filling bird feeders and scraping the walk to the mailbox. She knew, as always with the first snow, that in a few days autumn would return with its warm, sunny afternoons. This snow would all melt before subsequent snowstorms became part of the long winter landscape. The county snowplow with its blue flashing light would not be called out so early in the season; this was but a dress rehearsal.

The exodus of summer residents from Bear Lake occurred on Labor Day weekend or shortly thereafter. There were the usual weekend fishermen after that and an occasional follow-up visit to a cabin to check security or make a necessary repair. For the most part, however, Addie was the single year-round tenant on the lake. As the lone participant in the winter reverie she felt a sense of privilege in sharing this time with nature.

In spite of her love for family and cherished friendships, Addie enjoyed solitude and was in no way saddened by it. It was during these times alone that she felt the most recognition and understanding of herself and her God. The magic of being alone caused her to fear being forced into moving away. There was safety in the familiar repetition of what she knew, even if not shared with another human being. The thought of a building in the city, of traffic sounds and compartmentalized people with only walls separating their most private moments was frightening.

The knowledge that pushed at the back of her consciousness made this snowy day especially warm to Addie. This could be her last winter, her last season at Bear Lake. So she cherished it, like a child seeing her first snowfall and wanting only to bundle up and experience it firsthand. Addie swept the walk clear, sat on the covered porch in spite of the cold, and often stood in the doorway listening to the quiet and breathing in the pure, moist air.

It was from this hermitage just as darkness began to fall that Addie was startled by the sound of voices nearby. The noise was so unexpected that she wondered at first if she wasn't really losing it. Was her mind beginning to converse with her? Remembering the fear of being alone, which Joe and other well-meaning friends had placed in her, caused her to begin locking doors and pulling draperies closed. It was while reaching for the shade above the kitchen window that Addie located the origin of the voices. They came from the cabin closest to hers. It was on the side of the house where the kitchen and bedrooms were located. Her living area was across the back of the house facing the lake. The neighboring cabin was down the slope from Addie's home, which sat at the highest point on the hill. Even before her loss of vision Addie could barely see the other dwelling except for a small point of the rooftop. The sound of car doors closing and voices calling back and forth easily reached her now, although their conversation was not clear.

"What do you think, Rufus?" She scooped the cat into her arms from his vantage point on the counter where he was not allowed to be but often was anyway. Rufus was unmoved by the presence of neighbors, but Addie had a sense of impending danger. Henry and Elsa Roberts had owned the cabin next door longer than Addie had been at Bear Lake. The couple, now in their late eighties, no longer spent the entire summer at the lake each year. For the last two summers, their visits were rare and the cabin, for the most part, was closed up. Occasional family picnics or afternoon visits were the only times of late that Addie had heard voices there. At those times she had walked down to visit and exchange greetings with her old friends. Now both were in failing health and had recently moved to another state to live with their only daughter. Addie knew that they would not be visiting the cabin on a late October night with snow falling.

Henry and Elsa were considerate people who would have let Addie know if they had decided to rent or sell the cabin to someone else. Like so many others, they, too, had expressed their concern about her living through the winter by herself in the remote setting. So, who could be at their cabin?

I should call Joe, she thought and picked up the telephone receiver. Then, hesitating, she replaced it. No. That would only support his argument. The roads were probably slick; he'd race out here and insist that she return home with him.

She could call Bill Johnson, the sheriff. He would investigate and let her know who was there and if they were intruders. The Roberts would thank her if it was discovered that their cabin was being vandalized. Again she picked up the receiver. Again she returned it to its cradle.

"No, Rufus." Hearing her voice aloud gave her courage. "I'm being ridiculous. No one would break into a cabin on a night like this. Whoever is there has permission, and I'm being a silly old lady."

Addie went about the business of warming up leftovers for her evening meal. Later she tried to concentrate on the television, sitting close to better see the screen. It was to this that she first attributed the droning sound, a rhythmic thud, thud, thud. She turned her head, trying to see the TV with her peripheral vision, but she was unable to attribute the sound to the program. The noise grew louder until she seemed to feel the thudding inside her. She placed her hand to her heart, breaking out in a sweat. Was it a heart attack? She didn't feel sick, but the pounding sensation was real, although painless. In spite of her fear her breath came easily. She stood and, finding the remote to the television set, she turned it off.

The noise and the vibration continued and Addie realized it came from the next cabin. Cautiously, she opened the back door leading to the porch. The sound was louder and suddenly familiar to her. She had heard it behind her grandson Michael's closed bedroom door and experienced the pounding once when he had driven to the lake alone to pay her a surprise visit. It was the sound that had announced his arrival, even before she had seen his car blowing dust on the gravel road. "Darn that music!" Joe had complained that day at the house. "Michael, turn it down!"

Addie had laughed then. "I seem to remember someone else listening to rock and roll a few years ago. The Beatles, the Guess Who—wasn't that you, Joe?"

Sheepishly he'd grinned. "We were never that bad, Mom. Never that loud. And at least our music made sense. This stuff . . ." Exasperated, he threw his hands up in the air.

"History repeats itself," Addie had murmured.

She closed the door on a cold burst of wind. *Teenagers,* she thought. Perhaps they had broken in to have a party, or who knows what? On a Tuesday night? Then, as suddenly as it had started, the music stopped, and silence returned to the forest. Addie stood with her head against the door for a long time, listening, but heard nothing. No pounding, no voices. Again, she thought of calling the sheriff. But what if no one was there when he arrived? With the blowing snow and her poor vision she could not tell if light reflected from the hill below her. She returned to the television set and turned it on, louder this time.

It's nothing, she told herself. *Imagination? Maybe. But I'm not giving in to fear. Not this time.*

After a restless night Addie welcomed a new morning. It had stopped snowing and the wind was quiet; it seemed a different world than the night before. As soon as Addie was dressed, she went outside and listened for any signs of life at the neighboring house. Other than the honking of migrating geese flying above the lake, the morning was quiet. Whatever had startled her the night before was gone, and Addie could be at peace once again.

When at midday a timid knock sounded at the door, she assumed it was Fred Baca, the mailman, although she had not heard his truck arrive. Fred often left packages and oversized envelopes at the door. Occasionally, when he was ahead of schedule, he would stop for a cup of coffee and a treat. Addie liked him because he never discussed the dangers of living alone on the mountain. Like herself, Fred possessed a deep love for nature and thought that Addie lived in the most beautiful place on God's earth. He loved fishing and animals and the gentle people of the village. And this day he would be able to tell Addie if there was a car or evidence of people at the cabin next door.

When she opened the door, instead of the middle-aged mailman, the frame of a slightly built person stood before her. "I'm sorry to disturb you, ma'am." The voice of a young girl was as soft and small as she was standing in a bright ray of sunlight. "I wondered if I could use your phone. I need to make a collect call." She hesitated, and when Addie, surprised, didn't answer, she added, "It won't cost you anything. The phone's dead next door. Or shut off or something."

"You're from next door?" Addie's own small frame filled the space left by the partially opened door and she made no move to allow the girl inside.

"Yes. We're going to be staying there for awhile. My husband's looking for a job and . . . I hope we can get the phone fixed. I don't mean to bother you."

"It was your music I heard last night then?"

"Was it too loud? I'm sorry." The visitor fidgeted uncomfortably. "I really just need to use the phone, and I'll get out of your hair."

Was this the kind of danger Joe had warned her about? The vulnerability of being far away from help and an easy target for anyone who wanted to harm her? But how could someone even smaller than herself be a danger? The girl seemed frightened and shy, embarrassed to be asking for help. Against her better judgment Addie stepped aside and pushed the door open.

"Come in. It's still a little cold out there, isn't it?"

Relieved, the girl hurried past her into the kitchen. "Yes, it's cold in our house, too. Wasn't that snow wild? I mean, it seems too early to snow."

"We get an early snow or two here." Addie pulled a chair out from the kitchen table. "Sit down. Would you like a cup of coffee?" Addie always had a pot of coffee brewing, waiting for those visits from the mailman or other friends who might stop in unexpectedly, although such visits were infrequent now. "You're not from around here, are you?"

"No, ma'am. No coffee, and no, I'm not from around here. I like coffee but I'm pregnant and I'm not supposed to have caffeine. I like herbal tea," she hinted.

"I'll pour you a glass of milk," Addie responded. "Milk's good for you and your baby." Addie placed the telephone in front of her, thinking as she did so how young the girl seemed. She was but a child herself; it was hard to believe that she was expecting a child of her own. "Go ahead and make your call."

The phone beeped as the girl pushed the numbers, then a pause, before she said, "Collect" followed by "Sybil." Still another, longer silence, and then she hung up.

"Not home," she said softly.

"Here's your milk." Addie sat down facing her and shoved a plate across the table. "Have a cookie."

The girl obliged and it was obvious that she was hungry. Addie wished she had offered something more substantial. "Your husband's looking for a job?"

Gulping her milk, Sybil responded, "Yes. He's a good carpenter. He can paint, repair things, do almost anything, really."

"He may have a hard time finding work out here this

time of year," Addie said with concern. "It's off-season, and all the tourists are gone. Things get pretty dead here in the winter. He'd probably have better luck in Richmond."

When the girl did not respond Addie asked carefully, "Are you renting the place down the hill?"

"No, we're just staying there." Sybil reached for her third cookie. "It belongs to my husband's grandparents."

"Really? I know the grandchildren, but I'm afraid I've lost track. Which one is he?"

"Stoney." This she said with a burst of pride. "My guy is Stoney."

"I don't remember . . ."

"He's really like a step-grandson," Sybil explained. "His dad married this lady and her parents own that cabin."

"That's right, I remember now. Sharon remarried."

"That's her name, Sharon. Stoney doesn't like her," Sybil confided. "See, he lived with his mom in California, and his dad moved to Kansas to be with Sharon. It kind of bothered Stoney. Then his mom had all these different boyfriends, and it was really messed up." Sybil seemed relaxed and comfortable. She slid her glass out. "Could I have a little more milk? Those cookies really made me thirsty."

Addie obliged, half amused, half saddened by this little mother-to-be.

"Anyway, we're on our own now, so everything's good." Sybil said. "Oh, look!" She jumped up from her chair, rattling the table and causing Addie to gasp. "You've got a kitty cat!" Through her side vision Addie saw a yellow ball of fur fly for the safety of her bedroom. "Oh, I scared him. Oh, well. I like cats. I had one once but my mom got allergic. When I have my baby we're going to have all kinds of animals around. Stoney said we could."

Addie sighed deeply. "Your husband's grandparents know you're staying here then?"

"Of course. Oh, I'm sorry—I've eaten all your cookies!"

"Never mind, that's what they're there for." Addie thought for a moment, picking her words carefully. "You know, Sybil, it seems odd to me that the Roberts didn't call and tell me you were coming. We've always let each other know things like that. We look out for our neighbors. Everyone up here is that way."

"Oh, stupid me!" Sybil groaned. "Stoney always says I'm an airhead! That's the other reason I came over here. I wanted to use the phone and I was supposed to tell you who we are. Which I guess I did do, didn't I?" She laughed nervously. "We weren't sure when we'd arrive so they told us to come over as soon as we got here and let you know. And we just forgot to last night."

"I see."

"I guess I had my mind on making that phone call. I'm trying to reach my mom, you know, to tell her that we got here okay."

"But she's not home?" Addie asked.

"No. She's never home."

"Want to try again?" Addie asked gently.

At that moment the sound of a motor in need of repair could be heard in the distance. "Stoney!" Sybil jumped to her feet, banging the table a second time. "I've got to go!"

"Don't you want to try your mom again?"

"No, no. Maybe later." She raced to the door, calling as she went, "Thanks for the cookies and milk." The screen slammed behind her. "We'll try not to make so much noise, I promise." Like a frightened rabbit she raced down the driveway, cutting across the muddy ground to take a short cut down the hill.

51

★ ★ ★ ★ ★

A few days later, Joe showed up unexpectedly and announced to his mother that they were taking a drive back to the city to tour Gateway.

"I'm not saying you're moving, Mom. I just want you to see it, that's all."

"But I can't go today. You should have called first," Addie protested.

"You have plans?" Joe said half laughing but with a touch of sarcasm in his voice. "C'mon, Mom. You're stalling. It's a great day for a drive. I'll even spring for lunch."

"No, Joe, I really can't go." Addie went to the closet for her quilted jacket and her purse. She carefully placed them on a chair near the door. "Today's the support group meeting—you know, the vision class. Did I tell you about it? Dr. John thinks I should get involved in it. We talk about losing eyesight and learn how to manage living alone even if you're blind. I think it's good for me."

"You've been before?" he asked in surprise.

"Just once—last month. That was my first time. The leader comes from town so she doesn't get out here too often." Having had no real plan to attend the meeting, she ran her hands through her hair and brushed off her slacks, considering how she looked at that moment. Would she fool him into believing she had been prepared to go out?

"I'm sorry you made the trip for nothing. Maybe we can go on the tour another time."

"How are you getting there?" Joe asked. "The group meets in Pinecliffe, doesn't it?"

"Yes," Addie responded. "The county has that little bus for senior citizens and they use it to pick up anyone who needs a ride to the meeting. Do you remember Carol

Wilmont? She's the driver. She said she knew you when you were in high school and we came out to the lake for the summers."

"Carol Ashland, wasn't it?" Joe grinned. "Do I remember Carol! She married Herb, didn't she? He was a nice guy. A native."

"That's right. They've got three or four kids now. She's a talker!" When Joe still hadn't made a move to leave Addie said, "Carol will be out to pick me up soon. Maybe you'd better leave and we can get together another time. I'd hate to miss the meeting as much as I'd like to go with you."

"Now, Mom," Joe teased. "This is Joe, remember? I know you. What you meant to say was you're glad you have a meeting scheduled, because you'd hate to go with me. I can't believe you're excited about a support group. That doesn't sound like you! But then I know you don't want to check out Gateway either, even though it's for your own good." Addie flushed but didn't answer. "What the heck? Really, I'm proud of you. For going to the vision group, I mean. You're right. I won't interfere with that. We can drive into the city another time. Besides, I'm glad you're getting out of the house for a change. I'll take a day off next week and come out to make some repairs and winterize the place."

Relieved, Addie started for the door to see him off, but he stopped her. "Hey, it's early. I'll wait with you until your ride comes. Have you got anything to make a sandwich?"

Of course, the Old Mobile never came. When Carol Wilmont had called earlier to remind her of the meeting and take her reservation for the van, Addie had invented the excuse of a prior commitment. A knot had formed in her stomach at the mention of venturing to the village again for the support group. Now, when it became evident that there would be no ride, Joe cursed government programs that "can't even pick people up when they say they're going to." He insisted on driving Addie to the meeting himself.

When they pulled up near the community chapel, the van was also just arriving. "I'm going to give her a piece of my mind!" Joe exclaimed, but Addie quickly reached over and grabbed his arm.

"No, you don't, Joe. I'll take care of it. I'm sure there's an explanation."

"Mom, I just want to be sure this doesn't happen again. If you're relying upon these people for rides, they need to be there for you."

"And I have to fight my own battles." Addie hurried out of the car and then called back before closing the door, "You can leave now. I'll talk to Carol and she'll take me home. Go on!" She closed the door and patted it, then scurried toward the van to make arrangements for the trip home, embarrassment glowing in her cheeks.

After the meeting, when Addie was once again the final passenger in the van, she casually asked Carol if she knew one of the group members, a man by the name of David. "He wasn't there today, and I wondered if you knew anything about him."

"I know who he is. From Fremont, right?" Carol asked.

"I believe so," said Addie. "He probably doesn't ride the van, though. I don't think he's old enough to qualify as a senior citizen."

"That doesn't matter," Carol explained. "We bend the rules a little for programs like this one because we think it's important. We'll give anybody a ride that wants to attend. But David's never asked for one. His wife usually drops him off. I think he's just a few years older than I am, though. His youngest daughter just graduated a year or two ago. I don't know much about them."

Before Addie had time to think, Carol rambled on. "You know, it's strange. Most of the people in that group are seniors, aren't they? Why do you suppose that is?"

"Dr. Siegfried gave a talk at the class today and explained that." This time Addie felt pleased to contribute to the conversation. "The occurrence of blindness increases with age. It's something like two out of every one thousand people who are blind, and half of them are over sixty-five. That is, legally blind."

"Good God," moaned Carol. "I don't think I could handle that. But you're not blind. I mean, you see okay to step up on the van and walk to your door alone. It seems like most of those people aren't really blind, except that guy with the dog. He's been around here awhile. I know he's blind."

"That's a misconception people have," Addie explained. "People think if you're blind, you live in total darkness, and that isn't true. A person can be legally blind and still have some sight left. Dr. Siegfried told us only a small percentage are totally blind; you know, people who can't see anything. The rest are functionally blind even though they're partially sighted. You probably know that you're considered legally blind if your acuity is twenty over two-hundred or less with correction."

"I've heard that. As a matter of fact, Herb is legally blind without his glasses!" Carol said. "It must be hard for you, though, to have a condition that eyeglasses won't help."

"It is hard," Addie agreed. "I can see some things, but not others. I'm learning there are different philosophies concerning that, too," she continued. "Some people think you shouldn't struggle to use what little sight you have, that it just adds to your frustration. Others say you should work to use your remaining sight for as long as you can."

"What do you think?" asked Carol.

"I guess I haven't really thought about it much," admitted Addie. "I'm too busy being frustrated all the time!" She laughed, then said thoughtfully. "I guess what I think is you should use what you have but learn as much as you can about not relying on your sight. That makes sense to me."

"And is that what you're doing about it?"

"Sure, sure!" Addie laughed again.

Carol was easygoing and comfortable to talk to in this time they shared together. Yet Addie was surprised at herself as she educated Carol. She laughed with the realization that in spite of her reluctance to become involved in a support group, she had learned something from being there!

A week later, Joe returned as he had promised. Addie strolled through the cabin and yard with him, pointing out a squeaky hinge, a rattling shutter, and other minor problems. When Joe noticed a small stack of unread mail on Addie's corner desk, he asked if her bills had been paid recently.

"Hazel Siegfried has been helping out until Fran gets back," Addie explained. When Joe picked up the mail and began to shuffle though it, she hurried on, "She was supposed to come yesterday but got tied up at the office. She fills in for the receptionist, and then her grandchildren were out for a visit—but she promised to come tomorrow. You don't need to worry, nothing's overdue!"

"Maybe you need more reliable help, Mom," Joe suggested. "It sounds to me like Fran and Hazel are both too busy to depend upon."

"Perhaps," Addie conceded. "I'll check around. In the

meantime, can you reach a box on the top shelf of the closet for me?"

When he finished making needed repairs, Joe announced, "Now we're going to town for the afternoon. First, we'll stock up on groceries so you don't need to wait for Hazel to take you. And then," he paused, "we'll visit Gateway. We have a three o'clock appointment for a tour."

Addie did not respond. There was no point in arguing this time. He had given an entire morning to her. He had taken off work out of concern for her, and she knew this trip was inevitable.

"Just a tour?" she asked finally.

"I promise."

On the drive into town, Joe asked her about the support group meeting the week before. "It was good," Addie told him. "We had a guest speaker who talked about eye conditions and general health. You'll never guess who."

"From the city?"

"No." Addie laughed. "From Pinecliffe. It was our own Dr. John. We're so lucky to have a good doctor like him out here."

Addie thought back to the meeting as the car wove through the last stretch of tree-lined canyon before reaching the twenty miles of open prairie leading into Richmond. "I'm lucky today." That's what Walter had said when Addie had once again sat down beside him, and she had thought that she was really the lucky one. Flustered by her lie to Joe about attending the meeting, she had found comfort in sitting next to this amiable man who seemed so at peace with his world. When Gordon had laid his head across Addie's foot halfway through the meeting, she had smiled and remained still so he wouldn't move. Safe. Lucky.

After the meeting, Dr. John had sat down beside her.

"I'm glad to see you, Addie. This is a great program, but I didn't think you'd follow through. I'm really glad you're here!"

"It was a wonderful talk, doctor!" Addie had engaged him in conversation, avoiding Laura with her potential request for a home visit.

Before the meeting was over, she had volunteered to bring a chocolate cake to the Christmas party next month. Chocolate cake from scratch was an Addie Marsh specialty but during the last year, she had relied upon store-bought desserts. What had moved her to volunteer, Addie could not say. She knew she could no longer see the red lines on her Pyrex measuring cup to determine the proper amount of the ingredients for a cake. She had difficulty setting the oven's temperature dial and couldn't tell by looking when the cake was done. All previous efforts to do so had failed miserably. Maybe Hazel would find time to help her. Or she would just tell them she wasn't feeling well that day. Another lie. Thinking about all of these excuses and stories made Addie shudder. That was not the kind of person she wanted to be, but it seemed to be what she was becoming.

Joe and Addie arrived at Gateway just before three o'clock with a trunk full of groceries and an ice chest to keep them cold. Joe had foreseen that she'd worry about leaving them in the car and had left no avenue open for excuses today. He laughed lightly and joked with his mother as he took her arm and steered her up the brick sidewalk to the handsome oak entryway with double-glass doors.

"Isn't it beautiful, Mom? Wait till you see the yard out back."

"Fenced, I hope," Addie grumbled.

"What?" The clicking of high heels approached from a side hallway.

"A fenced yard, so we can't run away!"

"Mother!"

A sweet fragrance engulfed them as a young woman arrived and stretched out her hand to Joe. "I'm Kelly Jones, the social worker here at Gateway. You must be Mr. Marsh."

"Yes," Joe answered nervously, "and this is my mother, Mrs. Addie Marsh."

"Welcome, Mrs. Marsh."

"Thank you," said Addie extending her hand.

"Can I have you both sign our guest register?" Kelly asked as they stopped before a small podium.

"I can't see well enough to sign my name," said Addie. "Can Joe do it for me?"

"Of course. Do you need assistance on the tour?"

"I'll take Joe's arm if I do," responded Addie.

"I didn't realize that you're blind." Kelly fumbled through a stack of papers clipped into a folder.

"She says she's not. The ophthalmologist says she's legally blind," Joe stammered, before Addie could answer. "Will that be a problem in her admittance here?"

"No, of course not. Most of our residents have disabilities of one type or another. We'll just need a thorough medical history and an evaluation." She slammed the folder shut. "It's not a problem."

They began walking together down the corridor from which Kelly had arrived. She pointed out various rooms and "program areas." Joe nervously tried to maintain a conversation while Addie quietly absorbed the experience. She tried to picture herself living here and could only compare it to time spent in her sister's Denver mansion.

"Here's a sample of the private living rooms," Kelly announced as they turned down one of many side hallways from the main area. She opened a door and they entered a room with a large bay window. "You can have your bed here and other familiar furnishings from home. A special chair perhaps, and pictures. We encourage people to bring things that make them comfortable. And you have your own private bathroom. If you need it, we can provide assistance with bathing in a larger area, which I'll show you down the hall. We also do your laundry, and of course, we do the cooking. Everyone eats together in the dining room. It's a fun time, a time for fellowship. But you can have a small refrigerator in your room for snacks, if you like, and even a microwave for popcorn and things like that!"

Addie smiled, but she said nothing. Eventually they entered a large enclosed solarium where flowers and trees bloomed year-round. At one end a walled cage of finches and canaries provided entertainment with their constant singing. Park benches lined the walkways and a few of the residents sat visiting or wandered about amicably.

"Mom, would you like to sit here and rest a little?" Joe sensed her discomfort and gently led her to an unoccupied bench. Together they sat for a moment as Kelly stopped to answer a question from a woman walking in the garden.

"This is a pretty spot, isn't it?" Addie welcomed the chance to sit down. The atrium was peaceful and Addie knew that if she ever came to live here, this would be her favorite spot. It was not her porch above the lake, but it would relieve the claustrophobia of living in one small room.

"Are you okay?" Joe asked, almost in a whisper. "You're awfully quiet."

Resignation suppressed all of the replies she might have made. "I'm fine."

"Good." Joe squeezed her hand. "Then why don't you stay here a bit while Kelly and I check out some forms?"

"Forms?"

"To put your name on the waiting list," Joe said reassuringly. "It doesn't mean you're committed to moving here. It just means you have a chance when your name gets to the top. They call and ask if you're still interested. There are a lot of other names ahead of you. It could be a long time."

"But don't you think we should discuss it first?" asked Addie.

"We *have* discussed it, and we will discuss it some more." Exasperation crept into his voice. "Listen, Mom. You don't understand. I've done a lot of research on this. I didn't say much to you because I know how you feel about leaving home. I've been everywhere and Gateway is the best. That's why it takes a while to get a room. It's a model program. Everybody wants to live here. You don't leave here saying, 'I'll think about it.' You put your name on the list. It's the first of many steps. Believe me, they won't be calling you tomorrow. There's plenty of time to think it through."

"Well, whatever you say," responded Addie. "I just . . ."

"Wait here." Joe rose as Kelly joined them once again. "I'll be back in a few minutes, Mom." With that they were gone and Addie found herself alone among the trees and chirping of birds.

After a few minutes a man approached her. He used a cane but was moving at a good pace along the tree-lined walk. "Good afternoon!" He stopped when he saw Addie sitting on the bench.

"Hello!" she responded. "This is a nice place to walk, isn't it?"

"Indeed. I walk every day, rain or shine. That's what I

love about the garden. It's always good weather in here."

"I'm just a visitor," said Addie. "But this is a beautiful spot. I can see why you like it."

"Oh, I do. Enjoy your visit. Perhaps I'll see you again." With that he walked away, and Addie found herself alone once more.

She closed her eyes wearily and leaned back her head. A moment later another man approached from among the trees. This man she knew and relief consumed her. *Jacob.*

Hello, love. He was beside her then, present within that moment in time.

Oh, Jacob, she sighed heavily. *I don't want to move here. I want to be with you. It's time, I think, don't you?*

Don't be silly, he answered gently. *My dear, dear, Addie. You want to be where you can't be and you don't try to be a part of where you are.*

I don't know what you mean. A single tear fell down Addie's cheek and dropped from her chin.

I'll tell you then. Someday we'll be together again. I've always promised you that and it's true. But not yet. I'm looking out for you, darling, but you must do some looking out, too. Be the best you can be, Addie. You've always been that way. Why are you quitting now?

Because I'm old, Jacob. Because I'm blind. Because I'm tired.

Listen to me. Old is in your head. Tired just means you need more rest. And blind? If you've got to be blind, learn to live with it and get on with your life, Addie! It isn't over yet.

Chapter 4

Reminiscent of the earlier calamity with burned stew, billows of smoke filled Addie's tiny kitchen. Coughing and sneezing, she wondered how had this happened? She'd been so careful. She swung the kitchen door open, ignoring the below-zero temperature outside following yesterday's snow. Returning to the oven she murmured, "That cake hasn't been in there twenty minutes. It can't be done." But the pungent odor told her differently. As she retrieved the pan from the scorching oven, Addie knew that it was not only done, but charred. She dropped the pan into the sink.

"Now what?" As the smoke subsided, Addie grabbed a worn fleece jacket that hung on a hook beside the door and rushed outside. Earlier, she had cleaned the walk all the way to the mailbox and having heard the snowplow that morning, she knew the road had been freshly cleared as well. The newly packed layer of snow crunched beneath her feet as she strode down the drive and onto the road. The bright glare from the snow forced Addie to strain to keep her peripheral vision focused on the edge of the road as her guide. She knew the way from many walks over the years to visit Elsa Roberts.

Sybil greeted her neighbor with surprise. "Addie!" They had both agreed during a previous visit that "Mrs. Marsh" was too formal.

"I'm glad you're home, Sybil," Addie sighed. "Is there a chance you could assist me with a few things? I mean, would it be all right with Stoney? I'll gladly pay you for your time, dear."

"He's not here, but you know I'd be happy to help you." Her sincerity was real as she hurried in search of her coat. "Anyway, I get bored staying by myself all day. Stoney's doing some remodeling for a family over in Crestview. He won't be home until dark."

"Good! I'm trying to bake a cake for a Christmas party tomorrow and I'm having a hard time." Addie explained. "I need your eyes."

"My eyes?" Sybil locked a padlock across her door before lifting her legs high over the unshoveled snow outside. "I hope Stoney will get around to shoveling this walk soon. He won't let me, you know, because of the baby and all."

To Addie, the girl still seemed very young and small. She was lonely and had visited with Addie several times in the past weeks when Stoney was away. She'd even offered to help out around the house if Addie needed her. Still, she had no idea that her older neighbor was legally blind.

Her voice serious now, Addie said, "I don't see well, Sybil. And with this glistening snow, I can hardly see at all. Everything is so bright. I don't think I could have made it to your house if I didn't know the way so well."

"Would you like to take my arm?" Sybil held out an elbow.

"Please." Addie felt still more surprise at the frail, slender arm beneath the bundle of coat. "Are you eating right?" she couldn't help asking.

"Me?" They had reached the clean surface of the road, and maneuvered across a small ridge left by the snowplow, catching each other when one slipped. Sybil continued, "I'm eating right. I cook for Stoney all the time. He thinks I'm a good cook." Once again, pride crept into her voice. "He works long hours, Addie. He says he has to work hard for me and the baby. Isn't that sweet? I try to feed him good, so he'll stay strong and healthy."

"You feel so tiny to me, that's all," explained Addie.

"I don't show much yet. It's the way I'm built." Sybil was defensive and self-consciously pulled her coat closer.

"I'm sorry," said Addie. "I meant your arm. Your arm feels so tiny under your coat."

They walked on in silence, then Addie, remembering her plight, stopped suddenly. "Oh, Sybil, I must explain before we reach my house. I've made a mess of things. I need your help cleaning up if you don't mind."

"What happened?"

"Well, I was baking a cake, which I burned," Addie began as they resumed walking together. "And while it was in the oven I was cleaning up, and I knocked a bag of flour onto the floor. You know how flour drifts all over when you spill it? My kitchen is covered!"

"Oh, Addie!" Sybil giggled. "How did you burn the cake? Did you forget it with all the mess?"

"No, no," Addie shook her head. "I was watching it. I don't know what happened. I think there's something wrong with my oven. It runs away with itself and burns everything I try to bake. I need to get a repairman out."

"Maybe Stoney could have a look at it," Sybil offered. "He can fix anything."

"That would be great."

They had trudged back to Addie's house, and as they entered, Sybil laughed out loud, "Boy, you're not kidding that you made a mess! Oh, Addie, how on earth?"

Sheepishly, Addie joined her laughter. "Pretty bad, huh?"

"Addie, how . . . ?"

"I was wiping the counter and I knew the bag was there. I think it was closer to the edge than I realized, and I bumped it, and there you have it."

"Well, we'll clean it up, don't worry!" Sybil handed Addie her coat and pushed up the sleeves of her sweatshirt in preparation. She lifted the remains of the torn bag from the floor. "You've still got some flour left. Want to try again?"

"That's what I need you for."

"Rufus, get down now!" Sybil scolded as the cat thudded leisurely to the floor.

"On the counter again?" asked Addie. "I hope he didn't eat the cake."

"He couldn't eat this cake!" Sybil began laughing. "I'm sorry, Addie!" The more she tried to stop the harder she laughed. "I'm not making fun of you. It's just . . . this poor cake!" She lifted the pan a few inches and dropped it with a crash. "This isn't a cake, it's a boulder."

Addie joined her laughter until both had to sit down at the table to regain their composure. It was fun having Sybil in the kitchen on this cold, snowy day. She didn't scold or feel embarrassed for Addie. Through her kidding, she seemed to understand what Addie was feeling. It was as though they were children, Addie thought. It brought back memories of times with Sarah in the kitchen on Race Avenue, giggling at their blunders while their uncle was away from home. Even then, it had been Addie who created the bigger messes and Sarah who flew to the rescue.

As Sybil began to clean up the flour, Addie noticed intense heat from the stove. She asked Sybil to check it. "Addie, you left the oven on. Man, is it hot. I can feel it with the door closed."

"Well, I knew we'd be baking another cake so I didn't turn it off," Addie explained.

"I think we'd better let it cool off, anyway." Sybil

opened the oven door and reached for the control dial.

"That's what I was telling you," said Addie as a burst of heat filled the room. "It gets too hot, there's something wrong with it. We'll have to watch the next cake very closely."

"Why do you have it set so high?" asked Sybil.

"What do you mean?"

"I mean, you've got the temperature dial turned up most of the way. It's on about four-fifty," Sybil explained.

"That can't be," Addie muttered. "The recipe calls for three-fifty."

"Never mind." Sybil scrubbed the cake pan after dumping its contents into the trash. "We'll get it set right and leave the door open a bit to bring down the temperature. What do we need for the cake?"

"Here's the recipe." Addie handed Sybil a worn index card as she dried her hands on a towel.

After a brief silence, Sybil said, "Umm . . . Addie, this is for lemon meringue pie. Didn't you want cake?"

"Yes, yes. Here," Addie fumbled through a small stack of cards. "It's in these. 'Mom's chocolate cake', it should say. It was my mother-in-law's recipe." Then softly she added, "Jacob loved it, so did Jake."

"You really don't see well, do you?" Sybil placed a small hand on Addie's arm.

"No. No, I don't. I can't see things up close or to read. I guess that explains why I'm having problems cooking. I thought I had the dial on three-fifty, not four-fifty."

"It's okay. Like you said, I'll be your eyes today." Then she added playfully, "Together, Addie, we'll fight this old dragon and bake this cake in time for the ball!"

"And maybe you can take a small piece for your prince when he arrives," teased Addie back.

"My prince, yes!" exclaimed Sybil. Then, with shy speculation, she added, "And what about you? Your prince?"

"I'm too old for that!"

"You're never too old to be in love," Sybil said earnestly as she began to measure ingredients. "You said his name was Jacob? Your husband?"

"Yes, but he's gone now. He's been dead a long time."

"It's hard to think of that," said Sybil. As she talked, she measured and sifted. "I don't know what I'd do if something happened to Stoney. I mean, with a baby on the way. You had a baby, didn't you? You know what it's like."

"Oh yes, I've been there. I know exactly how you feel. We don't know how long we'll have the people we love." Then, sensing Sybil's uneasiness, she added, "Don't worry, Stoney's fine. Nothing's going to happen to you two. You love him very much, don't you?"

"More than anything."

"Is he good to you?" Addie felt that she was treading on sensitive ground, but her heart went out to the childlike girl who now busied herself in the kitchen.

"He *is* good to me!" Once again, Sybil was defensive. "It's not what you think. He'd never hurt me. He loves me as much as I love him. These bruises aren't his fault!"

"Bruises?" asked Addie.

"On my cheek. Silly me! You can't see them, can you?"

"No. I can see your hair and the shape of your face. But I can't make out your features or anything definite like that."

"That must be weird," said Sybil.

"It's an eye condition called macular degeneration that some people get as they age," Addie explained. "What did you say about bruises?"

"I've got a couple of bruises on my face," Sybil quickly

explained. "I was afraid that you thought Stoney . . . but it was just stupid me. I got up in the night to go to the bathroom and walked into a door. Guess I was the one that wasn't seeing too good!"

"You'll have to be more careful." A sad, uneasy feeling embraced Addie. "For you and your child, Sybil. Be careful."

"He's not that bad," Sybil said, as though compelled to reassure Addie. "I haven't had a great life." She paused thoughtfully. "Stoney is the first person who ever really cared about me. My mom drinks a lot. She's hardly ever at home. And my dad . . . would you believe I don't even know who my dad is? She tells me a different story each time I ask, depending on what mood she's in. I don't think she knows for sure." She laughed. It was a harsh, ugly sound unlike her usual happy giggle.

"But now I have Stoney, and nothing else matters. He's going to marry me and take care of us . . ."

"I thought you were already married."

"I guess I did say that before, didn't I?" Sybil opened the oven door and slid the cake inside.

"Yes," said Addie. "When we met, you told me that Stoney was your husband."

"He is, really. In our hearts and minds we're married! We just aren't officially married yet, but we plan to do it soon. How about being my bridesmaid, Addie?" She struggled to make a joke, but Addie remained serious this time.

"Does your mother know where you are?"

"She doesn't care. I can't even reach her."

The apprehension that filled Addie overflowed into the room. "I'm sure she's worried about you, Sybil. Why don't you try to call her again? Use my phone. It doesn't have to be collect."

"No, thanks, Addie. It's okay, really." The girl filled the sink with water and began cleaning the mixing bowls.

"I can do that part."

Sybil shrugged, trying to bring back the carefree feeling they'd lost. "I'll do it. I like to stay busy." Both were quiet with their thoughts for a few moments before she turned back to Addie. "Please don't tell anyone, Addie. As soon as the baby is born, we'll get married and be on our own. But until then, give us a little time, please?"

Addie was gentle and understanding, as Sybil had been earlier when they discussed Addie's problems. "You're runaways, then?"

"I don't think of it that way." Sybil wiped her hands on a kitchen towel. "We need to make some icing." She measured and stirred, testing the final outcome with a scoop of her finger. "It's really best for everyone if you think about it. Stoney and I both have pretty bad parents who don't want to be bothered. We need each other and we're going to make something out of ourselves. And the baby. Stoney really cares about this baby. He wants a boy, of course!"

"But what about school?" asked Addie. "Shouldn't you be in school?"

"I graduated." The lie hung heavily between them; Addie felt its weight but let it stand, unchallenged.

"What about the Robertses? Do they really know you and Stoney are living at the cabin?"

This time Sybil thought before responding. "Stoney's dad told him about Bear Lake when he married Sharon. He told Stoney he was sure it would be okay to use the cabin because they rarely visit it anymore. He even told him where the extra key was hidden. Stoney feels like that's enough permission."

As if she could read the struggle in Addie's mind, she

pleaded, "You won't tell them, will you? We're taking good care of the cabin. Stoney's fixing it up, and I promise, we won't hurt anything."

"But they're my friends," said Addie gently. "We have an unspoken agreement. I look out for their property, and they'd do the same for me. I can't lie to them."

"I'm not asking you to lie. I'd never ask you to do that!" She removed the cake from the oven exclaiming, "Look, Addie, it's done! Perfect! What kind of party is this cake for, anyway?"

"A support group." Addie's voice remained soft, yet stern.

"All right, all right," Sybil laughed nervously. "We'll tell them, Addie. We'll write Stoney's dad and stepmother tonight. Just let us do it, okay? It'll be better that way."

"Do you promise?" asked Addie.

"Promise! Icing." Sybil fixed her attention on the cake. "As soon as it cools, we'll spread the frosting and decorate it."

When the cake was finished and the kitchen cleaned, the two sat at the table sipping herb tea, which Addie had purchased for such an occasion after her new neighbors arrived. Brownies from the grocery store's bakery section were also offered and readily accepted. A comfortable level of conversation was restored as Addie silently convinced herself that Sybil would keep her word about writing to Stoney's dad.

"Would you tell me about when you had your baby?" Sybil's question took Addie by surprise.

"That was a long time ago, Sybil. Things have changed."

"Oh, I know that," she replied. "But I'd like to talk about it. I need another woman who understands. Stoney, he's not interested in that part of it. He just wants the baby

71

to hurry up and get here!"

Addie asked, "When are you due?"

For a moment, Sybil seemed flustered. "Well, I'm not really sure. In the spring or maybe early summer."

"Didn't your doctor give you a due date?"

Sybil shifted uncomfortably. "He's not real sure. An old-fashioned doctor, you know. He says the baby will arrive when he's ready."

"Sybil! You haven't seen a doctor, have you?" Addie demanded.

"Of course I have, Addie. Don't be silly. I'm taking care of this little guy." She patted her stomach. "I'm not very big yet. My mother said she hardly showed at all when she was pregnant with me. I think that's how my family is. Stoney keeps wondering when I'm going to get fat." She giggled. "I'll bet you've known people who didn't gain much when they were expecting, haven't you?" But before Addie could answer, she continued, "Tell me how it was for you. I mean, if you don't mind. Tell me what it was like having a baby."

Embarrassed, Addie collected her thoughts and was only starting to tell her story when they were startled by a sudden and unexpected pounding at the door. "Sybil, are you in there?" a husky voice demanded.

Addie rose and opened the door. She had met Stoney before when he and Sybil had been out walking one warm November afternoon. He had been cordial but distant then. Now, with a forced hospitality, Addie greeted him, "Well, hello there, Stoney. You startled us!"

Without a word he pushed his way past Addie and yanked Sybil from her chair. "What are you doing here?" he demanded.

"Stoney," she whimpered like a frightened child. "I'm just . . ."

"I'm afraid it's my fault," the older woman interrupted. In spite of her rising fear, Addie kept her voice calm. "Will you join us?" she gestured toward the table.

"No," he murmured, releasing Sybil. "But . . . thanks."

Addie hurried an explanation. "I needed help in the kitchen today, so I asked Sybil to join me. This time of year, you're my closest neighbors." As she spoke Addie walked to her pantry door and retrieved her purse from which she took a handful of bills. She guessed at the denominations, continuing her story unflustered as she handed them to Sybil. "I hope you don't mind. I really needed her assistance and thought perhaps you could use the money for the baby."

Stoney softened. "It's okay," he shrugged. "I was worried when I got home and she wasn't there, that's all."

"We didn't hear the car, Stoney. If I'd heard you, I'd have run right home." Sybil still sounded scared as she spoke. "Aren't you early?"

"The car broke down a mile or so up the road. I had to walk in this cold!" Anger again filled his voice.

"Can I help?" asked Addie.

"She can't see," Sybil whispered.

Stoney turned from Sybil to Addie, then back to Sybil, expecting an explanation. *Don't tell him that,* thought Addie, but she said nothing. When no clarification was given, he commanded, "Let's go. We've got work to do!"

Sybil dove into her coat murmuring an inaudible apology to Addie. As Stoney hurried her toward the door, Addie patted his back and said, "Don't you two overdo it. You've got that little one to think of." At this, Stoney released his grasp on the trembling girl. "Can I call someone to tow you or something?" Addie ventured.

"No, thank you, ma'am," Stoney replied. "I don't mean

to sound ungrateful, but my wife and I like to keep to our-selves."

"I respect that," said Addie and the couple disappeared into the fading afternoon.

For a long time Addie stood at the door wondering what she should do. There was no denying that she was fright-ened, for herself as well as for Sybil. She would call the Robertses, and if they felt it was necessary, she would alert the sheriff as well. She would not tell Joe.

Struggling, Addie dialed the private number Elsa and Henry had sent her after they moved in with their daughter. An answering machine informed her that they were unavail-able. Addie remembered that the couple often spent the winter holidays with Elsa's cousin in Arizona and would not return until after the New Year. She didn't have that number and not wanting to alarm them, Addie hung up without leaving a message.

Should she call Bill Johnson? If he interrogated them and did nothing, as she knew could easily happen since no law had been broken, would that just provoke Stoney more? Still, she would not tell Joe. She would stay alert and hope for the best. If anything else happened, she *would* call Bill. If not, she would call Elsa after the holidays and be sure she was aware of the couple in her cabin.

As evening fell, Addie restlessly rummaged through an old storage closet for a photo album which would take her back to that magical first pregnancy. When Sybil asked what it was like, a bittersweet recollection had surfaced. There weren't many pictures. It wasn't like when Michael was born and Joe and Judy photographed him waking and sleeping. But there were a few, etched in Addie's memory with both love and sorrow surrounding them.

At the bottom of a worn box, Addie found the album

and gently retrieved it. She took it out into the light of the kitchen and gingerly opened it. Perhaps she should have known, but she was not prepared. The yellowed pictures were only forms without faces. Blurs without names stared up at her. Pulling out a large, flat magnifying glass, she strained to distinguish them, but still the images were unclear. Tears welled up in her eyes with the realization that she could not look upon Jacob's or their baby's photographs and see those familiar poses. The pictures were lost to her, as were the two of them.

"We're going to have a baby, Jacob." Addie blurted the words, forgetting all the different ways she had planned throughout the day to tell him. Her farmer husband stood before her, a lack of comprehension in his ever-sparkling eyes. His tousled hair and dirty hands and trousers were evidence of his long hours in the field. The late summer harvest of 1941, was keeping him busy well into the evenings.

"Addie, I haven't had dinner. I haven't even washed my hands. And you tell me we're going to what?" Then he threw back his head and burst into laughter. He swung Addie up into his arms, kissing her. "A baby? Oh, Addie, really? A baby? Our baby?" Tears shone in his eyes as they stood in silence in the kitchen of the little house, clinging fiercely to each other.

"I hope he looks like you, Addie. Fair, with big blue eyes. We wouldn't want him to look like me."

"I disagree!" Addie responded. "I can think of nothing better than having a son just like you in every way, Jacob."

"But what if he's a girl? You don't want a girl that looks like me!"

Addie studied Jacob intently. "I want a boy and a girl who look like you, and one each who look like me, and

75

maybe a couple who are a good mix. How would that be?"

"I'll be an old man before we have all of those children. I won't be able to keep up with them."

"No one works as hard as you, Jacob," Addie said seriously. "I think they'll all have a hard time keeping up with you."

Jacob held her then, his big strong arms wrapped about her. A new person was to become a part of their lives, unknown as yet, but like Addie, protected and safe within Jacob's arms.

When the harvest ended, they busied themselves preparing for the baby. Jacob and his father added a room to the tiny house, giving them a separate bedroom of their own with an alcove for a nursery. An old wooden cradle, which hung from ropes in the barn, was lowered and prepared for another McNeil infant. Jacob's mother taught Addie to knit, a blanket first and later, tiny booties. Together, the women sewed a quilt coverlet for the cradle. With its new coat of varnish, it glistened as it waited patiently in the new bedroom.

As autumn turned to winter, Addie also changed. Her cheeks glowed constantly, and Jacob told her she was more beautiful than ever. When the weather permitted, their long walks together holding hands were filled with conversation about the child who would soon be joining them. They argued lightheartedly over names and what he or she would become when grown up. Addie painted a picture in their minds of a young ballerina who became an actress and brought fortune to her parents and fame to her home in southeastern Colorado.

Jacob insisted that their male offspring would become the president of the United States, thereby really putting their town on the map. "He'll be good and decent," said Jacob soberly.

"Like his father," added Addie, and he pulled her close to him.

"He'll be the man to put an end to all wars, Addie. No other man will ever have to stand and look at his wife bearing their first child and wonder if he'll have to leave them to fight a war."

"No, Jacob. Please don't say that. Try not to think about the war."

"You're right, I'm sorry," he apologized. "But he will be a great man, because his mother is Adeline McNeil if for no other reason."

"Adeline!" She laughed, remembering the confusion over her name on their first date. "I believe that she'll be a great woman because she will have such a fine father to look up to. I pity her husband, though."

"Pity a man for having a beautiful wife?"

"For her father's big shoes that some poor fellow will have to fill!"

At night as they lay in bed and listened to the first winds of winter shaking their home, Jacob held her even more tenderly than before. "I love you so much, Addie. You have brought me more joy than I ever dreamed possible."

"Sometimes it all feels like a dream, Jacob," she whispered back. "Can you imagine a baby here with us? Can you imagine it waking us in the night? And learning to talk with us and following you about in the fields? Oh, Jacob, think of it!"

"I am, darling. I can't stop thinking of it!"

Some nights they lay with moonlight flooding their bed and talked long into the dark. Now that the fields were resting, Jacob was with her often during the day. The crib began to fill with diapers and tiny nightgowns, some made and some given by excited neighbors and loved ones. It *was* a dream, a soft and glorious dream that began with Sarah's decision to ride in a roadster, while Addie took the streetcar with Jacob by default. It was a wonderful, blissful dream, until Pearl Harbor entered, cold and unexpected, waking them all from their slumber.

Sybil returned to Addie's a few days after the incident with Stoney. She apologized profusely for him, explaining to Addie that he wasn't really like that. He'd been working hard and was overtired and worried about her. Then the problem with the car hadn't helped matters any. But he had told Sybil he liked Addie and wanted his "wife" to help her out as much as she could. A few hours each week wouldn't hurt anything. She'd still have time to rest, Stoney thought. And was the cake a success? Was the party fun?

Addie assured her young friend that the cake was as good as any Mother McNeil had ever made and the party had bolstered a little Christmas spirit in her. This response prompted Sybil to insist on a Christmas tree with a chain of strung popcorn and homemade ornaments. Addie resisted. Spending the holidays in the city with Joe and his family would be plenty of Christmas for her. But Sybil would not be dissuaded. She arrived one morning with a three-foot-high scraggly pine, probably property of the U.S. Forest Service. Addie didn't ask where it came from.

The completion of the decorated tree took several days of Sybil's youthful chatter. Addie felt herself a sort of St. Nicholas, giving the girl the gifts of time and someone to listen without rebuke or criticism. Sybil's gift of her presence became a welcome break for Addie. Now that she could no longer drive or read a book for hours, she often found herself at loose ends, wishing for a diversion.

Sybil's visits lasted only two hours and she watched the

time closely, hoping that Addie didn't notice. When exactly two hours had passed, she made an excuse to return home, always followed by an awkward moment while she waited for the few dollars that she would receive for her time. Addie soon realized that she was Sybil's job. Stoney was allowing her to go to work, not to be a neighbor or a friend. This was acceptable to Addie, although it was not something she would tell Joe.

The tree was a source of comfort to Addie in the evenings before Christmas. Although she couldn't make out the details of the ornaments, a tiny strand of lights they'd found in the storage closet twinkled like distant stars. The white popcorn contrasted with the dark pine forming a wavy line around the tree. Nor was their work finished once the tree stood adorned. Each time Sybil came, they had the task of redecorating it after Rufus dismantled it while Addie slept. He seemed to particularly enjoy eating the popcorn.

Addie could predict Sybil's arrival to the minute, so it was a surprise when she heard a knock at the door late one afternoon. It was past time for both Sybil and the mailman, and she had talked to Joe on the phone only ten minutes before. A Christmas card from Fran, read and discussed thoroughly by Sybil, had informed Addie that her friend so enjoyed the warm climate that they had decided to stay in Florida through the holidays.

The dark form that appeared before her when she cracked the door was that of a man. In the fading light of day, Addie could tell little about him, only that he was large and had bushy hair, perhaps even a beard.

"Ma'am?"

"Stoney?"

"I'm sorry to bother you, ma'am," a deep, serious voice

said. "I'm missing my dog, a black Lab. Have you seen him about here by any chance?"

"Why, no, I haven't." Still startled by the intrusion, Addie remained in the doorway. Acknowledging for once Joe's warnings, she did not invite him in. "You're not Stoney? You're not my neighbor?" She stammered. "It's dark and the light is bad. I can't really see you, I can't tell, I mean . . ."

"I *am* your neighbor. I live across the lake. I just bought the old logging cabin where the mill used to be."

Addie remembered the run-down shack nearly lost among the trees and growth after years of neglect. The mill had not been operational in all of the years Addie had known the lake, and the property was surrounded by a high metal fence bearing "No Trespassing" signs. As intriguing as it had been to children, all of the youngsters in the area were forbidden by their parents to go near the place. Years before the Marshes had purchased their cabin on the lake, a twelve-year-old visitor had been seriously injured when a piece of flooring caved in while he and a group of cousins were exploring the camp. The county sheriff had imposed strict penalties for trespassing after that, and many meetings were held about having the mill torn down completely. But over the years politics and apathy set in. The logging camp deteriorated and was eventually forgotten as anything other than an eyesore.

Joe had managed to keep it alive during their summers at the lake by relishing in and repeating stories that the land was haunted by angry Indian spirits who objected to the plunder of the wilderness by the loggers years ago. In time nature saw to it that the dilapidated buildings and fixtures were swallowed up by the earth. Only the cabin remained, hidden from both the lake and the road above it by towering spruce and pines.

And so to this surprising new bit of information, Addie responded, "I didn't even know that place was still livable!"

"It will be when I'm finished. For now, I'm making do." The stranger shifted impatiently, then asked again, "Have you seen my dog? It's not like him to disappear like this."

"No, I'm sorry. I've been here all day, but I haven't noticed a dog."

"Thanks anyway." He turned to leave but with another thought came back again. "Listen, if you do see him, would you mind sending word over to me? I don't have a phone yet. No lines that far away. I probably won't be able to get a phone in until spring when the ground thaws."

"Yes, of course." Addie opened the door wider. He seemed kind enough, and she wanted to know more about his plans for the lumber camp. "Rufus and I will be on the lookout for him, and I'll send word if he shows up here." Rufus would indeed be very much aware of a black dog infringing on his territory.

"Thank you, ma'am." He turned a second time to leave.

"What's the dog's name?" Addie called after him.

"Blaze."

As he headed down the steps Addie called to him once again. "Would you like to come in for coffee and warm up a bit before you continue looking? It's awfully cold out there!"

"No, thank you." As the snow crunched beneath his heavy boots he added almost to himself, "I prefer to keep to myself."

For a long time, she'd had no winter neighbors. Now that she did, they all seemed to prefer solitude. Addie sighed remembering a time long ago on Bear Lake when no one turned down a good cup of coffee.

Chapter 5

The meeting room was particularly crowded, and a hum of conversation filled the air. After weeks of relentless cold and snow, a bright, sunny morning had dawned on Pinecliffe. Carol Wilmont's phone had rung repeatedly with calls from support group members who had canceled their ride due to the weather, but had a change of heart on awakening. Expertly, Gordon wove his way through the group, stopping at the empty chair next to Addie where she was already seated waiting for the meeting to begin.

"Well, Walter," Addie laughed. "Gordon's found your pew!"

"Is that you, Addie?" Walter joined her laughter. "He must know I like sitting next to you. Actually," he whispered, "I told him." As if in agreement with Walter's assessment, Gordon nuzzled Addie's hand until she gave in and scratched his head.

"I'm ruining your dog guide," Addie said. "He's so lovable, I just can't help it."

"He knows it, too! But it's okay. I'm seated now, and he's off duty."

As Walter turned to greet Susanna and her mother on his other side, the chair to Addie's left was slowly pulled back. "Hello!" she chimed. "Isn't it a gorgeous day for our meeting?"

"Hello," was the shallow response.

"David," Addie said, recognizing his lean frame and stoic voice. "We missed you at the Christmas party, and you missed a good time."

"I was out of town." Addie sensed his tension and wondered if she should leave him alone. Yet on this day, she, too, was experiencing a relief from the cabin fever that had held her hostage, when even Sybil wouldn't chance walking in the storm. After too many conversations with Rufus, she longed for human contact.

"You went away for the holidays?" she ventured.

For a moment, she thought he hadn't heard her or wouldn't respond. Finally, he told her, "My folks live in Iowa and my daughter is going to college there. So we all spent Christmas together in their home."

"You probably had better weather than we've been having here." Addie turned to face him now, hoping their conversation would continue.

His dismal response did not encourage her. "It was all right."

"Does your daughter like college?"

"Yes."

"I'll bet she's a good student."

"Yes."

The knot deep inside that often formed when she thought about blindness, returned. It was not for her own sake, however, that Addie's discomfort grew, but for the man sitting next to her. David was a farmer, like Jacob, but he could no longer work his land. The spirit that outdoor living had bolstered in both Addie and Jacob was tragically missing in him. Addie wished she had known David before his accident. Had there once been life beneath this shell of a person? Addie suspected that there had.

"I'm May Evans from here in Pinecliffe and I have glaucoma. It's stable, thank God for that!" The familiar introductions began.

"Quiet! Quiet, everyone!" Laura's voice rose above

May's. "The meeting is starting."

The din of conversation stopped abruptly as though the volume switch had been turned off on a radio. Jovial greetings faded away to the more serious business at hand. A new member was introduced, another longtime resident of the village, who lamented, "I guess time is catching up with me. Nothing works like it used to. My eyes, my ears, or my legs." A sympathetic murmur followed.

When Walter's turn came, he took a few moments to tell another anecdote of his childhood growing up with his over-zealous brothers. One summer, between fishing and swimming in the pond, they decided to teach him to play baseball. At a church social his brothers saw to it that he was placed on the opposing team. But their plans were foiled when he hit the winning home run, and he never let them forget it.

Next, Addie admitted the truth about her Christmas cake when she was complimented by Laura. "I had help baking it. The neighbor girl came over, and after cleaning up the mess and tossing the first cake, we got it right!"

"What happened to the first cake?" Cecil asked.

"It was charbroiled," laughed Addie. "I didn't think barbecue sauce would sit very well with chocolate."

As everyone laughed merrily, Laura commented, "We have a couple of lighthearted folks here today, don't we?"

"Well, it stops with me!" David's voice fell like ice over the room, and silence was immediate. He pushed his chair back to leave, but Addie impulsively reached over and touched him.

"David, we meant no harm," she said softly.

"Do you think it's funny?" he demanded. "Do you think that all of these asinine results of not having vision are entertaining? I'm sorry, but *I* don't!"

Addie felt him shake beneath her hand, and slowly she removed it. She tried to speak, but words failed her.

It was Walter who came to the rescue. "David, none of us thinks that being blind or visually impaired is funny. It is a fact of our lives; it's who we are. And that characteristic, which is part of us, sometimes produces consequences that are amusing. That's true of all people, whatever their special circumstances are."

"If we can't laugh, David, then all that's left is to cry," added Susanna. "I've been where you are now, and I know that. I truly know it."

"Humor is good medicine," interjected Laura. "Sometimes we all have to make that choice. As Susanna said, we can laugh or cry about our personal difficulties."

"Maybe crying is his choice right now. Leave him alone!" Leo called out. "C'mon, let's get on with the meeting." His fingers drummed impatiently on the table.

"Look, I'm sorry," David muttered as he scooted his chair back into place. Addie breathed a sigh of relief. "It's a hard time right now. Winter, the holidays. I don't even know why I come to these meetings. I suppose I'm feeling sorry for myself. Spring's coming. I want to be back out in the fields. I can't do it. I don't like who I am now. I liked who I was before I went blind." Then, his voice cracking, he added, "I don't mean to take it out on you guys. You're all wonderful people."

"That's okay, David. That's what we're here for, remember?" It was Alice who spoke this time. "Believe me, I've been there, too. I've been on both sides of the fence, the laughing side and the crying side."

"Which side is best?" asked Maggie, sitting next to Cecil.

"Oh, you know me," Alice laughed. "I thrive in sunshine."

The introductions resumed and were followed by the usual announcements and updates. The storm had passed for now, or so Addie thought. David sat quietly beside her, the familiar smell of English Leather dancing between them. When Laura suggested a discussion topic of coping with winter doldrums, Walter interrupted her.

"That's a great topic, Laura, and I think we all need it, especially after the last few weeks." His voice was kind and soothing. "But first, may I go back to something David said awhile ago?"

No, thought Addie.

"Go ahead," Laura encouraged.

"About working your farm, David," Walter said softly. "You said that you can't."

"I don't know how I could, like this."

"I know I'm an old codger," Walter laughed, "and farming's changed from my day. But I was a farmer and rancher my whole life, and I couldn't see. Sure, I had help. And yes, it was tough at times. But I did it. I think that you can do it, too. Maybe not everything, and maybe not the way you used to."

"I don't know, Walter," David hesitated. "I know you mean well, but—"

"Listen," Walter encouraged, "There's a way. I know there is. You can't drive, that's a given. But the rest of it, why not? There's technology out there that can help you. Computers with screen readers for your business files. Adaptations for your tools. Mobility. A cane, a dog guide, who knows?"

"That's right, David," said Laura. "There are 'agribility' experts who can evaluate your operation and give you suggestions. I'll find out whom to call and help you set up a meeting, if you want. You may not have to give up the career you've loved all of your life just because of the accident that robbed you of your sight. Walter's right. You've got to fight back."

David did not respond. Addie thought she heard him crying.

"How about it, David?" Walter encouraged. "Let Laura see what she can find out, and I'll get together with you and give you my dose of farm sense. I have all kinds of unorthodox ideas you can try."

"Okay." David said softly. It seemed to Addie that he relaxed a bit in his chair as her own spirits lifted in celebration for him.

The meeting ended, as always, with refreshments and fellowship. Laura joined Addie as she filled her coffee cup in the kitchenette and returned to the table.

"You know, Addie," she said, "You could have made that cake by yourself. Like we told David, there are ways of getting around obstacles that prevent you from doing what you enjoy when you lose your eyesight."

"Really, Laura, I'm doing well," Addie protested. "I have a lovely neighbor girl who doesn't mind assisting me."

"It's good to have help, Addie. At times it's more practical to let someone else help out. But there's so much you could be doing for yourself. It's a confidence builder to know you have that choice—to get help or to do it on your own if you'd rather. I'm not trying to push you, Addie, but I wish you'd let me schedule a visit with you sometime. I want to make you aware of the possibilities."

"Perhaps later," Addie said. "In the spring or summer. It's so snowy at the lake right now, and then we have mud season. I wouldn't want you to get stuck. I'll let you know."

"All right, but I can come sooner if you change your mind. I have a four-wheel drive, and . . ."

"Thank you," Addie stopped her. "Is Carol here yet? I don't want to miss my ride."

"Not yet."

"Hey, Miss Addie!" The tap of a long white cane against the table got Addie's attention. Leo slid into an empty chair nearby. He folded the cane into several sections and wrapped an attached band around it. "Leopold is here!" he drawled as Laura turned to speak to someone else. "I'm the youngest guy in the group," he said.

"And I'm probably the oldest," Addie conceded.

"You are not," he objected. "Some of these people are much older than you. But no matter. I have a question for you."

"What is it?"

"Why didn't you call me when you burned that cake? I would have eaten it, man. I live on burned food. Ask Laura." He raised his voice. "You there, Laura? Don't I burn everything?"

Her voice was further away now, but she had heard him. "You're doing a lot better, Leo. Much better."

"Aw, she's just being nice. I can't believe you threw a whole cake away, Miss Addie," he teased. "I live for desserts. That's why I come to these meetings, for the refreshments, you know?"

"Me, too," said Addie. "But that's a secret, so don't tell."

"You can count on me." He rose and turned away, flinging open the cane before him. "Yep, I come here for refreshments. That, and to argue with Cecil. He's my buddy, man. One cool dude."

Why did she come? Addie wondered. Why did she say 'yes' when Carol called her now? As if thinking out loud, she asked, "Why do you really come, Leo?"

There was a short pause before he answered, "Because I need this. Because right now, it's all I've got." The tapping of the cane resumed as he proceeded around the table. "Later, Miss Addie!"

Jacob McNeil, Jr. was born in a small rural hospital in southeastern Colorado in March of 1942. A healthy, robust child, he soon came to be called Jake so as not to be confused with his father. On the day of his birth, Addie's hopes were rewarded by his scraggly crop of brown hair and matching dark eyes—he was the image of his father. In those early days of life, a slight sparkle often filled his sleepy eyes, although in time it was a more serious nature that defined him.

Jacob McNeil, Sr. was fighting in Europe when his son was born in America. Addie's father-in-law sent him a telegram immediately following the birth. A few days later, Addie sent her own thoughts and feelings in a letter.

My darling Jacob,

I have just fed our little Jake and laid him in the cradle where he is already asleep. We arrived home from the hospital yesterday, and although it is wonderful to be here, I miss you terribly. I know Jake senses that something is missing, too. But we comfort each other—it makes me so happy to hold him and to touch him.

Oh, Jacob, he is beyond anything you might imagine. He looks just like you. I am amazed that you and I, in our love for each other, created this tiny new person. He's a good baby, not fussy or irritable. He has a strong voice and will use it when he has a reason, but those times are rare. His eyes twinkle just like yours, Jacob! I can't wait to share him with you. Win the war, darling, as quickly as you can! Your son wants to meet you and I miss you so.

Your father was here this morning on his way to the south field. As you know, all of the men from around here are off fighting in the war, and he's working the farm alone. He hoped to hire the Davis boys from down the road, but guess what? They've signed up, too. Only six-teen and seventeen years old! Can you believe that? They're just children. Since you are the only one of your father's sons who wants to farm for a living, I'm so glad that we now have a boy. We'll make a farmer of him soon enough! In the meantime, I promised your dad that I'd help him myself as soon as I am able. He looked worn out this morning. I've read that many women are working in factories to do the jobs of the men who are overseas. I see no reason why I can't assist with the chores around here. Your mother can watch Jake, or I'll strap him on my back like a papoose and take him with me. Stop scowling, Jacob! I can see you all the way from here!

I promise to write you every day, darling, so that you will know everything our little Jake does. Maybe that way you won't feel like you're missing so much. My love is with you wherever you go, whatever you do, and I know it is strong enough to bring you back home soon. I am proud of you for defending our freedom, and so is your son.

I love you always,
Addie

Addie pictured the few months each year when the

surface of Bear Lake froze and was subsequently dusted with snow. If she had not known a lake was there in the wintertime, it might have been an open meadow covered in white. In spite of the cold, devoted fishermen with ice augers and folding stools ventured onto the lake, dotting the landscape as forlorn solitary statues. But most of the time, Bear Lake was undisturbed by humans during the long quiet of winter. Addie knew that in time the snow-packed paths to the lake changed to mud and tiny green buds appeared to replace the brittle twigs of the previous year. She also imagined how the water began to shine through the ice in spots until it eventually gave way to the spectacular renewal of the lake.

One day at the beginning of spring, Addie sat on her porch while Rufus made a game of chasing a stray pinecone across the floor. It was good to sit outside again, to be an immediate spectator to the subtle changes in the world about her. The sounds and smells of nature and the blurred mass of budding green refreshed her spirit.

A voice calling up to her from the path to the lake inter-rupted her meditation. "Excuse me, ma'am?"

She had heard this masculine voice before but couldn't identify it.

"I'm sorry to bother you." He hesitated on the path, not wanting to intrude.

"It's all right. Who are you? I can't see you in the glare . . ." She shielded her face with her hand.

"Your neighbor. From the logging camp across the lake."

"Yes, of course. Please join me," Addie welcomed the visitor, although Rufus wasn't thrilled as he sauntered to the far end of the porch.

He approached the cabin, stopping just short of the

91

steps. "Is that your boat at the bottom here? Attached to the pier?"

"Yes, it's mine. Have a seat." She gestured to the other rocker, but he remained standing. "It's just an old rowboat. My son and grandson sometimes take it fishing."

"Well, it's come untied," he told her. "You're going to lose it. The ice must have held it in place all winter, but it's melting now and your boat's drifting away."

"Oh, dear," said Addie. "Can I trouble you to pull it back in and tie it up? My son may not be out for awhile and . . ."

"No problem. I didn't want to be tying it here if it wasn't yours."

"It's mine," she affirmed, "and I appreciate your help."

"Sure."

"Will you join me for coffee?" she asked hopefully.

"No, thanks. I like to . . ."

"Keep to yourself," she interrupted, and to Addie's surprise, he laughed.

"I guess you've got my number, all right!"

"Then I won't detain you," Addie promised, "but tell me before you leave. Did you find your dog?"

"Yes, I did. He's lying on my boat right now. We were fishing, and he preferred sleeping to walking up here with me."

"Rufus thanks him," said Addie.

"Your husband?"

"No, a good friend," she laughed, nodding in the direction of the cat. "One more question and I'll quit being a nosy old lady."

"You aren't," he responded good-naturedly.

"I remember you called your dog Blaze. What is your name?"

He approached the steps, climbing onto the porch. "I'm sorry, I guess I never introduced myself." Extending an unseen hand he continued, "I'm Paul Curtis."

"Paul, I'm Addie Marsh." He took her outstretched hand and squeezed it warmly. "How's your project with the logging camp coming along?"

"You said no more questions," he reminded her lightly.

"So I did."

"Let me explain." She saw the arm motions as he shoved his hands into his pockets facing her squarely. "I guess you'd say I'm a recluse. I served in Vietnam and the Gulf War. I'm not up to anything or intending to be rude. I've just reached a point in my life where I need time alone. Fortunately, I have the resources to do it, and this seems like a mighty good place to be a hermit."

"It is," said Addie. "I've been accused of it myself."

"Good," he sighed. "Then we understand each other."

"We do indeed." Addie thought a moment before saying, "I have veterans in my background. Vietnam. World War II. I've nothing but admiration for you fellows."

"That's good," he repeated. "Not everyone feels that way."

"No, I guess not. I believe you sacrifice much more than most people realize. Sometimes, you give everything."

"I'll tie your boat up tight," he offered, changing the subject. "It looks like it survived the winter. It could use a little paint, maybe a few repairs. One of the seats is sagging pretty badly."

"Thanks," said Addie. "We'll see to it."

With that he hurried back down the hill before Addie could tell him good-bye. In a few moments, she had another visitor.

Everyone's in such a hurry, aren't they? he asked.

93

Yes, Addie sighed and rested her head against the back of the chair.

I'll sit with you awhile. I'll be your eyes and tell you what I see on the lake, he offered.

She smiled, gently rocking back and forth. Rufus jumped into her lap, his motor purring loudly. *Thank you, Jacob. Tell me what you see.*

Addie awoke with a start, unsure for how long she had dozed. Rufus had left her lap for a new conquest. It was still daylight, Addie realized; she hadn't been asleep for long. The thought that had abruptly awakened her tugged at the back of her mind. What was it that was troubling her so?

Then she remembered. Paul Curtis had said that the boat had made it through the winter, but it needed paint and a few repairs. It occurred to Addie that if the boat was covered with its old canvas tarp, he couldn't have known that. Joe and his father had built the boat together the summer after his senior year in high school. It was the summer Joe was hurting with a pain that knows no healing. His father had used the project to distract him, to distract all of them.

Joe treasured that boat even more now that his father was dead. As Michael had grown up, it became a special bond between Joe and his own son as well. He took meticulous care of it and covered and docked the wooden craft before the first cold spell.

Last fall had been no different. Joe and Judy had visited on Labor Day weekend for a picnic. Michael had chosen not to join them, but to see a concert with his friends instead. Before they left, Joe had hiked down and taken the boat out of the lake, then covered it up because he feared his newest project at work would keep him from returning in the coming months.

Wistfully he'd said, "I'd drop it all in a minute if Mike would join me for a day, but that's pretty unlikely, isn't it?" Judy had soothed his ruffled feathers by reminding him that their son was in college and that hanging out with his parents wasn't exactly "cool."

It was Michael, Addie now realized, who had left the boat uncovered and not securely tied. He and two other boys had surprised Addie one unseasonably warm Saturday late in October. Michael asked his grandmother's permission to take the boat out on the lake. They had retrieved several poles and other pieces of fishing gear from the shed where Joe kept them stored. They had rushed off in high spirits down the hill to the pier. Addie reminded him that his dad had already covered the boat for the winter, and he had promised to leave it as they found it.

After dark, she had heard them trudging up the hill, full of laughter and noise. They had been famished and she'd warmed soup from a can and made sandwiches. "Did you cover the boat again?" Addie had asked him as they sat down to eat.

"Oh, gosh, Gram. I forgot!"

"We left the poles in it, too," one of his friends reminded him.

"Well, eat your dinner. Then you'll have to take flashlights and run back down. Your dad will have a fit if it's left like that."

"I know, Gram. We will," he'd promised. "As a matter of fact, Dad will have a fit if he even knows we drove out here and went fishing today. We're supposed to be spending the night at Pete's studying for midterms next week."

At Addie's disappointed frown, he shrugged sheepishly.

"It's okay, Gram." Tenderhearted and sensitive, Michael was not as responsible as his father would have liked. He was so different from Addie's own two sons that he was a constant source of adventure and surprise. Michael could melt her heart with a simple smile, and he loved her deeply in return.

"I don't like you hiking down there in the dark, but it must be done. Be extra careful," she'd warned. "I'm too old to be pulling you out of the lake."

"You know, Gram, the guys and I were talking out on the boat. It's a great night outside and we've got sleeping bags in the jeep."

"From a camping trip in July," one of the others said, holding his nose.

"We thought we could sleep on the porch tonight. That way we'd be up first thing in the morning to cover the boat. You know, take care of it in daylight so it's done right. What does my lovely grandma think about that?"

"You are a charmer, aren't you?" Addie had laughed. "Your lovely grandma wants to know what about your midterms?"

"We studied all yesterday afternoon and again this morning. How about it, Gram?"

"All right, you win. But you'd better call your parents, Mike, and let them know where you are."

"Do I have to, Grandma? We told Pete's mom we were driving out to see you. She's cool. So if anything happens, they'll be able to find us. But if nothing happens, why bother them with details?"

"Michael . . ."

"Please, Gram?"

And so, they had stayed. The next morning they had slept in, startled to learn what time it was when Addie finally woke them. They'd hurried about frantically preparing to leave, since Pete had to be to work by 10:00 a.m. In all the confusion, everyone had forgotten about the boat.

Now, all these months later, Addie remembered. She realized with dismay that the boat had remained uncovered throughout the winter. She also knew that the fishing gear had been equally exposed to the elements, if it had survived at all. She would be partially to blame when Joe made the discovery. One more reason to be unhappy with his son and one step closer to Gateway for Addie.

Sitting in her rocker above the lake, she contemplated what to do. When Sybil returned at the beginning of the week, she would ask if Stoney might be willing to have a look at the boat. Maybe he could find some paint in the garage and touch it up so that Joe wouldn't notice. If she managed somehow to bring the fishing poles and gear up to the house, perhaps she could clean them herself and return them to storage before Joe missed them. And she would give Michael a good scolding the next time she saw him.

It was Saturday. Sybil never visited on the weekends when Stoney was home. Another thought occurred to Addie. Perhaps Paul might still be on the lake fishing. If so, she'd flag him down and explain her dilemma. Perhaps he'd carry the gear for her and cover the boat until Stoney could work on it. With luck, Joe might not be aware of the condition of his boat until everything had been attended to.

Her decision made, Addie pulled on her rubber mudboots. As she headed down the murky path she was encouraged by her progress, however slow. Her peripheral vision allowed her to maneuver fairly well, although she realized that her depth perception was becoming increasingly distorted. She could not see the path at her feet at all. Still, the dark line of the distant trail against the grass, dotted with patches of unmelted snow, created enough contrast that she followed it to the bottom. When she reached the lake, Addie found the boat neatly tied alongside the small wooden pier that jutted out from the end of the path. She tried to scan the lake, but with her limited sight, no forms were visible. All was quiet except the occasional call of a bird from the trees overhead. Cupping her hands, she shouted, "Hellooo! Paul? Anyone out there? Hellooo!"

The only response was from Rufus, who had gingerly followed her to the end of the dock. "Where did you come from?" Addie asked nervously. "Never mind. Today I wish you were a dog, or a pack horse, or something useful! Now what have I gotten myself into?"

Carefully, Addie lowered herself to a sitting position, dangling her legs into the boat. Her neighbor had tied it at its regular spot against the dock. "Well, there's no turning back now," she murmured. "I might as well get this over with." Gently, she slipped into the boat, running her hands across the seats and floorboards to inspect it. Three scattered fishing poles were located, along with an open tackle box. As she ran her hands under the wooden benches, Addie also retrieved a net and two empty pop bottles.

"Damn it, Michael!" she cursed, then felt a pang. "I love you, but damn it again!" She sat squarely on the middle seat and lifted the items one by one from the boat to the dock. When this was accomplished, she carefully climbed out, clinging to the end of the pier for stability.

It was beginning to grow dark as Addie searched but could not locate the cover. She crawled across the pier, using one of the poles to prod the edge of the shore. Nothing. This she would have to leave to Stoney. In spite of her present predicament, it amused her to think that she was pinning her hopes on a young man she didn't trust, whose repair skills might not live up to Sybil's fantasies.

Addie bundled together the poles and net laden with trash. Carrying them in one hand and the tackle box in the other, she found it more difficult to maneuver. Slowly, cautiously, she began climbing the slope back to her home. She was relieved that there was still adequate daylight away from the dense brush of the shoreline. Long before she'd realized how much her vision was deteriorating, she had noticed it was difficult to see at night without light.

Rufus ran ahead of Addie, stopping occasionally to wait for her. One step at a time, deliberate, careful, not much further . . . Later, she remembered that one of the poles had slipped, and her legs had become tangled in it. She remembered falling and crying out, before hearing the tackle box roll down the hill and darkness swallowed her.

Chapter 6

"Addie, Addie?"

Addie struggled to open her eyes to the dim light. Her mind was heavy and thick, unable to comprehend. The smell of disinfectants floating on stale air hinted that she was in a hospital room.

"Addie?"

"Dr. John, is that you?" As the man reached toward her, Addie's eyes fell shut and she was once again engulfed in blackness.

"Addie?" The profile of a uniformed soldier filled the doorway of the farm cottage where she sat rocking her baby to sleep. He knocked lightly, even after he knew she'd seen him. For one moment her heart told her what her mind knew could not be true.

A telegram had arrived several days before informing her that her husband had given his life in service to his country. But the glare from the afternoon sunlight surrounding the visitor was deceiving, and Addie whispered, "Jacob?"

Quietly she studied the fair, broad-shouldered man who stood before her with only a screen separating them. Freckled, with deep blue eyes, everything about him was different from the man whose death she could not accept. She watched him remove his cap, and fumble it nervously in his hands. In spite of his size, he seemed timid, almost frightened. Against a rising sense of panic, she wished he'd disappear and leave her alone with the gentle breeze outside her door intermingled in the soft hum of her lullaby. Jake opened his eyes, questioning the song's sudden end and the tightness in his mother's arms.

"Addie McNeil?" the man repeated tentatively. "I'm sorry if I startled you."

When she did not respond, he added, "I'm Sergeant George Marsh. I'm a friend of your husband. May I come in?"

"Why are you here?" she answered, cold and distant.

"Please, may I come in?" The sergeant's soft, sad eyes met hers and held them.

She sighed in resignation, "Yes, come in."

He remained standing, blocking the outline of the door. "You *are* Addie?" he reaffirmed, but continued before she could speak. "Yes, I know you are. It's exactly as Jacob described. You, this place, and—the baby."

"Will you sit down?"

"Thank you." He lowered himself onto a chair as though exhausted, resting his head briefly in the palms of his large hands. He sighed, then sat straight and tall, as he remembered that he was a soldier representing his country. Still, the words did not come easily. "I, uh, I've . . ."

The baby, now fully awake, sat up in his mother's lap and grinned shyly at the stranger before placing a small, wet thumb into his mouth.

"I fought alongside Jacob and got to know him well in the time we spent together," he began.

"He told me about you in his letters." Clinging to the hope that the message had been a mistake, she leaned forward and looked beyond the sun-filled doorway. "Is it possible . . . ?"

The pain in the young soldier's eyes answered the question for both of them. "I wish it were so," he said. "As you were notified, Jacob was killed in action. He saved my life

101

and the lives of others. I was wounded and sent home immediately. I asked to accompany his remains and be with you. It was what he would have wanted."

A moan escaped from deep within Addie, then rose into the air as a wail. The soldier jumped up and gently took the startled baby from his mother, who had nearly dropped him in her despair. Just as quickly, the whimpering child was returned to her outstretched arms, where she enfolded him and broke into long, muffled sobs. "Oh, Jake! Oh, Jacob! Oh, dear God, help us!"

Addie did not know when Jacob's parents entered the room or who took the baby from her and rocked him to sleep. She remembered the sergeant asking if he could stay with them until after the burial. He asked to be called George and offered the story of Jacob's last battle. But as he began, Addie had left the room and disappeared into the field, to walk alone where she and Jacob had strolled many, many times before.

Later, when George was helping Mr. McNeil harvest the last of the summer broom-corn, Addie realized that the size of his upper body was due, in part, to thick-layered bandages around his chest. In spite of the elder farmer's objections, the young man worked tirelessly and refused to rest. At times, he seemed possessed by a silent rage that only hard, physical labor could dispel. As sweat covered his face, his hair curled into tiny childish ringlets. A teddy bear, Addie thought, as he cuddled Jake one evening after dinner. She could understand why Jacob had liked this strong, gentle man. He *was* a contrast to the man she so loved. At times awkward and uncomfortable, he was not as easy with people as Jacob had been. But his efforts were always sincere. He pushed himself to help, to partially fill the void Jacob's death had left.

Miles away from the farm when his friend was laid to rest in a veteran's cemetery, George spoke of Jacob's heroic actions, simply but movingly. His hands shook as he helped Addie into the car for the long drive home. When she buried her head and cried as they left the graveyard, he wiped his own eyes before carefully taking Jake from her lap and entertaining him on the way back to the farm.

As unexpectedly as he'd arrived, George Marsh left them a few days after the funeral. "I'm going back," he told them. "I owe it to Jacob, to all of you."

During the months that followed, Addie busied herself caring for Jake and working on the farm. She tried not to think, not to realize that her husband wasn't coming home. She refused to listen to reports of the war and cried herself to sleep in the loneliness of the bed they'd shared together.

The end of 1942 brought more bleak news. In spite of their efforts, the crops had not produced well; the farm was failing. Age and grief had taken the strength from the elder couple, and no amount of encouragement or long, hard hours of work from their daughter-in-law could revitalize them. Gradually, Jacob's mother spent more and more time in bed, unable to care for her home or the little grandson she adored. The war raged on, both in Europe and on a small farm in southeastern Colorado.

One evening, Addie's father-in-law arrived unexpectedly, with the same heavy air about him that had brought George Marsh to her door months before. "I've something to tell you, Addie." He was a man of few words, especially since his son's death and Addie waited for him to get to the point. "I'm selling the farm."

"You can't—" Addie began, but he held up his hand to stop her.

"Hear me out. It's for the best." He explained that he'd

had a substantial offer for the property, and both he and his
wife wanted to sell and move to Missouri, where their only
daughter lived. "I'm worn out. You've been a godsend to
me, Addie—all your hard work—but it isn't enough. Jacob's
brothers are enlisted and neither of them wants the farm
when the war is over."

"I'll work harder!" Addie insisted. "Jake's getting older
and I'm growing stronger and learning more every day.
Don't give up, Dad! We can do it! The war will end, and
we'll hire more help. Men will come back looking for work,
and . . ."

"Addie, Addie, stop!" He studied her with sad, tired
eyes. "It's for her," he said slowly, nodding his head toward
the big house. "Mama can't stay here any longer. There are
too many memories, too much pain for her here. All of her
children are gone now, and Jacob in his grave. I can't lose
her, too, Addie," he apologized. "You're welcome to come
with us to Missouri. You're like a daughter to us," he
added, his head ducked in embarrassment. "Or," he raised
his eyes and cleared his throat, "we'll see to it you're taken
care of. Part of the proceeds will be yours. It's only right,
after all. It was to be Jacob's farm when he returned."

"Who's buying the place?" Addie wanted to know.

"Just a man, no matter to me," he'd told her. "A man
who can look past the war and see the potential for this
farm. That's for a younger person now, not me. It's too
good an offer to pass up. If we try to run this place alone as
you and I've done this last year, there won't be anything left
to sell in a few years."

Lightly, he touched her arm and left, the door squeaking
behind him. Addie sat down, feeling old and tired herself.
Defeat hung like a rain cloud about to burst. She could
fight it no more.

In the end, she'd packed what belongings she could take, including the cradle, and the rest was sold at a farm auction before the new owners arrived. Addie boarded a train with her one-year-old son and moved to Denver. As they pulled out of the station, her in-laws waving from the ground below them, Addie remembered the last time that she had ridden a train. Feeling alone in spite of little Jake, she recalled how different that trip had been. It was two days before her marriage and Jacob had ridden with her from Denver, pointing out the familiar landmarks as they neared his home. It had been a magical time of love and expectation.

That was a distant memory now, and the long ride to Denver seemed endless. Exhausted by grief and the trip, Addie handed her crying toddler to Sarah, who stood with Daniel on the station platform at the end of their journey. A white-haired chauffeur whisked their belongings into the trunk of a long, shiny car. The driver would return for the larger items later. Two small nieces, who had been produced by Sarah in quick succession, eagerly greeted their relatives in the mansion that would be their new home. A nanny dressed in a crisp white uniform took immediate charge of Jake, despite Addie's objections.

"Now, now," cooed Sarah. "It's okay, Addie. She's very, competent. Nothing but the best for our daughters! You need your rest; you've got to get your spirit back. Oh, Addie, look at you, my poor little sister! You're home now. Let us take care of you. You're home." She pulled Addie into her arms, where the younger sister wept. Soon she slept.

"Mom, are you awake?"
"Joe, is that you?"

105

"Thank God!" Joe sat on the edge of the hospital bed and took his mother's hand in his. "How do you feel?" he asked gently.

"I'm all right." She tried to turn on her side. "Ouch!" she cried reaching for her chest. "What's happened to me?"

"You've cracked a rib," Joe told her. "That's what's hurting you. And you have a mild concussion. I hope that's all."

"I fell, didn't I? I remember. Down by the lake."

"Yes, what were you doing? Do you remember?" Turning away, he scowled. "Judy, see if the nurse can find Doc Siegfried and tell him Mom's awake. I don't think he's left the hospital yet."

"I was checking on the boat and got tangled up in the fishing poles," Addie recalled sheepishly. "I was trying to carry too much, I think."

"You stepped into a ten-inch-deep hole, Mom. I'm sure you never even saw it! What did you think you were doing out there?"

"It's my fault!" called another voice from the corner of the room. "Gram, I'm sorry! I forgot all about the boat. You shouldn't have—you should have called me."

"Michael, come here." Addie reached out for his hand. "I guess you and I are really in the doghouse now!"

"It's not funny, Mom! You could have been killed. Do you know how lucky you are?" Joe scolded.

Choking back tears, Michael continued, "It *is* my fault, Grandma. I was too busy thinking of myself and my fun, I wasn't being responsible. I'm glad you're not seriously hurt! I don't know what I'd do if something . . ." he broke down.

"What's this? No tears now. All is well!" Dr. Siegfried marched into the room, bringing sunshine with him. "Addie, old girl, how are you feeling?"

"I think I'll live, John," she smiled.

"I should hope so," he agreed. Then on a more sober note he added, "You've sustained a cracked rib. There really isn't much we can do for it except to let it heal. We don't bandage them anymore—just let nature take its course. The healing will take awhile, and it will remind you from time to time that it's there. Is the pain very bad right now?"

"It's tolerable." At that moment, Addie silently promised herself to endure it without complaint, no matter how bad it was.

"I can give you something for the pain."

"I can manage without, thank you."

"Let me check you over then." The doctor gently examined her before announcing, "You look good, Addie. I'm not seeing any residuals from the concussion. You were out for awhile."

"That explains why I don't know how I got here!" she laughed.

"Exactly. Are you having any dizziness or pain in your head?"

"No, nothing," said Addie. "Sign on the dotted line, and I'm ready to go home."

"Wait a minute, not so fast!" Dr. Siegfried laughed with her. Then seriously, he added, "I want you to spend the night in the hospital for observation. You'll need to see me for a follow-up. If you notice any changes—headache, nausea, anything like that—call me right away."

"Will do."

"Aren't you going to tell her not to try anything like that again?" Joe's tone was pensive.

"Well, I would hope she already knows that," the doctor said, gently patting Addie's arm.

"Now, wait a minute!" Joe demanded. "We're all acting warm and fuzzy here, as if nothing happened at all! Is everyone forgetting my mother hiked down to the lake on her own when she can't even see, trying to do God knows what?"

"Joe," Judy began, but he interrupted her.

"Are you saying, Doctor, that she should go home and resume business as usual?"

"What are you suggesting, Joe?" Dr. Siegfried turned to face the younger man.

"You know she shouldn't be living alone anymore. It's not safe! Why am I the only realistic one here?" Joe took a deep breath, looking squarely at the physician. "Tell her!" he demanded.

Dr. Siegfried walked to the bed table where he'd laid Addie's chart and studied it thoughtfully for several minutes before responding. At last, he said, "You were very lucky out there, Addie. You could have been seriously injured or even killed. You're lucky that you seem to have bones of steel."

"And a brain to match," added Addie.

"Mother," Joe warned, "will you please just listen for once?"

"Joe," Judy whispered again.

Dr. Siegfried cleared his throat before he continued. "What you did was foolish, Addie. I don't have to lecture you like a child. You know it yourself." Turning back to Joe he said, "You're right that your mother isn't altogether safe living on her own out at the lake. But I'm not going to tell you to put her in a home, either. We're all getting older, myself included. Your mother is fiercely independent, Joe, and that's not a bad thing. I don't have a crystal ball I can look into that says to me, 'Now it's time for this person to give up her home and move into a more structured setting.' I believe in my heart that each person has to reach that conclusion on his or her own, unless of course there are neurological implications affecting the thought processes." He raised his voice slightly. "That is not the case here."

"You're telling me to take her home?" asked Joe.

"She shouldn't be home alone yet. She'll need temporary assistance. I can prescribe home health care, nurses who come in daily to monitor her condition." Dr. Siegfried's voice remained calm. "We'll see from there how she does."

"No!" said Joe. "She's going to live with us for awhile. I don't want strangers in her home taking care of her. We can manage better if she's at our house."

"We?" asked Judy.

"It won't be for long. Please, hon," he said softly. "You'll be off for the summer in a couple of months and Michael can help out." Then, glaring at his son, he added, "I think he owes her that!"

"Joe, it's my decision, not yours. Please try to remember that," Addie said sternly.

"Mom," Joe said, "I don't trust your decisions anymore."

A cloud fell over the room as each person collected their thoughts. Dr. Siegfried was the first to speak again. "Joe's made you a kind offer, Addie, and you should consider it," he said gently. "But you're right, it's *your* decision. There is nothing to keep you from doing anything but what you choose to do."

Addie sighed. "I feel like I've created enough trouble and I know you'll only worry if I return home alone. I'll go with you, Joe, but only until I feel better."

They settled Addie into the sunroom on the back of the

house, which had been added on along with a family room a few years ago. It was a cheerful room with its own adjoining bathroom. Judy had decorated it in soft yellows and blues and it was warm and inviting. With the exception of an occasional visit from her sister in Seattle, however, the room was seldom used. For a time, it would be Addie's home.

The morning after her arrival, when Judy had already left for school, Joe sat with his mother before leaving for his office. "Are you comfortable here?" He was self-conscious, ashamed of his behavior at the hospital.

"Very," Addie responded. "This is a lovely room."

"We've got it covered so that one of us will be here as much as possible," Joe explained. "Michael's in his room studying now, but he'll check in with you later."

"I'm fine." Then, to make conversation, Addie asked, "What did you think of my next-door neighbor when you asked her to feed Rufus?"

He snickered, "She's homely, just skin and bones."

"Skin and bones? I know she's tiny, but she's pregnant, Joe."

"If she's pregnant, I'm Napoleon. Is that what she told you?"

"Yes. I thought I couldn't see well enough to tell if she was showing," Addie sighed. "You don't think she's pregnant at all?"

"She sure didn't look like it to me," he said. "Anyway, I was glad she offered to take care of Rufus. Judy's allergic to cats, you know."

"It's fine," said Addie. "I think Rufus will enjoy Sybil for awhile and vice versa."

"If he hadn't saved your life, I'd probably have found him room and board at the animal shelter."

"Joe!"

110

"No, really, Mom," Joe continued. "If he hadn't tromped over there whining to your neighbors, it could have been a long time before anyone found you."

"I know," Addie said. "Good old Rufus."

"Sybil said that he sat outside their door and cried like a baby. It was so strange that she realized something was wrong and they decided to check on you."

"He's been good company," Addie said fondly.

"I'm sure she'll take good care of him. You know, Mom, that's a pretty weird outfit next door to you. That guy, what's his name?"

"Stoney."

"Yeah, Stoney," Joe continued. "He is one strange character. He was nice enough about the cat and all. But still, there's something about him—"

"He *is* a little different," Addie acknowledged. "Sybil usually comes over to help me when he's at work."

"He said he was a relative of the Robertses. Do you believe him, Mom?"

"He's the son of Sharon's new husband. I don't know how well he knows Henry and Elsa. They're living with Sharon in Kansas now, did you know that?"

"I think you mentioned it once." Joe took a long swallow from a mug of coffee. "I guess they won't be back to the cabin much then, will they?"

"I doubt it," said Addie. "Neither of them are in good health."

"And they realize they shouldn't live alone anymore," he emphasized his point.

Addie had no response to this. She had resolved to avoid any future arguments with Joe. She had also resolved to be honest, to have no more secrets. And so, his next question tugged at her conscience.

"Do the Robertses know those kids are living there? I don't even think they're married, although they say they are."

"They said Stoney's father gave them permission to use the cabin, but I honestly don't know." Addie took a deep breath. "Maybe you should call them, Joe. I tried once but got an answering machine and I didn't want to leave a message that might alarm them. After that, there didn't seem to be any problems, so I never called again."

"I'll do that," he agreed. "As soon as my life calms down around here, I'll get in touch with them."

"Are things tough at the office?" asked Addie sympathetically.

"No, with my mother!" He reached over and squeezed her knee affectionately.

They sat silently, as Addie summoned up the courage to ask, "Joe, you're not thinking I'm going to Gateway from here, are you?"

"No." She breathed a sigh until he explained, "I wish you were. That's no secret. I still think it's best for you and I think you would see it, too, if you moved there. Unfortunately, it's so popular that your name is still several slots down on the waiting list. There aren't many openings. I wouldn't be surprised if another facility was built soon. I wish I had the money to invest in one myself."

"Here's a start for you," said Addie as she reached to the carpet and retrieved a shiny penny.

"I don't get it, Mom!" Joe exclaimed. "You say you're blind and you failed to see a big hole that you stepped in. Then you lean over and pick a penny up off of the floor. It doesn't make sense!"

"It's confusing to me, too," admitted Addie. "I saw that penny out of the side of my eye, so I knew where it was.

When I turn to view it directly with my central vision, it was gone. I can no longer see my feet when I look straight down, so of course, I never saw that hole."

"That must be frustrating for you."

"It is," agreed Addie. "Close your eyes, Joe, and feel the penny. Can you tell what it is without looking?"

"Sure," Joe said, "it's a penny. Or if I didn't know, I might think it was a dime."

Addie reached inside her purse. "Keep your eyes closed now." She handed her son a dollar bill. "What's that?"

"It's money, of course," he laughed. "I don't know how much. I mean, how could you know without looking?"

"Exactly," said Addie. "That's what it's like for me."

"Wow, Mom, I'm sorry. I didn't realize simple things like that could be so difficult."

"Don't feel sorry for me," she said. "I know how to tell a dime from a penny and a one from a five dollar bill."

"Really?"

"They showed us at group. You feel the edges of coins when you aren't sure. A dime is rough, a penny is smooth."

"I never noticed that before," he said.

"You never had to."

"You've got me there," he sighed.

"We also learned to fold our paper money different ways and pay attention when we're getting change."

"I'll be!" Joe laughed. "That's so simple when you explain it, but when I had my eyes closed it was another story." He stood up. "Look, I have to get to work. Do you need anything before I take off?"

"I'm fine. Thanks, Joe."

When he returned home that evening, Joe surprised Addie with a stack of mail. "I had the post office forward it from Bear Lake," he explained. "I'll read it to you and take care of the bills." He began opening the parcels, one by one. "Hey, look at this. It's a get-well card from your support group." He read the verse to her, then stated, "They must like you, Mom."

Smiling, Addie inquired, "Did Gordon sign it?"

"Uh, let's see. Yeah, here it is, Walter and Gordon. Who's Gordon, your boyfriend?"

"Sort of."

"Really?"

"Go on. Read the rest of the names to me."

If Addie had been asked to find one word that described her feelings for Joe's wife, it would have been "respect." Judy Marsh had been a part of Addie's life since her marriage to Joe the summer after they both graduated from college. Although the relationship between her and her daughter-in-law wasn't really close, it was a good one built upon mutual regard.

Judy was a quiet, intelligent woman who taught sophomore English at the same high school she, her husband, and their son had all attended. She was a loving, supportive wife to Joe and a caring, attentive mother. She had also found time to work in a master's degree and was active in church and civic affairs. She had nursed her own mother when she'd had cancer years before and continued to see her regularly since the death of her father.

Perhaps most important to Addie was Judy's devotion to Joe, who was surely not the easiest man with whom to share a life. Judy, like Addie, could see beyond Joe's idiosyncrasies to the good, hard-working man he was. For that, more than anything else, Addie loved her.

Moving into her home was another matter. This was unfamiliar turf to Addie, a lifestyle very different from her terribly missed routine on Bear Lake. She knew that the present situation was difficult for Judy, too. Although they maintained a kind and proper demeanor toward each other, Addie knew it would be best for both women if this arrangement ended as soon as possible.

With Addie's next visit to Dr. Siegfried only a few days away, Joe was unexpectedly called out of town to perform an audit. "Can you get away and take Mom to Pinecliffe to see Dr. Siegfried on Wednesday?" he had asked Judy.

Amicably, Judy had agreed. As the school year was winding down her students were suffering with spring fever, and she looked forward to the prospect of a quiet drive to the mountains. After Joe left, Addie surprised her daughter-in-law by joining her in the kitchen. Normally, Addie remained in her room except for meals, unless invited out by the family. Addie knew they assumed she was most comfortable alone and were respecting her privacy. In reality she felt sequestered and bored.

"I wondered if we could have a talk?" Addie asked upon entering the room.

"Why, of course, Addie," Judy pulled out a chair for her. "Is something troubling you?"

"Judy, I want to go home," Addie began. "I feel fine now. It's almost summer, so there will be people around if I need something. Take me home, Judy, while Joe's gone. Let's pack my belongings, and if Dr. John says I've recuperated enough, let me stay at Bear Lake after my appointment."

"Oh, Addie," Judy sighed. "You're writing a prescription for my divorce!"

They laughed together. "I'm putting you on the spot, Judy, I know, and I'm sorry. But I'm determined to spend one more summer at home. I truly don't know how much longer I can live alone in Pinecliffe. For now, it will be easier for all of us if you'll take me back to the cabin. I need time to sort things out in my mind, and I don't want to get into an ugly fight with Joe."

"Forgive me, Addie. I don't want to hurt you," Judy said. "Please listen to me. The reality is that your problems haven't magically disappeared while you were convalescing. You cannot cook adequate meals for yourself. You need help to read your mail and pay your bills. You can't even walk around your yard without getting hurt." A momentary pause gave both time to consider these words. "You can't shop for your own groceries, Addie. You rely upon Hazel, who is too busy to help, and that little teenager who's probably a fugitive in that cabin next door." She paused, and when Addie didn't reply she asked, "Have I said too much?"

"You've said nothing that isn't true," responded Addie. "I asked for it. By all means, finish. I want to get our cards out on the table."

"But you didn't know I had a loaded deck, did you?" Judy tried to soften the impact of her words. "Since you lost your sight, Joe has tried very hard to be there as much as he can. He drives out to see you, calls frequently, and worries constantly that you're not safe and you're not eating properly. Whether you agree with him or not, he's spent a great deal of time researching alternatives for you, besides keeping your name on the list at Gateway. Then his worst nightmare comes true. You walk down to the lake and end up falling into a hole because you can't see where you're going. He loves you, Addie. *I* love you! How can we let you go back there when it's not working? What will be different?"

Tears filled Addie's eyes, and for a long time she was silent. Eventually, she said, "Me."

"What?" asked Judy.

"Me," Addie repeated. "I think it's time for me to make some changes."

"In what way?" Judy probed.

"I have to take charge of my life again. I'm learning in my vision meetings that there are different ways to do things when you can't see. I've put off using them because I couldn't accept that I need to. But, I'm ready now. I'll do anything to be able to stay in my own home."

"What kinds of changes are you talking about?" asked Judy.

"Just a minute." Addie went back to her room and returned with a small business card that was worn and frayed on the corners. "We can call Laura Benning to begin with," she said handing Judy the card. "She said she has some ideas for me. That's her job—teaching people who've lost eyesight the skills they need to remain independent. You can talk to her, too. And I'll quit being so stubborn. I'll quit taking chances and acting like I'm invincible."

Judy tossed her hair back and laughed. "Now there's a promise I'd like to see you keep!"

"How about it?" Addie smiled.

"I'll make you a deal," said Judy.

"Okay."

"You work as hard as you can and learn as much as you can to be safe. If you'll truly do that, then I'll try to convince Joe that you can live on your own at Bear Lake," Judy challenged. "It won't be easy, but we can do it, if we work together."

"You've got a deal!" Addie said with delight.

Judy rose from the table. "Let's start gathering your things together," she said.

Chapter 7

"Addie, you're back! We missed you!" Alice Mumford threw her arms around Addie, almost lifting her off the ground in her enthusiasm.

Harriet Stevens scurried forward, chattering as she approached. The sound of her voice was like the welcoming babble of a summer brook. "Addie, are you well now? We heard about your fall, you poor thing! But you didn't break your hip, thank goodness for that. I had a friend over at Fremont who broke her hip and it was . . ." Her voice trailed off in the throng of well-wishers who stunned Addie with their warm greetings.

"I've never been missed like this!" she giggled.

"You just don't listen, do you, Addie?" Leo's unmistakable voice joined the others.

"Don't listen?" she asked.

"I told you if you ever wanted to go fishing, Cecil and I would take you. But no, you had to try it alone!"

Against a roar of laughter Addie quipped, "I promise next time to call you guys first!"

Maggie Parks put an arm around Addie's shoulder and murmured sympathetically, "Laura told us the story of how you got hurt. Believe me, there's not one grandparent here who wouldn't have done the same thing. We're always covering for them!"

"I hope you don't mind my telling them what happened, Addie." Laura joined them. "People wondered why you'd walked down to the lake by yourself with so much mud still covering the ground."

"She'd gone fishing!" Leo insisted, tapping his cane with a frolic.

"Fishing for trouble!" said Addie. "No objection Laura, and Maggie's right. We do spoil our grandchildren, don't we?"

A chorus of voices agreed. "Addie, over here!" It was another familiar voice. "I've saved your seat. I wouldn't let anyone else sit in it while you were gone."

"Thanks, Walter." Addie and the rest of the crowd moved towards their seats. "Where's my buddy?" To Addie's delight a warm tongue on her hand answered the question.

"Let's get started!" Laura called out. "Introductions. Who's here today?"

And so, the now-comfortable routine began. For the first time, Addie felt peaceful among these friends. She hadn't realized how much she had missed them, how much she cared and wanted to be there for them as they had been for her. More than once, she wiped a stray tear from her cheek as the meeting progressed.

"I'm David, from Fremont. I'm blind from a retinal detachment due to an accident. No, wait," he went on. "Let me reword that for Addie. She's missed a couple of meetings." He cleared his throat, although his voice shook as he spoke. "I'm David from Fremont. I took a long vacation, but I'm learning again how to do the work of a farmer. I took time from my busy day to be among all of you, my special friends." A hush fell over the group as Addie impulsively squeezed his arm.

"Oh, David," she whispered, "I'm so happy for you!"

"I'll tell you all about it after the meeting," he promised, unable at that moment to say more.

The focus of that day's program was the upcoming

county fair, in which some of those present had entered arts and crafts in the past. Ideas for adapting hobbies and continuing involvement in the fair were presented by several people. Marie Reinholdt shared her success in crocheting a rag rug that she hoped would win a ribbon. She explained that, although she continued to enjoy crocheting with yarn, she found that using strips of cloth and larger hooks was easier to do by feel. She could no longer rely upon her sight but could locate her mistakes by touch. "And I still make plenty of them!"

Cecil explained the struggle he was having in his attempts to complete a wood carving entry. "It used to be so easy," he lamented. "But mama here, won't let me quit!" Maggie blushed and said nothing.

David offered some suggestions to Cecil on identifying and handling his carving tools safely. He was intent and serious as he tried to troubleshoot with the older man, and Cecil thanked him warmly.

"Walter's going to try to pass Gordon off as a pig and win a blue ribbon!" Leo teased.

"He's fat enough!" Walter remarked good-naturedly.

"Are you entering produce, David?" asked Addie. She had disliked the awkward moments in the past when David refused to participate in group discussions and was enjoying his refreshing involvement.

"Not this year. I'm just starting again, but give me time."

"We've only got a few minutes left," Laura said.

"Time for refreshments!"

Laura ignored Leo's interruption and continued. "There's someone else here today who's experienced some real achievements in the last few weeks. Addie, do you want to share with us what you've been up to?"

The flood of red moved from David's face to Addie's. "I'll try." She had been more of a listener in the past and hoped she would find the words.

"Well," she began softly.

"Speak up! Marie can't hear you!" May called out.

"Well," she started again, "I'm cooking now. Laura came out and marked the dials on my stove and microwave and electric skillet. I can set them by touch now, and not burn my food. I'm also using a timer with big numbers I can feel and other tools that help. And measuring. Laura showed me how to measure without having to see the lines."

"Aren't those marks on the dial a help?" asked Susanna with enthusiasm.

"They make all the difference," said Addie.

"Have you tried talking books yet?" asked Walter, referring to the audiocassette program sponsored by the National Library Service.

"Oh, yes! I don't know how I lived without them," Addie replied. "I used to love reading, and now I can sit out on my porch and listen by the hour. It's wonderful to read again!"

"We told you so!" teased Harriet. "But you wouldn't try them before."

"She never listens!" Leo reminded them.

"What else, Addie?" asked Laura. "I know we still have a lot to accomplish."

"Let's see," Addie continued. "We marked my laundry dials and my thermostat. Sometimes it gets a little chilly at night and I like to turn the heat up. Before, I was either too hot or too cold because I was always guessing."

Muffled murmurs of understanding went around the table.

"Oh, yes," Addie went on, "we're going to look at low vision devices to see if there isn't something that will allow me to read my mail. Down the road my son, Joe, wants to get a computer with a scanner and software that reads the screen for me. My daughter-in-law and grandson have offered to help me learn to use it. I can scan my mail and have it read aloud to me. I might even be able to write checks and pay my bills with the computer. Until then, I'm going to hire someone to read my mail and keep records for me, if necessary."

"I didn't like my kids paying my bills," Harriet empathized. "I felt like nothing was private anymore."

"The computer adaptations have been great for me with my agricultural business," added David. "I'm still learning, and you know, it's kind of fun as well as challenging."

"Look out!" warned Leo. "Addie, does this mean no more burned cakes? I like 'em the way you used to make them."

"I'm afraid so, Leo. I've reformed!" Then an afterthought came to her. "I almost forgot. My daughter-in-law is going to record my favorite recipes for me on tape so I can listen to them when I want to bake. I'm real excited about that!"

"When are we invited to dinner?" asked Cecil.

"Any time!" laughed Addie. "My door is always open!"

As the meeting ended and the social time began, a few group members carried refreshments to the table. The local sheriff entered the room looking for Marie. "No emergency," he reassured them. "She locked herself out of her house this morning but she can get back in now."

"What's that?" Marie cupped a hand over her ear.

"I've got your lock fixed," he spoke slowly into her ear.

"I had to make a new key," he enunciated, placing a shiny gold object in her hand.

"Thank you, Bill," Marie said gratefully. "You're a good man."

Bill Johnson had been the county sheriff serving Pinecliffe and the surrounding small villages longer than anyone remembered. Each time his term ended he ran for re-election unopposed. He was a tireless man devoted to his job to the point of living it. He had never married and often commented that the community was his family. He was never without several offers for holiday dinners or a place to visit on Sunday afternoons.

Like most longtime residents of the valley, Bill had spent many hours fishing at Bear Lake and, over the years, had developed a friendship with Addie. Many times in the long winter months when she was alone, she would hear his patrol car driving past her cabin. He'd check the surrounding area, then honk his horn three times to let her know he'd been by. On this day when he spotted Addie sitting among the others, he joined her.

"I heard you were back home. Saw the lights on at your place. I should have called before now, but we've been busy," he apologized.

"Thank you, Bill. It's good to be home."

"I kept an eye on your cabin while you were away," he assured her. "Talked to those kids next door to you, too."

"Have they been a problem?" asked Addie, remembering that Joe had forgotten to call the Robertses after their conversation and she had deliberately chosen not to remind him. Addie turned her chair slightly toward him.

"No, not at all. The girl seems nice and says she's been helping you sometimes."

"That's true," Addie responded. "She was good

company this past winter."

"Say, Addie, another thing." He pulled a chair closer, to talk quietly.

"What is it?" she asked turning to face him.

"Are you aware that there's a fellow living at the old logging camp across the water from you?"

"Yes, I am," she responded. "He's a veteran. Retired army, I believe. He bought the place and plans to fix it up."

"So he says," said Bill. "He's not too friendly, is he?"

"What do you mean?" asked Addie.

"Well, I've tried to strike up a conversation with him, but he says he likes to mind his own business. Of course, that's fine with me, but I guess he won't be much of a neighbor. Not like most people around here."

"He's been nice enough to me," Addie protested.

"You know him?" Astonished, Bill leaned closer.

"Not well," Addie admitted. "He's stopped by a couple of times."

"What for?"

"Well, once he was looking for his dog. And the day I fell, he came up to tell me my boat was untied."

"That's why you went down to the lake?" he asked.

"Oh, no. He fixed it for me. I went down later to check on it," she told him. "After he left, I remembered that it was loose because my grandson had used it and left it uncovered. I went down to cover and clean it, and that's when I fell."

"Well, I'm glad to hear he was good enough to tell you about the boat and tie it up for you. I wouldn't have thought he'd go out of his way to be neighborly," Bill responded. "But listen, Addie, you *are* vulnerable living out there all alone the way you do. Don't be too trusting with people you don't know. Things aren't like they used to be

124

when everybody knew everyone. Be careful. And remember
that you can call me anytime at all, okay?"

"Thanks, Bill."

"All right, then. I've got to take off." With that he disappeared into the bright sunny day, leaving Addie to wonder
again about Paul Curtis. He did seem nice enough to her,
but Bill was right. Paul wanted to be left alone and wasn't
interested in being neighborly.

In sharp contrast to the previous months, Bear Lake was
full of activity. The shores were lined with fishermen and
the water was dotted with rowboats and rubber rafts, sometimes late into the evening. Children could be heard
chasing about through the trees, a bittersweet reminder to
Addie of days past when her own boys, and later Michael,
made summer memories while staying at the cabin. A trip
to the mailbox could sometimes take over an hour as old
friends and new acquaintances stopped to visit with Addie.

As with the changing of all the seasons, Addie was now
sure that this was her favorite. As much as she relished the
quiet serenity of winter and the freshness of springtime,
Addie loved the energy and excitement that the summer
people brought back with them. They were mostly kind,
considerate people who shared with Addie a passion for the
mountains and the lake.

She thought back to the first day she'd come home when
she and Dr. John had convinced Judy that she was ready.
After settling in and helping to put away her clothes, Judy
volunteered to walk next door and pick up Rufus. Because
of Judy's allergies, Sybil carried Rufus back to the cabin and
the three of them laughed as the old cat welcomed Addie
home.

Sybil set him down, but as Addie leaned over to pet him,

Rufus promptly turned his head and walked away, deliberately ignoring her. He then hopped onto the back of the sofa where, with his back still to Addie, he stared out the picture window as if she wasn't there. When Addie tried to pick him up again, he jumped away from her and busily began licking himself from head to toe, oblivious of everything and everyone.

Addie got right in front of him so he'd have to acknowledge her. At this, Rufus had promptly closed his eyes. Judy, Sybil and Addie had laughed until they nearly cried. Hours later, when Addie was enjoying her first evening of solitude at home, Rufus found her lap and purred loudly. She had thought, at last he's forgiven me for going away.

Now the two were settled into their routine. Rufus was enjoying the attention of all of their summer visitors. He also liked Laura, who visited often. He recognized the Old Mobile when it turned up the lane to take Addie to the group meeting or to run errands. Carol thoughtfully planned these trips when she had time to accompany Addie into the stores. Rufus discovered that if he jumped through the open door of the van, its affable driver and any other passengers would reward him by scratching his head. They sometimes had a little trouble convincing him to leave so they could start for town.

The cat had an especially close bond with Sybil after their time together when Addie was staying at Joe's. Whenever she came to help Addie, as was their continued arrangement, he ran down the walk to meet her. Interestingly, he never followed her home, perhaps out of fear that he might have to stay there again.

"Good morning, you sweet old cat!" Sybil called lightly as she arrived one day. "Are you staying out of trouble?"

She greeted Addie with equal zeal. When Addie had first

returned home, Sybil was like a lost puppy, staying close until Addie literally tripped over her. It was this evident need that prevented Addie from bringing up the fact that Sybil was not on the verge of childbirth as she had predicted in the fall. Like a porcelain doll, Addie feared that the girl would crack if upset.

Sybil watched the clock more closely than ever these days. It seemed to Addie that she dreaded being the cause of anything that might upset Stoney.

"He's so tired, Addie," Sybil defended him. "If I don't get things done at home, he gets real cranky. But who can blame him? He works so hard, he can't be expected to put up with a messy house when he comes home."

Addie did not respond.

"I try to have his dinner warm when he gets there. He hates it if it's the least bit cold. And he's so funny about dust. If there's dust on one little thing—but then he's got hay fever. You can't blame him."

Finally Addie ventured, "What does he do? I mean, what happens if his food is cold or there's dust on something?"

Sybil fidgeted uncomfortably. "Well, he just doesn't like it, that's all. If he's real tired, he gets pretty upset."

"Does he hit you, Sybil?"

The concern in her voice caught the girl off guard and softly she responded, "Sometimes."

"I was afraid of that."

"It's my own fault, Addie!" Once again, Sybil fervently defended him. "If I didn't make him angry he'd never do it. It's me who needs to change, not him!"

"Oh, Sybil," Addie sighed heavily. "It's never right to hit someone you love. There are better ways to work out your problems. You can't let him keep doing that."

"It's not like it's all the time!" she maintained.

"What about the baby?" Tenderly, Addie introduced the forbidden topic.

Sybil again fidgeted and for a time, Addie thought she wasn't going to answer. "There's no baby," she finally muttered.

"What happened?" Addie's voice remained soothing and calm.

"I lost it. Again."

"You've had two miscarriages?" asked Addie.

"Yes," Sybil began to sob as she spoke. "After the first time, right away I got pregnant again. It means so much to Stoney to be a father. Then I lost the second one—right after you went away."

"Did Stoney hit you, knock you down? Could he have caused it, Sybil?"

Still sobbing softly, she answered, "I don't think it was his fault. He says it's mine!" Her crying became louder and Addie sat silently with her for a long time, holding her hand, but not speaking.

When she'd stopped crying and had blown her nose, in a very flat voice Sybil told Addie, "Stoney says I'm not a woman. He says I can't even have a baby like other women. He's going to leave me, Addie. I know it. He hints about it all the time. I'm trying real hard to get pregnant again, but nothing happens. Sometimes I have pain down there," she added shyly.

"Oh, Sybil," Addie sighed again. "Please, listen to me."

"I always listen to you, Addie," she said with childlike innocence. "You know, you're like a mother to me. I never really had much of a mom. You're the first woman I could ever talk to like this. You may be a lot older than me, but you're the best friend I ever had in my life! You're the only friend, really."

Addie's heart ached with the sincerity of her words. "That's a real compliment," she said at last. "I'll always remember it."

"It's true," Sybil smiled faintly. "What did you want to tell me?"

"Many things," Addie sighed. "To begin with, have you seen a doctor since you had the last miscarriage?"

"No," she confessed. "We don't have health insurance. We can't afford it."

"You could get help through Social Services," suggested Addie.

"No," Sybil objected. "They'd find out we're not married yet. They'd make me go back to California."

Ignoring this confession Addie said, "Maybe not. I could call them or go with you to talk to them . . ."

"No thanks," Sybil said, "You're nice, but you don't understand. If I try to get on welfare, they'll check me out. Then they'll send me home. Home—to another foster parent. Addie, you wouldn't believe how many different foster homes I've lived in. I've been in foster care more than I've ever lived with my own mother."

In spite of herself, Addie was shocked at this revelation. Her heart went out to the impotent child before her.

"Don't get me wrong," Sybil went on. "Some of those people were real good to me. But just when I'd get settled in, they'd move me or send me back home. Then there would be trouble again, and I'd be back in foster care. Most of those people were great. But a few were just in it for the money—they didn't care about me. I won't do it again. I don't have to," she said brightly, "I have Stoney now!"

"But he beats you, Sybil. You're no better off with him," Addie confronted her. "You're only kidding yourself. You can't stay with Stoney, not this way!"

"He doesn't beat me!" Her voice rose in anger. "I told you what happens. It's my fault! If I didn't make him mad, we'd be fine. It's not so bad. I'm trying harder. I want to have his baby. I *will* have his baby!"

"All right, calm down, Sybil. It's okay." For a moment Addie feared not only for the hysterical girl, but for herself. She'd been warned about being too trusting, and yet . . .

"Listen, Sybil." Desperately, Addie tried a different approach. "If you want to have a baby, you need to be seen by a doctor. Maybe the reason you're experiencing pain has to do with the miscarriages. Sometimes if you don't see a doctor after that you can get an infection, and that could keep you from getting pregnant again."

"Really?"

"Really. Now, I have a very good friend who's a doctor in Pinecliffe. He's kind and gentle and I know he'd be happy to take a look at you. I'll go with you if you'd like," she offered again. "I'll even pay the bill, and you can work in exchange for it."

"Addie," Sybil paused, "I can't."

"But why?"

"The same reason I can't go to Social Services. He'll ask too many questions."

"He's not that way, Sybil," Addie insisted. "I know him well. He can be trusted. Please, at least do this much."

The girl patted Addie's hand softly. "I promise I'll think about it. But let me decide. You won't tell anyone what we've talked about, will you, Addie? I can trust you, can't I?"

As Addie struggled to respond, Sybil expertly changed the subject. "We've got tons of work to do! No more time for this. I told you I'd catch up your ironing today. Put on that talking book we were listening to, about the dog, okay?

I really liked that." She began to hum and busy herself about the house.

When her time came to an end Sybil abruptly announced that she was leaving, calling as the screen slammed behind her, "Remember, Addie, you can't tell what we talked about today, okay?"

For a long time after she left, Addie turned their conversation over and over in her mind. "What should I do, Jacob?" she said out loud. "I'm the only person in her life she's ever trusted. If I violate that trust she may never have faith in another human being. If I don't, she may pay a terrible price for my silence. And if Joe knew about all of this . . ."

For once, Jacob was silent.

"Could Jonathan take us past the old house on Race Avenue, Sarah?" Sitting in the back seat of the limousine next to her sister, Addie felt a release from the unfathomable claustrophobia that she often experienced within the walls of the mansion. It felt good to have a day away from Daniel, his stuffy parents, and the innumerable servants who filled every corner of the house. Even a break from the children was needed from time to time, as Addie rarely let Jake and his cousins out of her sight. Unlike her older sister, Addie refused to allow a nurse, no matter how qualified, to raise her son. And she enjoyed Jake. He was the bridge to her past that she could cross over with the sound of his laughter or a look into his eyes.

"I don't see why not," Sarah responded amicably. "I told you, this is your day out, little sister. A drive, shopping, some lunch—whatever you like."

"Why am I so lucky today?" Addie asked.

"Because I needed an excuse to get away just as badly as

you did!" exclaimed Sarah. "I'm ready to explode—in more ways than one!" She pointed to her protruding belly and they both broke into a fit of laughter.

"Not in the car, Sarah," Addie begged. "I mean, could you see Jonathan . . . ?"

"Oh, Addie, stop!" Sarah giggled. She was different away from the house on these infrequent excursions with Addie. She was the old Sarah, the fun, easygoing beauty whose little sister had always adored her.

With the small inheritance Addie had received following the sale of the farm, she and Jake had been able to live comfortably in her sister's house. Daniel refused Addie's offer to pay for rent and food. Her only real expenses were personal items and Sarah often returned home from shopping with clothes and "little boy things."

Sarah leaned forward and slid open the small window separating them from the driver. After giving Jonathan brief instructions, she leaned back again. She was flushed with heat, even though it wasn't a particularly warm February day. It was 1946, and as they could see upon returning to their old neighborhood, Denver was changing. "This town's growing too large," Sarah sighed. "Now that I'm not allowed to drive myself about, I don't know my way around anymore."

"I'm lost, that's for sure." Addie pressed her face against the window, trying to gather a sense of direction. When their old home came into view, Sarah signaled Jonathan to slow down while each sister took it in.

"It's been painted green!" Sarah moaned. "Nobody paints bricks green!"

"I can't believe it!" Addie gasped. "And the rosebushes—they're overgrown. I'm glad Uncle William can't see this."

"He would turn over in his grave!" cried Sarah. "Green!"

Slowly the limousine rolled on with Sarah providing a new set of instructions. "I miss him, don't you?"

"Sometimes," said Addie. "He was good to us. We were lucky he took us in."

"I'll say." Sarah struggled to find a comfortable position. This was her fifth pregnancy in almost as many years and it was the most unbearable one thus far. With four beautiful daughters, Daniel was determined to continue trying until he could produce a male heir.

Sarah's energy level dropped quickly as the day progressed, and although Addie wished to stay away as long as possible, she feigned fatigue herself and the two headed for home early. Jake was in his mother's arms almost before she could take her coat off. At four, he was a handsome little boy, with a sharp mind and serious spirit.

"You have company, Mommy!" He announced proudly before a butler could break the news formally.

"I do?" she asked, surprised. Addie never had company. The only visitors to the rambling old house were friends of the family from whom she shyly maintained a respectable distance.

"You do, Mommy," Jake whispered after receiving a scolding glance from the nurse. "It's a man."

"Mrs. McNeil," one of the butlers stepped forward. "You have a visitor in the west wing sitting room. I told him you were out for the afternoon, but he insisted upon waiting."

"I think he had nowhere else to go!" The nurse murmured putting a hand on little Jake's shoulder. "Come with me, young man. Your mother has a guest and you are not invited."

"I'm inviting him now," Addie said calmly, taking her son by the hand. "If I have a visitor, so does Jake." The nurse scowled and turned to the back of the house to report yet another incident of disrespect for her authority from Addie. From the day of her arrival, Addie and this determined woman had been at odds with each other. It was the one and only aspect of her life in the mansion where Addie refused to compromise. She, too, felt extremely capable of directing the course of her son's upbringing.

When they entered the sitting room, Addie was surprised to see George Marsh rising to greet her. "Hello, sir." Little Jake ran ahead of her, extending his small hand as any gentleman might do.

"How do you do?" was the response.

Addie reddened and grinned at her son. Looking back to the visitor, she too, extended a hand and said, "George, what a surprise!"

"How are you, Addie? It's so good to see the two of you again." He seemed taller than Addie remembered but not as heavy. The absence of bandages, perhaps? His shyness was still apparent in the dampness of his hand and the slight quiver in his voice.

It must have been hard for him, she thought, *to sit in this house waiting for me.* "We're doing well," she answered politely.

As soon as they were seated, another servant arrived with a tray containing coffee, tea, soft drinks, and a variety of snacks. "Only one, Jake," Addie cautioned her son, who often attended parties with his cousins and enjoyed filling up on cookies and cakes.

"Yes, ma'am," He studied the tray intently before making his choice.

"Someone's grown up quite a bit now, hasn't he?" the

soldier said admiringly.

"That he has," Addie agreed. "A great deal since you saw him last. He was only a baby then."

"Do you know me?" Jake asked shyly.

"I knew you when you were very tiny," Sergeant Marsh said. "But I think I like you better now. You don't cry as much as you did then."

Jake laughed with delight and Addie beamed. "What brings you to Denver?" she asked. "And how did you find us?"

"Well, I just got out of the service," he explained. "I liked Colorado so much that I came back here to try to find work. And I guess I've been successful. I found a job in a factory in Richmond, in the southern part of the state. I start in a few weeks."

"Good for you!"

"I found you through the McNeils. We've stayed in touch, and I stopped to see them in Missouri on my way out. They seem to be doing well."

"Yes, they are," Addie agreed. "We write regularly. I hated to see them give up the farm, but now I know it was best for them. I think they're happy. Last summer Jake and I rode the train out to visit them."

"You rode the train that far?" he exclaimed turning his attention to Jake.

"Yes, sir!" Jake answered proudly. "Just me and my mom!"

"That sounds like fun."

"It was," said Jake. "And you know what?"

"What?" asked the man with a wide grin.

"I got a toy train just like the one we rode on. Want to see it?"

"Boy, do I!"

The little boy sped from the room leaving both Addie and her guest laughing.

"He's a beautiful child, Addie," he said. "Jacob would have been proud of him."

"Yes. He's a lot like his father," she acknowledged. "I'm so glad you came, George! Won't you stay for dinner?"

Chapter 8

In the weeks before starting his new job, George remained in Denver and saw Addie and Jake almost daily. There were trips to the zoo, and movies, and long, chatter-filled afternoons in one of several rooms in the mansion. When snow covered the play yard it was George who joined Jake and his two oldest cousins in building a huge snowman, complete with a carrot nose and charcoal eyes. When it became evident that George was to be a regular visitor before heading south for his job, he was offered a room in the home. This he politely declined. At first, he was referred to by members of the household as Addie's deceased husband's friend. But in a short time, he was simply George.

The servants liked this kind, gentle man who treated them with the same interest and respect as he did the other residents of the house. Sarah and Daniel, however, were reserved and avoided acknowledging him whenever possible. George Marsh, after all, was not their peer. He was a common man, a laborer, a soldier. He did not fit in with their lifestyle or society. It had been Sarah's hope that Addie would eventually marry one of Daniel's eligible bachelor friends. Many evenings had been spent playing cards or visiting with these prospects, with Addie behaving courteously but showing no true interest.

Sarah had decided it was too soon for Addie to care again. Although she had never quite understood her sister's love for the young, handsome farmer, she respected the tragedy of her loss and was willing to give Addie time. Therefore, Sarah was not prepared for Addie to accept

George Marsh's obvious interest in her, and she let her feelings be known.

"Addie, he's not right for you," Sarah began abruptly one afternoon when the couple had returned from a lunch date.

"What?" Addie watched George retreat down the walk toward the driveway, where Jonathan insisted on opening his car door despite the young man's attempts to wave the servant away.

"That George. Addie, he just isn't your type! If you're ready to date, let me and Daniel find someone, you know, more suitable," pleaded Sarah.

"You mean richer, don't you?" Addie bluntly turned from the window, then softened at Sarah's hurt look. Impulsively Addie hugged her sister as she had when they were children. "Sarah, we aren't dating. You're making too much of this. It's just refreshing to be with someone who knew Jacob, someone who was with him . . . at the end."

"That's the last thing you need!" Sarah insisted. "You need to be with someone who can help you forget, not dredge up all the pain again. Listen, there's a new young attorney in town, and Daniel says he's perfect for you. What do you say to dinner Saturday night, a nice evening on the town?"

"I say no!" Addie giggled and hurried to change the subject. "Let's see what the children are up to."

Someone who was with Jacob at the end. It was George who finally broached the subject. Addie had avoided the topic since that day at the farm when he'd first related the story of Jacob's death and she had left the room. From the moment he had returned to her life, George and Addie had talked endlessly of Jacob's life, but never of his death.

Once Addie had commented, "Jacob is a hard man to get out of your system, isn't he? You seem to think about him as much as I do."

"I guess it's true, I do," George had answered. "I didn't know him long, but he sure had an impact on me. He was a good, loyal friend. A great soldier."

"Is it wrong to dwell on someone who's gone?" she asked him.

"I don't know," George studied Addie. "I think maybe it's okay. Jacob will never die for you and me, and why should he? We'll always remember him. And you're lucky," he nodded toward Jake who was playing across the room with his cousins, heedless of the adult conversation. "A part of Jacob lives on in that little guy." With tears brimming Addie had reached out and squeezed his hand, grateful for his understanding.

When George started his new job, he and Addie frequently arranged to be together. Either he would make the long drive north, or she and Jake boarded a bus late Friday afternoon to visit him, spending a good part of Sunday to return. The owner of the boarding home where George lived welcomed the visitors. She could see a relaxed change in her favorite tenant when Addie and Jake arrived and provided special accommodations for the widow and her young son.

It was almost summer and George was spending the weekend in Denver. On this particular day, Jake was attending a birthday party at a neighboring home and George had suggested that he and Addie drive to the nearby mountains to enjoy the beautiful weather. They parked the car at the side of the road, and made their way across a brook on a makeshift log bridge to a trail that wound into the foothills.

The day was lovely, and they were in good spirits as they

139

climbed high above the stream, until both the water and the car were specks next to the winding ribbon of road. Here they crawled atop a flat boulder where they found shade in a pine tree jutting impossibly through the hard stone.

"It's so peaceful here," George remarked as he lowered himself, then offered Addie his hand to sit beside him. "It's like the rest of the world has disappeared."

"It was like this on the farm sometimes," said Addie. "Surrounded by nature, the changing of the seasons. Even when I was alone, I found comfort in it."

"Do you miss it there?"

Addie thought for a time before answering him. "I miss what Jacob and I had there," she said finally. "I miss our little house and his family, the simple way of life we lived. But the war took all of that away from us. One by one his brothers and sister left the area. Then, of course, he died. And then his parents gave up." She sighed heavily. "It could never have been the same after that. No, George, I don't miss it. Not now. That's all behind me now."

An uncomfortable silence followed, and Addie searched restlessly for something to fill it. "Look!" she grabbed George's arm. "A chipmunk!"

Paying no attention he stared into her eyes. "See—" she pointed, then turned her head away.

"Addie, let me tell you how he died. You can't put it behind you until you know." His voice was soft and kind.

"What difference will it make?" her voice shook.

"For me it made all the difference. Your husband didn't give his life without purpose. I want you to know about it. For your sake, for Jake's."

"All right then." Still she looked away, staring into the distance at the infinite panorama before her. "Tell me."

Gently George draped an arm over Addie's shoulder as

he spoke. She shivered, then moved closer to him. "There were six of us who'd kind of stayed together," he began. "We'd been in battle for days, trying to defend a little town. Women and children were there, and we were trying to evacuate them before the Germans came. But all hell broke loose.

"We thought we had them all loaded on trucks. You could see those little kids peeking out from under the tarp where we told them to hide—they looked so scared. Kids don't understand war and bombs and guns. They don't know why they have to hide on a truck and leave home. Some of them cried, and I don't know how, but their mothers stopped them real fast. It was so strange."

"Did you get them out?"

"We thought they were all out when one of the women with several children became hysterical because she couldn't locate her two oldest boys. Our captain asked if Jake and I and our four buddies would do a quick sweep of the main square to see if we could find them. We agreed, thinking it would only take a few minutes."

Addie turned to face George, sensing that he was in the village as he told the story. "The six of us set out. It was dusk, and we hid in the shadows. We saw German troops marching into the village from the other side. The rest of our unit rushed to move out the trucks and hide in the countryside. We were separated from them. The Germans were between us and our platoon, so we didn't try to rejoin them. It would have given them away. As a result, our backs were up against enemy territory."

"Did you make it to safety before they saw you?"

"We did, finally. We saw a little house on a side street with the door hanging open. It was pitch dark and we were tired and wet—it had started to rain. We took a chance and hid inside. We were scared." His voice shook as he whispered, "I was so scared."

He did not continue until Addie prompted, "Were there people in the house?"

George shook his head. "No one was there. It was empty."

"What about the missing boys?" asked Addie.

"It turned out that they were on another truck with some friends. Everything was so disorganized in our rush to round them up that the mix-up wasn't discovered until the next day when the trucks reached safety."

"And you were left behind," mumbled Addie.

"That's right," said George. "The risk was too great to the refugees. Our captain needed everyone left in the squadron to escort them out of the area. And the town was empty."

"The Germans left, too?" she asked.

"Not that night," answered George. "There was a covered area in the square and they stayed in it all night. The next morning they started searching, looking for people I guess. I think they were wet and tired, too. When they realized all of the people were gone, they just more or less went through the motions."

"What happened to all of you?"

"We stayed in hiding in that house. It was open all around, and to reach the main road and safety we needed to go the opposite way through their camp. There was no other route to escape. Since we were outnumbered, we decided to wait it out. I figured they'd find us and we'd all be killed or taken prisoner. But it was weird. They were also seeking shelter and I think they checked out every house around but the one we were in. A couple of guys came close, one even peeked in the window. But nobody came in.

It was like it was invisible. Nobody bothered."

"So you stayed there, waiting for them to leave," Addie offered, wanting to keep Jacob alive in the story a little longer.

"They weren't in any hurry, that's for sure," George continued. "We spent a couple days in that house, slipping out at night to drink rainwater from some pots that were outside. I lost track of time. I guess the house had been empty for a long time, because there was no food in it. We had a few rations on us, but after a while we didn't know if we were going to die from bullets or thirst or starvation."

"It must have been awful."

"It was," he nodded with the memory. "We couldn't even talk much. But I guess I don't have to tell you who kept us going."

"Jacob?" she murmured.

"Jacob. That guy. You'd have thought we were just taking a little break from the war. He never doubted we'd get out. He wouldn't let anyone get down. He was our senior officer and he took that seriously."

Addie felt a tear slide softly down her cheek and brushed it away. "Then why . . . ?"

George straightened before finishing the story. "There were a lot of them, but slowly they started to clear out. We were cold and hungry. We all knew we were running out of time. There was a fellow with us by the name of Charlie Dowds. He was barely eighteen, and he was starting to lose it. He was a good guy, always tried hard. But he was just a kid, Addie. He didn't have any business in the Army. He belonged back in the States in high school—he and a lot of other kids just like him. I think that's why he went with us. He thought as long as he stayed with Jacob, nothing could hurt him. And, of course, Jacob was great with boys like that. He built their confidence."

Addie remained silent now, her arms wrapped tightly around her knees. "Most of the enemy moved out and there were only a few left that we could see. I don't know why they stayed behind or what they were waiting for. It was dawn and they were gathering in the square. That damn rain never had let up."

Slowly he continued. "I think if we could have hung on a few more hours they would have left and we'd have all made it out alive. But Charlie cracked. He burst out the door before any of us could react." George sighed wearily.

"Jacob shouted at us to run out the back and cover him. He'd try to get Charlie and join us. We couldn't stay in the house any longer—they'd seen Charlie and they were coming. It happened so fast." George strained with the memory.

"I offered to hold back, too, but Jacob pulled rank on me. He ordered me stay with the others. I shouldn't have gone, Addie," he whispered.

"Go on."

"The last thing he said before we went out the door was, 'I'll see you on the other side.' And then everything fell apart. The Germans took aim as they marched toward us. Jacob dodged through the street, shouting commands and trying to reach Charlie. As he ran, he returned their fire. I got hit racing for cover. The other guys didn't discharge their weapons because they feared hitting Jacob or Charlie. And for a second, we thought Jacob got all of them."

George took a deep, shaking breath before he continued. "It's all such a blur—after I was hit, I could hardly tell what was happening. I found out later that Jacob caught up with Charlie and tackled him to the ground. He held the kid down until he stopped struggling, then rose and signaled our troops to advance. But another shot was fired and before we could back him, Jacob was killed."

Addie covered her mouth, gasping.

"My comrades all fired then. And the last one, the one who shot Jacob, was taken down. When it was over everything was quiet, except Charlie Dowds. He was curled up on the ground crying. Somebody ran ahead to help Jacob, but it was too late. And Charlie, he just kept crying and crying."

"Was he wounded?" Addie's voice was flat and distant.

"No," George sighed. "But he had wounds of a different kind, the kind that will never heal."

The two sat quietly for a long time. The wind rippled gently through the trees, offering a soft romantic melody incongruous with the somber mood hanging heavily upon them. George's arm remained draped about Addie as she huddled, motionless. She said almost in a whisper, "Is that all?"

"Yes," George nodded slowly. "I don't remember much about the next few days. We made it back to an aid station." He added thoughtfully, "I remember wondering if Jacob knew he was going to die. I mean, I kept thinking about that when it was over. I think he knew that somebody might have to die to save me and Charlie and the guys. Even though he had so much to live for, he wasn't afraid if it was him. I'll always respect him for that."

Silence again embraced them. It was a story Addie would play over and over in her mind for years. But at that moment, her thoughts were frozen. Every question she would later ask herself, every alternative her imagination could develop to change the awful outcome, was buried on the mountainside that day.

Slowly, the two rose as the sun began to set. Hand in

hand, they retraced their way down the shaded path. When they reached the stream, George bent and washed his face in the cold water. His blue eyes glistened as he turned back to Addie.

"Thank you for telling me," she said and gently wiped his face with the sleeve of her jacket.

He caught her hand and held it against his cheek a moment. His eyes urgently searched her face. When he spoke, his voice was husky and broken. "Addie, is it my fault that Jacob died? Could I have saved him?"

"Oh, George, no! Don't ever say that! Don't even think it!" She pulled him into her arms and felt his body shake heavily against her. "You did what he ordered you to do. You did nothing wrong."

Then, ever so gently, he kissed her and buried her within the shelter of his own strong arms.

They married that summer in a small wedding in the garden at the mansion. Jake stood proudly between them, carrying on a small velvet pillow the two gold bands that symbolized their union. Sarah, holding her infant son, stood with her brood of children. The servants beamed, even the nurse who would soon be saying her final good-bye to young Jake.

It was to be one of the last times the Marsh family visited the mansion. As Addie left Denver and headed south with her family to her new life in a blue-collar town, she knew that the sisters would never really overcome the differences in the lifestyles that they had chosen.

Addie placed her hand gently around Maggie Parks's arm just above the elbow. "Ready for takeoff!" she laughed.

Maggie proceeded nervously, "Well, here goes. Tell me if I do something wrong."

"Relax," Laura instructed above the mixture of voices that filled the Pinecliffe community room. "This is just a learning exercise. Make it fun."

Addie adjusted the sleep shade across her eyes, which shut out any remaining vision that might have helped her. Slowly Maggie started out, and together they explored the room. Addie tried to concentrate above the occasional laughter or comment from other partners nearby. By walking in unison with Maggie and using nonverbal signals that Laura had taught them, the two soon became efficient at traveling together. They maneuvered expertly through a narrow maze of chairs that Laura had set up. They opened and passed through doors together, closing them behind without missing a step.

They ventured outside to the front steps and down the sidewalk to the curb. They crossed the street twice before making their way back to the building. With Maggie pausing before the steps to allow Addie to find them with her foot, with changes in arm positions, and by her warnings about doors and obstacles, the two were able to walk comfortably together.

"Thanks, Maggie," said Addie pulling off the shade.

"You did great!" Maggie responded.

"Only with your help," Addie assured her.

"It's like dancing," Laura said. "With practice you can travel with someone's help without worrying about doors and stairs and obstacles. It sure beats having someone grab you by the arm and drag you along!"

Murmurs of agreement responded. "I've been doing this since I became blind," interjected Leo. "I don't see what the big deal is. I don't need to be taught this stuff!"

"But I do, Leo," said someone else. "So bear with me, okay?"

"Sure, I know. But, hey, I need a chick, man. Give me a good looking woman's arm, and I'll follow her anywhere!"

"Oh, Leo!" Alice laughed. "Always a joker. What are we going to do with you?"

"I think we should be serious during our lessons!" May Evans shouted from across the room. "Laura's trying to teach us things to help us, and we all need to pay attention."

A tense silence filled the room interrupted only by Leo's muffled, "Oh, God, here we go . . ."

"All right, everyone." Laura began to dismantle the obstacle course and push the chairs back toward the center table. "Some of you, please help me with this, and let's get back into the group and discuss what we've learned today."

"Well, I don't think Gordon thought much of this exercise," Walter began once they were all seated. "He thinks he's a much better guide than a human."

"I'd have to agree with that sentiment," remarked David.

"But I think it's good," Walter continued in a more serious tone. "I don't always take Gordon, for a number of reasons, and this will be a big help. Sometimes when you're in an unfamiliar place with sighted people, they want to help you in the wrong ways. I love my nephew dearly, but whenever I'm with him, he wants to grab me and drag me or push me in front of him. It's very uncomfortable. He's even run me into a door or two!"

"Can I relate to that!" Addie laughed. "My son, Joe, is forever grabbing and directing me. I know he means well, but I feel so unsure of myself when he does it. If he'd use this method, we'd manage a lot better when we're out together."

"And Joe's not here. And Walter's nephew isn't here. So

what are you going to do Addie . . . Walter?" asked Laura.

"Teach them!" the two said in unexpected unison.

"You've got it!" Laura laughed. "This technique of walking safely with another person is called 'sighted guide.' The only way you will get your family and friends to use it with you is to teach them. They haven't magically learned what to do just because you lost your sight, so they do what they think is best. Unfortunately, it's often the wrong thing."

"Sighted people are stupid!" Leo muttered.

"Yes, we are," Laura agreed good-naturedly.

"That reminds me of something else," Susanna said. "I think some people believe that when a person is blind, they can suddenly hear better and their sense of touch and smell are more acute."

"I wish!" the person next to her responded.

"It's not true," she went on. "I think that now my other senses are much better than when I could see, but it didn't just happen. I had to work at it. You start relying more on hearing and smelling and touching when your vision is gone. But it sure isn't automatic. You have to practice and pay more attention than before."

"Being blind isn't easy, that's for sure," said David.

"Another perception that people with sight seem to have about the blind," began a new member of the group, but he was interrupted by Leo.

"I told you sighted people are stupid!"

"Now that's about enough!" May half rose from her seat.

"Wait a minute. Hold on you guys! One speaker at a time," Laura said as May eased back into her chair. "Let Tom finish."

"What I was saying," continued Tom, a retired teacher from the Pinecliffe High School, "was that in the movies or in literature, blind people are sometimes depicted as having super-human capabilities."

"Not always. Sometimes it's assumed that blind people are pathetic," said David.

"And we can never hear." Cecil yelled from across the room making his point. "People often shout at me because I'm visually impaired. That makes sense, doesn't it?"

Heads nodded as knowing laughter supported Cecil's contention.

"What it really comes down to," Susanna concluded, "is that we're just regular people who happen to have trouble seeing."

Laura said, "You folks have to be the teachers. You have to let people know what you need and what you don't need. If you don't recognize your friends in the grocery store, you must let them know why. You literally have to teach them to identify themselves. You need to teach the people you are with how to be sighted guides. They aren't going to figure these things out on their own."

"Because they're stupid!" Leo hissed, not willing to let it go.

"Leo, that's enough!" May's voice was cold. "We are so fortunate to have this support group and for Laura to give us her time each month. I come here to learn, not to listen to someone else being rude and disrespectful." A silence filled only with shifting chairs flooded the room.

"Listen," Addie's soft voice broke the tension. "I know what you're saying, May." She proceeded in spite of the discomfort of speaking before a group, a task that had never been easy for her.

With her face flushing in full Addie style, she somehow continued, "I know that sometimes when a person is trying to hear and others are talking or being silly, it's hard." Like the first day she had attended a meeting, she clung to the edge of the table. "Sometimes Leo gets carried away, and we have to let him know that, especially when he's keeping someone else from speaking. But we're here to share *all* of our feelings, and that includes being angry or silly or sad."

For once, no one interrupted. Addie could feel a roomful of sightless eyes upon her. "I don't know what caused the act of desperation that took away Leo's sight. But for him to reach within himself and find the ability to laugh again, even if that laughter doesn't always fit the occasion—well, I don't know if I could ever do that."

Addie took a deep, shaking breath above the hush of the room. "I guess what I'm trying to say is this: We are friends, and friends listen to whatever needs to be said. We have to remember what's important," she said. "We are here for support. Support for May. Support for Leo." She felt Walter's hand cover her own clenched fist and squeeze it gently until she relaxed. "I guess that's all I have to say."

An unexpected round of applause broke forth and Addie felt her body tremble. Walter was still holding one of her hands as Gordon's cold, wet nose searched for the other. Maggie leaned over and placed an arm around May.

"It's all cool, May," Leo stood awkwardly and stretched. "We're still friends, okay?" His cane bounced across the rungs at the back of the chairs as he made his way around the table. "C'mon, Laura. Let's get those refreshments going! That's what we all really come for. Hey, whose turn was it to bring them today anyway?"

An afternoon summer shower had brought the bustle of a busy day at Bear Lake to a halt. Addie was not concerned. A veteran to all weather, she knew how quickly this would change and she settled into the solace of her little cabin.

Rufus shook himself indignantly as he rushed past the open screen door after calling to Addie to let him in. Apparently the storm had interrupted an important adventure and wasn't as agreeable to him as it was to Addie. As they settled in together to wait it out, Rufus licked away the drops of rain from his shiny coat.

"May I use your phone?" Addie was startled by a dark form filling the opening beyond the screen.

She reached back to the small table by her chair and turned off her cassette player, which had become a staple of summer afternoons. "Sure, come in. I didn't hear you knocking."

As the man entered her kitchen, Addie could not make out his face, but recognized a tall, broad frame and the deep, hollow voice accompanying it.

"Paul Curtis?"

"I'm sorry to bother you," he replied. "Could I use your phone?"

"Yes, certainly. It's right here. Isn't yours working?"

"I still don't have one," he said. "I've been waiting for the installation crew all day."

"I don't believe there was ever phone service to your side of the lake," sympathized Addie. "They must be having to run new lines all the way."

"Well, whatever it is, it sure is taking a long time. Sometimes I think if you're an outsider around here . . ."

As he made his call, Addie prepared a new pot of coffee and placed a freshly baked pie on the table, ignoring the sheriff's concerns about her unfriendly neighbor. "Any luck?" she asked when he was finished.

"Tomorrow," he said. "They say they'll be out tomorrow for sure." Studying the preparations on the table he carefully chose his words. "Mrs. Marsh—"

"Addie. Everyone calls me Addie."

"All right, Addie. This is very kind of you, but I can't stay. I have too much to do. I am grateful for the use of the phone, and I'll try not to bother you again."

He was gone before Addie could object. Wearily, she sat alone at the kitchen table. Her first thought was not of the intrusion or even her neighbor's refusal. Her primary concern was that he had gone back into the rain without a hot drink to sustain him. That had never before happened in Addie's home on Bear Lake.

That night Addie couldn't sleep and was aware of every sound the dark produced. More than once she was startled, only to find Rufus sleeping soundly at the foot of her bed. Unable to discern what was troubling her, Addie scolded herself for being foolish. She even practiced changing her thoughts, remembering happy times, praying for sleep to come.

After finally drifting into a restless slumber, Addie again awoke suddenly. Rufus, too, lifted his head in surprise. This time Addie heard a distinct, unmistakable sound. Someone or something was prying at the bedroom window. Without thinking Addie shouted out, "Hello! Who's there?" She remained in her bed, too frightened to move.

A scrambling sound was followed by a thud as the intruder hit the ground. Addie was certain she heard footsteps running toward the lake. A moment later, all was still. Was she dreaming?

Creeping to the window, Addie remembered her sight was useless in the dark. She spent the rest of the night in the living room sipping tea and thinking hard about what to do. It was a familiar problem, only this time there were promises she had made to others to be sensible when in trouble. Still, a call to Joe or Bill Johnson was a step closer to Gateway. This was her summer. She was starting to take charge of her life again. Even with the events of the night, Addie could not bring herself to summon help.

At the first signs of daylight, she moved to the porch knowing there would be no more sleep this night. A chorus of birds welcomed her and a blanket of moisture still on the air filled her lungs, chasing away the remaining traces of fear. The morning was new, and though no one stirred about the lake, Addie was aware that she was not alone.

Jacob, she breathed.

Good morning, my love.

Oh, Jacob. What am I to do?

Lock your doors.

Lock my doors? Addie laughed out loud. *Is that all you have to say? Lock my doors!*

My dear Addie, he sighed. *You're making this harder than it needs to be. Yes, lock your doors. Be smarter than the world around you. It's not the same as when we were young. Do what is necessary to be safe. Then sit back on this porch and enjoy your mountains, darling. It's really very simple.*

Chapter 9

The Old Mobile wound its way up the familiar road to Addie's home with Carol Wilmont's incessant babble rising and falling melodically with the hum of its motor. This time, however, instead of picking up or returning Addie, a delivery was to be made. As the van came to a stop in a cloud of dust, Walter stepped down from the side door, his hand clasped firmly around a sturdy leather harness. The driver's parting remarks as she retreated to the road were not acknowledged by the yellow dog within the apparatus as he seriously attended to his duties.

"Hello there!" Addie called from the doorway. "Welcome to Bear Lake."

"Hello, Addie!" Walter called congenially waving his free hand. "Gordon, Forward!"

"I hope my cat doesn't distract him," said Addie as they approached the door.

"He's okay with cats," Walter laughed. "He'd probably rather not be, but his education included a feline tolerance class."

"But the feline in residence here went to a different school," Addie teased.

"He'll be all right. As a matter of fact, Gordon told me on the way out here that he just wants to spend the afternoon lying on that famous porch of yours."

Holding the screen door open for the pair, Addie asked, "How does Gordon know about my porch?"

"Well, don't forget, he comes to Group, too. You probably think he's always sleeping under the table. But the truth is, he's a horrible eaves-dropper. He's knows every-thing about everyone!"

"I'll have to watch what I say in the future!"

"Boy, something sure smells good in here, Addie. What have you been up to?" Walter stood in the center of her kitchen, and Addie thought how easily he fit in, how he seemed to belong here.

"I've made stew. Do you like it?"

"Like it? I think this must be my lucky day."

When Gordon was comfortably settled on the porch and Addie had given her guest a tour of her home, the two sat at the kitchen table and enjoyed the meal. They discussed Bear Lake and its history and significance to the Pinecliffe area. Walter had been there only a few times for picnics and summer outings in the five years he had lived in Pinecliffe.

"What brought you here?" Addie asked when he told her that he was a newcomer.

"Actually, it was my nephew, Mark." He pushed aside his plate as he spoke. "That was a wonderful lunch. You should find trouble and need me more often."

"Don't even think it," Addie moaned. "I seem to be able to get into trouble without even trying."

Walter laughed. "You keep things interesting all right. As I was saying, my nephew introduced me to Pinecliffe. You see, I'm a widower. Unfortunately, my wife and I were never able to have children, so I'm very close to my broth-ers' kids."

"Didn't you say at one of our meetings that you spent your working life farming?"

"Yes. It was a great way to live," Walter went on with his story. "When Mark's father died and my other brother and I decided to retire from working the farm, we passed it on to his boy. By then Mark was employed as an engineer here in Colorado. I didn't want to stay out at the farm. For one thing, I wouldn't have been able to quit working; I'd have been in everybody's way. And I believe the kids needed a chance to make it on their own without me scrutinizing their every move."

"I can't imagine they wanted you to leave," Addie ventured.

"Oh, no, they didn't," he assured her. "I was welcome to stay. I still go back once a year to visit. My remaining brother and his wife were heading to Arizona to move into a condo, and they also invited me to live with them. But, I guess I was ready to 'do my own thing' as the kids say. Anyway, when Mark invited me out for a visit, I decided this is where I wanted to live."

"You said he lives in Richmond?"

"Yes, he and his wife and kids wanted me to stay in the city with them, but that's not for me. I'm a country boy and I wanted a place of my own. I like family, but not too close."

"I do understand that!" Addie chuckled.

"One day while I was still visiting, we took a drive to Pinecliffe and I fell in love with the village. I got lucky. I met a lady who was just preparing to move and hadn't even officially put her home up for sale. I bought it on the spot, and here I am!"

"You were never sorry?"

"Not at all!" Walter exclaimed. "I love it here! I hope to spend the rest of my life in Pinecliffe. The people are nice and everything I need is in walking distance. I feel so—"

"Lucky!" Addie finished for him and they both laughed.

"Now, we've got more serious business to discuss, don't we?" Walter asked as Addie refilled his glass with iced tea.

"I'm afraid so, Walter. I can't thank you enough for

coming out to help me today. I didn't know who else to call."

"I feel honored," Walter said. "You said you were afraid. What happened?"

Addie told Walter about the noise she had heard the night before and how sure she was that someone was trying to pry open her bedroom window while she was sleeping. Walter expressed concern over this possibility, but wondered why she hadn't called Sheriff Johnson.

"Calling Bill is putting out the red flag, Walter. My son is pushing to move me to town, and I'm not ready to do that."

"You thought if you called the sheriff your son would find out and put more pressure on you?" he asked.

"Exactly!" Addie sighed. "I know I need to take some precautions to be safe. It's not the same world out there anymore, not even at Bear Lake. Joe's awfully busy, but he tries to keep things up pretty well around here. He came out the weekend after I got home and filled in that hole I stepped in and inspected the paths front and back. Still, I'd feel better if you could check things for me. I can't ask him to do it without telling him what's bothering me."

"I see." Walter rose from his chair. "Well, let's get started, Addie. I'll do everything I know to help you secure your home, but it may take several visits. Your cooking's better than mine."

"No problem!" Addie felt an abrupt rush of pride in her accomplishment.

"You'll need to show me all the windows and doors, any place that someone could enter. I didn't bring my toolbox. Do you have equipment?"

"A shed full." Addie placed the back of her hand against Walter's, and he immediately took her arm just above the elbow. "Just tell me what I need to do. I want to help!" she insisted.

They spent the afternoon examining Addie's home. Walter expertly ran his hands around each window sill and door jam making repairs as needed. Screws and bolts were tightened and inside locks were installed or repaired. After years of farming, Walter had a miraculous ability to make do in the absence of necessary hardware. They visited harmoniously as they worked together, and as the afternoon progressed, even Gordon and Rufus were lying within a few feet of each other in no apparent distress.

Twice Carol phoned to return Walter to the village, and twice she agreed to extend the visit. When it was close to the driver's quitting time, Addie and Walter were finished and began to put the tools away.

"I think you're in good shape now, Addie. I don't think anyone could break in here without quite a bit of effort."

"I feel so much better," Addie replied.

"Good," said Walter. "I'm glad I could help you. Support. Isn't that what that nice lady in the group said it was all about?"

"What nice lady was that?" Addie reddened.

"Seriously," said Walter. "That was a kind thing you did for Leo. I think it was something all of us needed to hear."

"Oh, well," Addie brushed away his compliment. "Let's wait outside for Carol."

Walter fastened the harness back around Gordon who immediately resumed his sober posture. "A couple of other things you might want to do, Addie," Walter suggested as they waited. "You should consider starting a 'buddy system' with someone else who lives out here. You know, check in with each other regularly, and if one of you doesn't respond the other can get help right away. We talked about it at Group while you were at your son's. It's obvious, really."

"I suppose it's best if your 'buddy' isn't living in Florida?" Addie teased.

"It could get expensive calling long distance!"

"You don't know anyone who'd be interested, do you?" She asked as Walter bent to adjust the harness.

"Well," he feigned a serious response. "Gordon might be." They laughed together before Walter said, "I'll call you in the morning. And another thing. Nobody should be without smoke detectors. Do you have one?"

"I did, but it's obviously not working," Addie lamented. "There have been a couple of times it should have gone off and didn't."

"The famous cake episode?" he laughed.

"And others."

"I'll pick one up for you and we'll get it installed," Walter offered.

"Oh, no, Walter, Joe can . . ."

"It's no trouble, Addie. Red flags, remember?"

"Thank you so much for today, for everything." Addie walked down the driveway alongside Walter and Gordon as they heard the familiar rumble of the Old Mobile approaching.

"Don't be afraid to call the sheriff, Addie," Walter warned. "Sometimes that's what you have to do. Don't take chances."

"And Addie," he called from the window as the van pulled away. "Lock your doors!"

"Yes," she whispered. "Someone else already suggested that."

Addie had barely returned to the kitchen and was busy cleaning up the dishes that she and Walter had left in their hurry to get to more important work, when a sudden knocking at the screen interrupted her reflection of the day's events.

"Addie! Why is this door locked?" It was Sybil in her usual burst of youthful exuberance.

"Sybil! Come in, come in."

Before Addie could explain the door, she had unhooked the latch, and the girl was in the kitchen full of enthusiasm and excitement. "Who was that guy with the dog? Oh, Addie, I raced up here as quick as I could when I noticed that dog. I wanted to see him so bad. Was that one of those blind dogs?"

"No, Sybil. If that dog was blind he wouldn't be much use to my friend, now would he?"

"Oh, Addie," Sybil laughed. "You know what I mean!" She automatically began to help Addie stack the dishes and carry them to the sink. The older woman did not object. Sometimes it was best to keep Sybil occupied.

"He's called a dog guide," Addie explained.

"And that man, Addie. Have you got a boyfriend?" Sybil teased. "Have you been holding out on me?"

"No, dear," Addie smiled. "He's just a friend. A wonderful friend."

The Fourth of July at Bear Lake was the busiest day of the summer at the mountain resort. Every year for as long as Addie had been at the lake, the Pinecliffe Chamber of Commerce held a picnic in the park next to the community building. Then at dusk, wagons pulled by tractors and loaded with hay and full of excited townspeople and visitors made their way to the shores of Bear Lake. On the way to the lake everyone joined in singing patriotic songs in honor of the holiday.

As the wagons arrived, the summer residents of Bear Lake welcomed their neighbors, providing them with more food, conversation and games, until darkness fell and the moment everyone was waiting for came at last. The Pinecliffe High School marching band emerged from among the trees, drawing the spellbound attention of everyone. With boisterous music they proudly introduced the fireworks display, a spectacular program which turned the blue water into rainbows of light flashing high above its shores. The program originated from a floating platform in the middle of the lake, keeping fire danger confined to the water.

Addie always had a front row seat to this magnificent event from her porch high above. This year was no different. The entire week prior to the holiday, she had planned for the celebration which was to include her family from the city. She had cleaned the cabin, and had insisted on doing all of the cooking, allowing many hours for preparation. When the day arrived, she felt more like the Addie of years past than she had in a very long time.

"Grandma!" Michael was the first to enter her home after Addie heard the car pull up out front. "I want you to meet someone."

"Michael!" Addie caught the boy in her arms cherishing the clean, soapy scent of him. In doing so she realized his hand was entwined with someone else who followed closely behind him.

"Gram, I'd like you to meet Beth. She's my—well, she's a friend of mine from college."

"Beth!" Addie exclaimed. "Welcome to Bear Lake. What a nice surprise. I'm so glad you came."

"Michael's told me all about this place," a fresh, timid voice replied. "I couldn't wait to see it!" Although Addie could not distinguish the girl's features she could manage wisps of reddish blond hair, and she was sure the girl was blushing. Addie liked her immediately.

"Mom!" Joe's voice boomed as he set a cardboard box filled with contributions to the feast on the kitchen table.

"How's my Addie?" The soft caring voice of Judy caught her by surprise as her daughter-in-law slipped from behind Joe and gave her a hug. "You've been busy preparing for this, I can tell."

"Judy! Joey!"

"Joey!" Michael burst into laughter and Beth giggled. "Okay if I call you Joey, Dad?"

The father took a playful swipe at his son as the young couple ducked, then raced toward the porch. "I'm going to show Beth the lake," Michael called over his shoulder.

After having their fill of Addie's banquet, the family sat lazily on the porch watching the sun set over the water. Michael and Beth sat on the steps, his arm wrapped around her. Occasionally they joined the others in conversation, but for the most part they whispered softly, giggled, and fell into quiet moments when her head rested on the boy's shoulder. Addie's heart pounded with this tender surge of young love before her. More than once she fought to control a rush of bittersweet joy which brought tears to her eyes.

It was good to be together with all of them. For once, there was no scolding or discussions about the future. The family was mesmerized by the magic of the mountains, the lake, and the celebration.

"I've got something I want you to have, Judy," Addie announced reaching into her apron pocket. "You've been such a help to me these last few months, and, well . . . I just wanted to show my appreciation." She pushed a small box forward and awkwardly Judy took it. "I guess I'm lucky, Judy." Addie borrowed a familiar line.

"Lucky? Why?" Judy held the box tightly but did not open it.

"To have you for my only daughter." Addie smiled, then went on softly. "I love you."

"Oh, Mom!" Judy rose and pulled Addie close to her. "I'm the lucky one."

Embarrassed, Addie laughed, "Open it. Open it!"

Inside the box Judy found a small gold locket in a heart shape with a tiny latched door. It was quite old but had been freshly polished for this occasion. Gingerly, Judy pried the tiny door open and looked upon the faded black and white photo of an infant. She sent Addie a questioning look.

"That's your husband," Addie confided. "He was just a few days old there. His father gave me the locket when Joe was born, and now I want you to have it."

The other family members crowded around to examine the gift as Judy whispered, "Thank you, Mom. This means so much to me."

Addie did not reveal to her family that this was not the original gift she had intended to give, although it fit the occasion. The idea of giving Judy a piece of her jewelry had come to her one day when she and Sybil were going through some old boxes in the extra bedroom. With all the talk of her moving, Addie had begun the process of sorting her things. She was determined that no one else would go through her belongings and stoically wished to be involved in the dispensing of them.

They had come upon a box of old costume jewelry, and Sybil had admired a string of sky blue beads. They had an interesting hue to them, which sparkled and caused the shade to change in various types of light. "Oh, Addie, these are gorgeous!" Sybil exclaimed holding them up to her neck and studying them in an old dressing table mirror. "Why don't you wear them anymore?"

"Oh, I guess I'm too old!" Addie laughed.

"You're never too old for something like this!" Sybil insisted.

"You take them, Sybil," Addie said impulsively. "I want you to have them to remember me by."

"Oh, Addie, do you mean it?"

"Of course I do," Addie gave the girl a quick hug. "Please take them."

"Oh, Addie," she repeated. "No one's ever given me something like this. I will treasure them," she said passionately. "I'll always think of you when I wear them. They're the color of your eyes, the color of the lake."

Later when Sybil had left, Addie thought of Joe's wife and decided upon a special piece of jewelry for her to have as well. What Addie had chosen for Judy was a tiny gold cross that George had given her the day they were married. The cross had been found lying in the dirt next to Jacob's body and had been given to George as he prepared to return to the United States. She had worn it for years until the chain became old and tangled, and she feared she would lose it. It was one of her most treasured possessions, and she knew that Judy would understand that and take care of it after she was gone.

Addie had stored these special treasures in a small ivory box that the Judge had given her when she was still a girl. This box was kept in the bottom of her chest of drawers. But when Addie had gone to retrieve it, she found the box missing along with most of its contents. The only items left behind, that had apparently fallen into the drawer as the box was being removed, were a medal awarded after Jacob's death, the golden locket and a small quartz stone. The stone was the first gift her son, Jake, had ever given her when he was just a toddler. He had found it in the yard and run straight to his mother, proudly presenting it to her. "Kissmus. Mommy's kissmus!" He had cried happily, memories of Christmas and gift giving still fresh in his young mind. And as the day the stone was given, Addie treasured it again upon finding it that afternoon.

Addie had searched frantically through all of her belongings for the other missing items. As she did so, she became vaguely aware that many of her belongings had been handled. Other things that she recalled having in the past, could no longer be found. The back parts of drawers and cupboards were untidy and disorganized—not the way she remembered leaving them. It was then that Addie realized her home had been burglarized. Someone had been inside and taken many of her keepsakes which she realized would now have value as antiques, when seen through the scrutinizing eyes of a dealer.

The thought of these things missing—her cross, the wedding ring which Jacob had given her, the tiny bracelets the hospitals had used to identify her sons—had been devastating. Her home had been entered and violated by some unknown person or persons. Who could it be? And when? Had she slept through it, or had she unwittingly been sitting between Walter and David at a support group meeting while someone stole away a part of her life?

Addie had not reported the theft. She had not even told Walter. A part of her rationalized that it was her own fault, she had misplaced them. But deep inside she knew that wasn't true. More red flags.

The band was playing and the fireworks were beginning

to dazzle the lake below. The Marsh family crowded close together in anticipation, Judy still clinging to the small, cherished box.

"Mom, can you see the fireworks?" Joe asked placing his arm around her shoulders.

"Parts of them. They're blurry, but bright!"

"Wow! Would you look at that?" Michael called out, and the others *ooed* and *awed* in excitement. No matter how many years they stood on this porch, each Fourth of July was new and thrilling to the spectators.

"I can hear them, that's for sure!" Addie covered her ears and Joe hugged her.

Hours later, when the visitors had left Bear Lake, Addie sat quietly on the porch. A frightened Rufus now snuggled securely in her lap and purred to the familiar creaking of the tattered rocker. A few distant voices lingered on the night air, but for the most part the raucous world was finally still. Addie could smell the faint gun powder fragrance of the evening's colorful inferno. It lingered softly among the pines bringing a wave of memories from years gone by.

Back then, she and George and the boys mingled among those on the shore. Because he was a gifted trumpeter, Jake had been allowed to join the Pinecliffe band for the event, even though he attended school in the city. George had been the master of ceremonies for the night several years in a row, although he had struggled each time with his shyness and the butterflies that kept him on edge for days in advance.

Another familiar face joined her quiet reverie and Addie's contentment fused with her cat's delicate slumber. *Hello, my love,* he said tenderly. *You've had a nice day, haven't you?*

Perfect! Addie sighed.

Did I see a distant memory rekindled tonight? he asked after a long silence.

The children? Addie flushed.

Us, he whispered.

It was like that, wasn't it? I can think of nothing more wonderful for my dear Michael than to have what we had, Jacob.

Nor can I, dear Addie, he whispered. *Nor can I.*

"Mrs. Marsh?" A slight tapping on the perpetually locked screen door drew Addie's attention from where she sat at the kitchen table, her fingers moving across the open book in front of her. "May I come in?"

"Paul?" She recognized him in spite of his uncharacteristic timidity.

"It's me. I don't mean to startle you, but I'd like to visit if you have time."

Addie hesitated. Time was a commodity of which she had plenty to share, but maybe not with Paul. After several abrupt encounters with him, she was startled by his request for a visit. Across the gravel road, she could hear a group of youngsters playing volleyball in the side court their grandfather had put up that summer. It had become something of a gathering place for teenagers who found themselves vacationing with relatives at the lake. Addie welcomed their laughter and even the traces of their music, which reached her doorstep from time to time, playing from a portable radio. It comforted her to know that she was not alone.

"Mrs. Marsh?"

"I'm busy!" Addie blurted and immediately felt remorseful for a tone of voice that was foreign to her.

"I don't blame you." His voice remained amazingly soft and kind causing Addie even more discomfort. "Addie," he paused. "I know I've been rude to you, but you and I have always been friends. Please let me in."

"It's not that," she began. "You see, I'm studying for my vision program. I really am busy, Paul."

He stood quietly, not leaving the doorway.

"Out of bounds!" Came a scream from across the road, followed by, "No way!" and a conglomeration of referees giving their individual opinions in unison.

"Addie, I've come to apologize to you," her visitor said when the noise subsided. "At least let me do that. I'm a man with far too much pride. It wasn't easy for me to come over here. Give me a break, okay?"

He was gentle, almost pleading with her. Addie rose and unlatched the door. "I can only visit for a few minutes."

"Thank you!" Telling Blaze to lie down outside the door, he entered the cabin. "Can I sit here?" he asked pulling back the chair opposite hers, and Addie flushed with the awareness that she had not even offered him a seat.

"Yes, of course, my manners," she mumbled. "Would you like something to drink, Paul? I made these cookies this morning." She slid a plate across the table.

"Now that's more like it!" Paul laughed uneasily. "Do you have coffee made?"

"Always. I'm addicted."

"To coffee, or people dropping in?" he asked. "I seem to remember a time when I was the one avoiding you. You were asking me to stay and I was rushing away."

Addie's face again reddened acknowledging the truth of his words. "I keep the coffee pot going for Fred, the mailman, and in the summer there are always morning visitors ready to share a cup with me." She spoke more easily as she poured two cups. "I enjoy the visitors, of course, but I'm afraid I do have a weakness for coffee. I guess if I was going to avoid caffeine, I'd have quit long ago."

"Perhaps this is one visitor you'd rather not have drop in, though?" he asked tentatively, not wanting to spoil the beginnings of relaxed conversation.

"I'm sorry, Paul. I like you, and that's the truth. But lately," she drew a deep breath as her neighbor interrupted her.

"Hold on, Addie! I'm the one who came to say I'm sorry, remember? You don't owe me any apologies."

"Let's put it behind us," Addie said, pushing to the back of her mind the confusion of her missing belongings and the repeated warnings of family and friends to be careful.

"I'd like to try to explain myself, if you'll listen," he pleaded.

"All right then."

"I've been trying since I moved out here to get assistance from the county. You know, utilities, telephone service, road graders. It's been absolutely impossible! They tell me they'll be out but no one comes. I feel like I have the plague or something! It's said you can't fight city hall and I guess it's true. The more I demand, the more I'm put off."

"That doesn't sound like Pinecliffe," Addie said with surprise. "Maybe in a bigger city you'd get that kind of treatment, but usually out here, everyone tries to help each other. I can't imagine why you're being treated like that."

"Can't you?" he sounded cold and hollow now.

"No, I can't." Uncomfortably Addie adjusted the books on the table in front of her.

"I guess it's my battle to fight," he said. "But this morning I realized that there is at least one person in this community who has shown me kindness since I arrived, and that is you. I want you to know how much I appreciate that."

"Thank you," said Addie waving her hand to dismiss the

subject. "Your apology is not necessary, but accepted. We won't mention it again. Now, I really do have to get back to this, Paul."

"I'm sorry." He rose from his chair. "I'll get out of your way. Thanks for the coffee, and the cookies were great."

"You're welcome."

"What is it you're working on anyway?" He turned back unexpectedly.

"Braille," Addie responded. "I'm trying to learn Braille. My teacher who visits from the city shows me a little each time she's here, and I'm supposed to study between lessons."

"That's neat!" Paul responded with enthusiasm. "It looks hard to me. Do you think you'll ever know it well enough to sit down and read a book by touch?"

"Oh, I don't know about that," Addie laughed. "I'm learning it more for myself than for reading books. I have my tapes for that."

"What good will it do you then?"

"If I learn it, even the alphabet and numbers, I can do all sorts of things. I can put telephone numbers and recipes and my grocery list in Braille, so I can read them back." Her enthusiasm returned, and for a moment she forgot her fears. "I can make labels for food and sew Braille tags into my clothing to tell me what color they are when I'm not sure. Dark blue and black look the same to me."

"I never thought of that," Paul said. "All those things the rest of us take for granted can be a little tough for you, can't they?"

"They can," Addie nodded, "but there are ways. I'm even going to be able to play cards again when I learn Braille. Large print cards are available, but they don't help me. My teacher showed me how the suits and numbers are written in Braille on the cards so they can be identified."

"That's right!" Paul laughed. "I remember playing cards with a blind guy once. He beat the socks off of me!"

"You're kidding!"

"No, I'm not." Paul had opened the screen door but pulled it shut again as he told his story. "Not long after I enlisted, I couldn't get home one Christmas. This guy who lived off base invited me to spend the holidays with his family. It turns out he had a brother who'd been blind from birth. We got snowed in and spent a lot of time playing poker. That guy got a good chunk of my paycheck for Christmas!" Paul laughed and this time Addie joined him.

"I'll tell you what, Addie. I'm challenging you to a game of poker when you get good enough at this. How about that?"

"You're on!" Addie giggled. "Only don't tell my teacher. Somehow I don't think she'd see a poker game as proper motivation."

"It's our secret. Study hard!" And with that he disappeared into the late morning sun.

Addie latched the door obediently and returned to the table where she dropped her face into her hands, shaking her head back and forth. "Now I've invited my reclusive neighbor that no one seems to know anything about back to my home to play poker," she sighed. "What would Joe think about that?"

Chapter 10

"Jake! Joey! Come in! It's time for lunch!" The young, aproned mother stood in the doorway of the tiny bungalow and watched as two boys slowly broke away from a game of football in the middle of the dead-end street. Everyone who lived on this block, shadowed by the tall smoke stacks of the adjacent mill, was aware that the pavement was a miniature football field and drivers should proceed with caution.

"Just a minute, Mom!" called the older boy who dove back into the game for a desperate catch. He maintained his balance, his feet hardly touching the ground, until he passed an imaginary goal post and surrendered his body to the laws of gravity.

"Touchdown! We won, fair and square!" shouted a freckled neighbor boy with a mop of brown curly hair.

The younger of Addie's two boys, now standing on the curb, beamed with pride at his brother's accomplishment. Only six, he was the youngest boy in the game and would not have been allowed by the others at all, except . . . he was Jake McNeil's kid brother, and Jake wouldn't have it any other way. Because Jake was a prized friend, you accepted Joey with him. This was one unspoken rule of neighborhood politics for which there was no compromise.

Addie found a sense of peace in this. Joey would be fine in twelve-year-old Jake's protective silhouette, and the older boy truly didn't seem to mind. From the day of Joey's birth, he had latched onto the child with fierce devotion and love. It was Jake who had prompted Joey's first words and steps. It was Jake who taught Joey the ways of school and the importance of study from the first day the two walked hand in hand into the old brick building two blocks from their home. It was Jake who too easily took the blame for his younger brother's mistakes. And it was Jake whose scolding could do more to reform the youngster than any words or punishment their parents could render.

Sadly, those reprimands were too often necessary. For it was Joey who clumsily blundered through each day. It was Joey who could tear a new pair of trousers the first time they were worn. And it was Joey's loud, eager voice that burst forth at the wrong moment and had to be hushed in disapproval.

This particular summer had been unusually warm and Addie was grateful for the hours the two brothers spent together in the house or playing outside with the other boys. With Jake, Joey could venture to the schoolyard or ride his bike to the market, crossing a busy street along the way. Without his brother, Joey demanded constant entertainment and balked at the discomfort of the relentless heat.

When she and her sons finished eating lunch, Addie began to clear the dishes away. The boys retired to the living room floor where they began putting together the pieces of a board game. Moments later Joey bounded to the door hollering as he ran, "Dad's coming! Dad's home!"

Unconsciously, Addie removed her apron and pushed her hair away from her sweaty forehead. She quickly surveyed the tiny home that she and George had purchased after their marriage eight years ago, and was satisfied that it was sparkling and clean. He was never critical of her, in fact, George often commented on his wife's hard work to keep their home nice. She had sewn and starched the curtains. The furniture, while worn, always glowed with fresh polish. It was important to Addie to have things nice for

George in return for the backbreaking labor he performed daily for his family in the nearby mill.

Each morning Addie packed George a plentiful lunch in the dented, old, black box that he carried. There was never time to come home for the noon break, which was announced by the factory with a long, blaring whistle that could be heard throughout town. And so this day, Addie was surprised at Joey's announcement. It was indeed George who swung open the iron gate into their yard, just in time to catch Joey in his arms. Jake sauntered onto the front porch and leaned against a thin, wooden pillar, interested, but more reserved, in his early adolescent maturity.

"Daddy, what are you doing home?" Joey demanded as his father swung him high into the air, then landed him safely back on the front walk.

"I got the afternoon off!" George's face radiated as his wife came through the door and joined the older boy in anticipation. "And we're going on a picnic!"

"A picnic?" Joey gasped. It was an accepted fact to the family that weekdays were strictly for work, and weekends would include family outings when the chores were finished and extra money was available.

"Are you off?" Addie asked in amazement. "Should I pack a picnic dinner? Where are we going?"

"How did you get the afternoon off, Dad?" Jake joined in.

"Can we fish, Dad? I'll get the poles together and—" Joey chimed.

"Hold on, now. Everybody just hold on!" George laughed. "You are so full of questions, a man can't even think!" He wiped a damp brow as wet hair framed his jolly face. "Now, I'm going to change out of my work clothes and get cleaned up. And yes, we need dinner packed. And maybe pajamas and extra clothes, too. It's Friday—I'm off tomorrow. We can have a long picnic!"

The threesome stood in shocked silence, and the man exploded with hearty laughter. "C'mon! C'mon! There's no time to lose. Let's get ready. Yes, Joey, you can fish. Jake, help him get the poles." He planted a kiss on Addie's forehead as he rushed past her into the house.

George maintained his air of delight and mystery as they loaded the station wagon and closed up the house. He refused to give a hint of their destination as they piled into the car and pulled out of the driveway. No one was surprised when he headed southwest toward the mountains. It was a favorite destination of theirs, and the fishing was good in the streams beyond the little town of Pinecliffe.

At Addie's insistence, he revealed that his foreman had given him the afternoon off for time owed when a piece of machinery had stopped production, and George had stayed past midnight to repair the equipment. He refused, however, to respond to their concerns that they hadn't brought a tent in which to sleep, and where would they be spending the night, if not in their own home?

Again, no one was surprised when they drove through Pinecliffe and turned west toward the picnic areas bordering the stream, which had its beginnings in Bear Lake above the mountain community. Joey whined for a moment when his father didn't stop for ice cream at Scottie's, a landmark diner in Pinecliffe, but one look from Jake brought silence to the younger boy. The surprise came when George turned the car away from the creek bed and headed up a rough gravel road toward the lake itself. In moments, the glistening water welcomed them, and the quiet of the afternoon was broken only by the hum of their car and the occasional distant pounding of a hammer.

176

"They're building homes up here," Addie said in surprise.

"Summer cabins," George corrected her. "The forest service sold some of the land for private use. It's really going to be nice. That's why we came up here. I want to show you something."

George continued to drive to the highest point above the lake where he turned into a driveway overgrown with wild grass and weeds. It led to a small log cabin at the top of the hill. When they reached the end of the driveway, he turned off the motor and opened his door, signaling to the others to get out.

"Is it all right?" Addie asked cautiously. "We're on private property, aren't we? Do you know the owner?"

"Of course I do," George answered. "I know him well. Do you want to see the inside?"

The boys were now enthusiastic and peered into windows as their father dug into his pockets for the key. Inside, the cabin was cool and smelled of wood and a soft wisp of pine. Addie ran her fingers over a newly installed counter top, as Jake stuck his head into the fireplace to stare up the chimney. Joey at once was retrieved from a bed in a sparsely furnished adjacent bedroom, as he began jumping wildly upon it in his excitement.

"Now, settle down!" George commanded. "Come and look at this view." A window across the back of the house framed Bear Lake below. Addie felt her heart stop, overwhelmed by the beauty, the peace of this magical place.

"Do you know the owner, Dad?" Jake asked in almost a whisper. "Do we get to spend the night here?"

"I told you, I know him well. And, yes, we're spending the night here—the whole weekend if you want."

"Yeah!" shouted Joey who raced back to the door to

begin exploring his new world.

"Wait a minute, son. Not so fast!" George caught him by the shoulder and turned him back toward his mother and brother. "First, I've got a story to tell all of you."

They sat together on an overstuffed couch, neatly placed between the window and the fireplace. Addie could not take her eyes from the view of the lake. A blue jay appeared before her, breaking the scene for a second in a teasing dive, causing a smile to cross her face as George started to speak.

"The man who built this cabin works with me at the mill. You've heard me mention John Andrews, haven't you?"

"He's the man you often eat lunch with, isn't he?" asked Addie.

"Yes, and I'd like for all of you to meet him before he leaves," George went on. "He's older than I am and plans to retire at the end of the year. John and his wife built this place over the last few summers. They had hoped to retire here, but won't be able to now."

"Why not?" asked Jake. "Too cold in the winter?"

"Not the way John planned it," said George. "It was intended for these acreages to be used for summer cabins, but John built this place sturdy enough for year-around living. It even has a furnace. He figured as long as he didn't have to work anymore, it wouldn't matter if he got snowed in once in awhile. But, unfortunately, things aren't working out for him. And it's too bad. John's a good man."

"What happened?" asked Addie.

"His wife is having some health problems, and her doctor feels the only way she'll improve is to move to a warmer climate. Her heart is bad, and she struggles with breathing at this altitude."

"What a shame," Addie murmured.

"They're disappointed all right. But they've got to do what's right for her," said George. "In the fall, she's moving to southern California, to a town at sea level where her sister lives. John will join her when he retires. They've vacationed there a number of times, and both of them like it, so it's not all bad. It's giving up this place that gets them down."

"I can imagine," Addie sympathized. "To build a dream and not be able to live in it."

"Exactly," said George. "When John told me about it, well . . ." his voice faltered as his eyes met Addie's. "He offered to sell it to me—almost at cost. Just what he's got in it. I guess I couldn't pass up a deal like that. It seems to mean something to him to know that his cabin will be in good hands; that it will be loved and cared for the way he would have done."

"You mean you're the owner?" Jake exclaimed in disbelief.

"No, Jake, we're the owners. All of us."

"We're going to move here?" asked Joey. "Where will I go to school?"

"No, we can't move here," George laughed. "We'll still live in Richmond, and you'll go to your same school. I have to work, so I've got to be close to the mill in the winter. This will be our cabin—our second home. We'll spend our summers here. You boys can fish and play in the mountains all day if you want to. Your mama won't have to work over a hot stove in the city. And I'll drive back and forth every day. A few months of commuting out of the year will be worth it."

George studied the quiet, disbelieving faces of his family. Reluctantly, he fixed his gaze on Addie, knowing her thoughts before she spoke them. But as she opened her

179

mouth, her words were quickly drowned out by the eruption from her two sons as the reality of their father's gift sunk in. They were full of questions, answers, and plans all at once. They wanted to fish and swim and hike all within that moment. Their father was reciting rules, and Joey needing to stay with Jake, and Addie stared in silence as he tried to calm everyone at once.

"We can't afford this, George." Addie rose from her chair and went to the window, her back to all of them. "What on earth are you thinking?"

"Addie, the children . . ." he whispered.

Respecting this, she waited until George allowed the boys to make a short climb to a pile of rocks nearby. He promised that he would accompany them on their first hike to the lake as soon as he and their mother were settled.

When the boys were out of earshot, Addie began again, "Oh, George, I'm sorry. I know this must mean a lot to you, but we barely get by as it is."

"Addie," his voice shook and he cleared his throat. "Let me worry about that. I've saved a little here and there, and I'm due a raise, maybe even a promotion, in October. Let me do this for you, Addie. Don't you want it?"

"Want it?" her eyes glistened. "I love it. I can think of nothing more that I could want. You know I hate having the boys cooped up in town all summer, and you know better than anyone how much I love being out in nature. I need space and trees and a big open sky. In all my dreams, I couldn't have imagined a place as grand as this! Want it? Oh, George . . ."

"Then it's yours," he whispered pulling her close to him. "I love you more than anything, Addie. This is for you. For us. I can manage it."

They kissed, their first kiss in the cabin at Bear Lake as

their sons' laughter bounced among the trees. Hand in hand the young family took their first walk to the lake and later ate their first dinner and spent their first night in the cabin. A quick visit home to retrieve more belongings began the first of many summers on the lake. And George's first addition to the new place was a huge, wooden porch across the back of the cabin, where Addie could sit and watch the children as they played.

"That's it, Addie, that's the way! You've got it!" Laura walked a few steps behind her, the soft tap-tap of the long white cane steady and rhythmic. The tip of the cane dropped over the curb bringing Addie to a stop. "Found it, didn't you?" Laura beamed.

"I guess you've made a believer out of me," Addie sighed lifting the sleep shade which covered her eyes and prevented her from using her residual sight. "It still feels strange. What do you suppose people who have known me all these years must be thinking when they see us out like this?"

"They probably think you're learning to use a cane. Either that, or that some strange woman is chasing you down the street!"

Addie laughed as she pulled the sleep shade down again. Immediately, her serious demeanor returned as she listened for traffic and determined when it was safe to cross the street. Once on the other side Laura suggested, "Let's take a break."

The streets of Pinecliffe were lined with trees intermingled with park benches. When the two were seated comfortably beneath a shady cottonwood, Laura asked, "Does using the cane bother you that much, Addie? Are you self-conscious?"

"Honestly? Yes, I am. I know I don't see well, and there's no doubt this cane helps me to be more self-reliant. Even though I've been in Pinecliffe a long time, things change and I don't think I could get around on my own unless I was using a cane. I don't feel I need it at home. I know my house and my yard well enough. But still," Addie continued, "I feel embarrassed having people see me. And I guess I feel a little defenseless, too."

"Try and think of the cane as a tool, Addie," Laura encouraged. "It helps you to find your way around in unfamiliar areas. If anything, it makes you more safe than vulnerable. Motorists recognize that the white cane means you have impaired sight, and they're more cautious. It also gives you identity. If you need help finding articles in a store, the clerk will understand your situation, and give you the right kind of assistance instead of just pointing and saying 'over there.' If you run into old friends, but you don't speak because you don't recognize them, the cane will tell them why, and they'll speak to you."

"I guess that's better than having them think I'm rude."

"That's right," Laura agreed. "Remember, Addie, all of the discussions we've had at the support group. Your vision loss is just a part of who you are. It is nothing to hide or be ashamed of."

"I know," Addie nodded. "Old man pride just keeps raising his ugly face!"

"And you just keep knocking him down, okay?"

"Okay."

"You know, Addie," Laura sighed after a few moments of peaceful silence had passed between them, "I like it here. I mean, this little town, the mountains, Bear Lake. It's so different from the world forty miles down the highway."

"I like it, too," Addie replied softly. "In fact, I love it.

It's the only place that will ever be home to me."

"It's you, Addie," the teacher laughed. "Peaceful, yet rugged. A survivor of life's storms."

"I'll take that as a compliment!" said Addie.

"It was intended that way." Laura rose from the bench. "All right then, do you want to try walking over to the grocery store before we end today's lesson?" she asked.

"Yes. I'd like to shop by myself later this week," responded Addie. "Do you think I'm ready?"

"Yes, I do." Laura reassured her. "Remember, too, Addie, that you have a folding cane because you may not need it all the time. You still have some good peripheral vision, so when you feel you don't need it, just fold it up and put it away. But keep it with you when you're away from home. You never know when you'll be in a strange area or encounter glare or darkness—or need to cross a street by yourself."

"I suppose the more I use it the better?"

"Absolutely! Practice makes perfect, right?"

That evening Addie used the cane at dusk to walk down to the edge of the lake. Laura had put an oversized tip on the cane, which allowed it to easily handle the rough terrain of dirt paths and gravel roads. Addie remembered the last time she had ventured to the lake alone and was determined to challenge the fear.

Once on the shore of the lake, she took a deep breath, enjoying the solitude of early evening. Already, fall was in the air as the end of August approached. It felt good to stand there alone. She was happy here, and tonight she had given the greater boundary of her home back to herself. The quiet lapping of the water bouncing against the shoreline was a welcome refrain. For several peaceful moments the silhouette of a woman with a cat sitting faithfully at her side blended with the trees along the lake's rocky border.

As the first stars began to glimmer in the sky, Addie carefully maneuvered her way back up the hill. When she safely reached her cabin, she sank into the familiar arms of her waiting rocker with relief and confidence.

The next day she called Carol Wilmont and asked for a ride into Pinecliffe. There was no point putting it off any longer; she would go to town alone, buy her groceries, and maybe even browse around the hardware store. She would do all that she could for herself and ask for help only when needed. She would be a part of the community again. She would talk to people and feel the warm afternoon sun on her face. She would relish the smell of popcorn from the small corner confectionery and the sound of traffic in the street.

To Addie's pleasant surprise, Carol made no comment when she announced her intention to shop alone today and unfolded the long white cane before stepping out of the van. With a quick wave of her hand, the driver merely called after her departing passenger, "See you in a while Mrs. Marsh—and stay out of trouble!"

Holding her head high, Addie walked into the small grocery store and approached the check out stand. "I need help finding a few items," she said. A high school boy stocking shelves nearby was summoned, and he dutifully assisted Addie in locating her purchases, reading labels, and giving prices.

Addie had finished her shopping and made arrangements to have her groceries placed in the store's cooler until she was ready to ride home, when she ran into Fran Wallace. After so many months of referring to Fran as her invisible helpmate, her sudden appearance on the street was like that of a ghost.

"Fran!" An astonished Addie cried as her friend called out to her. "Are you finally back?"

"Oh, Addie, you poor dear!" Fran embraced her. "How have you managed? I'm so sorry to leave you like that. We got down to Florida and Wally got sick and had to be hospitalized. One thing led to another, and we ended up staying there and I—well, I should have phoned you, but it was all so mixed up."

"Fran, I'm fine!" Addie laughed. "Really, I'm doing fine. I've missed you, of course. Is Wally okay now?"

"Oh yes, he's well. He's waiting in the car for me now. Poor Addie. I heard your vision failed you fast and that you fell in the lake. And someone told me that Joe wants to put you in a nursing home."

Addie laughed again. "It's a small town, Fran. Don't believe everything you hear."

"I can start helping you again next week if you'd like," Fran offered, ignoring Addie's comments. "I don't know how much longer we'll be in town, but I can help until Wally decides to take off again. I guess you aren't in the nursing home after all."

"No, Fran, I'm still here," Addie teased.

"I can see that. But you must need my help!"

"Really, Fran. I'm fine." Addie insisted. "I can't think of anything I need right now."

"You don't need me anymore?" Fran finally seemed to grasp the message Addie was sending.

"Yes, of course I need you." Addie softened and put an arm around her friend. "I will always need your wonderful friendship. Call me and we'll go to lunch. We can talk about old times and catch up on all the Pinecliffe gossip. You can tell me all about your trip. And if you insist, I'll tell you the true story of how I fell *near* the lake, not in it."

185

"I'd like that, Addie. Next week, for sure!" Fran hurried away and Addie found herself laughing still. It was odd. After all this time, Fran was home. Help had arrived, and Addie didn't need it.

She wandered through the hardware store comfortably, speaking to old friends and neighbors and visiting with a few lingering tourists. Two college students, who had been locking their bikes in front of the store when Addie came in, had been deferred to her by the manager when they began asking questions about the history of the area. The three stood in an aisle between the paintbrushes and flowerpots on half-price, and talked for what seemed hours. The students were genuinely interested, and Addie had plenty to share with them. When they thanked her and Addie turned to venture down another aisle, she was stopped again.

"Miss Addie, is that you? I thought I heard your voice."

"Leo?"

"In the flesh!" the young man before her responded. "What are you doing in here?"

"It's my shopping day," said Addie, "And you?"

"I'm helping my grandmother buy some paint. She wants me to smell the colors."

"Leo—" Addie warned as he laughed.

"You didn't know I could paint, did you, Miss Addie?"

"Leo, I believe you could do anything you set your mind to," she said with sincerity. "Except drive. Don't try that, okay?"

He leaned close to her and whispered, "Because you'll tell May on me, won't you?"

"Leo—" she threatened again.

"Seriously, Miss Addie." He straightened up and Addie felt him tower over her. "I do have something I've been wanting to say to you." His voice held a quality Addie hadn't heard before, genuine, yet determined.

"What is it?"

"Thanks," he responded. "Just thanks."

"Thanks?"

"You know," he stammered, "what you said about me at Group. I mean, it meant a lot to me."

"I'm glad," said Addie softly. "It meant a lot to me, too."

"Come with me," the teasing side of Leo returned. "I want you to meet my Grandma. I've told her all about you, the cake mess, everything!"

A pleasant woman, Leo's grandmother, like Addie, could see only good in her grandson. They visited for some time, and before they finished Leo had secured a lunch invitation at Bear Lake for the two of them. His grandmother promised they'd come and bring, of course, a cake. Addie left the hardware store with a package of batteries in one hand, her cane in the other. She pushed the button on her talking watch. An hour remained before the appointed time when the Old Mobile would take her home. Casually, she walked to the end of the block, then deliberately turned away from the diminutive bustle of Main Street. Maybe she'd go see what Walter and Gordon were up to.

As was so often his style, Joe arrived unexpectedly one Sunday afternoon. "Pack your overnight bag, Mom, you're going to the big city!" With cooler autumn temperatures, Addie kept the storm door closed and locked, quietly absorbed in a novel blaring from her talking book player. Joe had let himself in with his key. He seemed not to understand how this might startle her, and Addie avoided conflict by not mentioning that he'd scared her right out of her chair.

Instead, her mind raced to his current plan with guarded

suspicion. "Not another trip to Gateway, I hope?"

"No, Mom, for crying out loud! I said overnight bag—just one night." He caught his impatience and hurried to explain. "I'm sorry. I wanted to surprise you. Michael's doing a paper for an American History class he's taking this semester. It's on the effects of war, and he's doing a graveyard slant. It's a pretty creative idea for him."

"I've always known he was creative, Joe," Addie said.

"Ah, Mom, here we go. That's not what I meant—let's not fight, okay?"

"Sorry," Addie murmured. "Tell me about the project."

"Well, he's going to drive out to the Veteran's Cemetery tomorrow. He's got an appointment to interview an administrative officer out there, and he wants to take a few photos. I thought maybe you'd like to ride along with him. He'd like your company, and I think you can give him some insights about war." Joe paused, choosing his words carefully. "Anyway, how about it, Mom? It's been awhile since you've had a chance to go out there."

"Too long," sighed Addie. "I'd love to go, and I appreciate you thinking of me. I really do, Joe. Why don't you go with us?"

Joe shrugged, fiddling with an object on the table. "I don't know," he said. "You know how I feel about all that. Anyway, I have an important meeting tomorrow. Michael wants to get an early start. He'll have to miss some classes to do this, but I think it will be good for him. It might make him think a little."

Addie remained silent.

"There I go again, huh?" Joe sighed. Addie patted his arm gently. "I can't win. You want me to lay off of Mike; Judy tells me to quit bugging you about Gateway. Am I really that bad?"

"No, Joe, you're not bad. Maybe you care too much, could that be?"

"I do care—about all of you," he answered. "Go pack your bag, okay? I'll put out some extra food for Rufus. He'll be all right for one night, won't he?"

"One night's okay, but I wouldn't want to leave him longer than that." Addie went into her bedroom and began to put a few things together. She could hear Joe rummaging in the kitchen, and she hesitated before calling out to him. Trying to keep her tone even she asked, "What is the status of Gateway anyway?"

He did not answer immediately, but appeared momentarily in her bedroom door. "You really want to know?"

"I think I should, don't you?" She immediately regretted the insolence that filled each word.

"All right, but I didn't bring it up, okay?"

"Okay."

"Your name is very close to the top of the list. They've pretty much promised me that something will be available by the holidays."

"Which holidays? Thanksgiving, Christmas?"

"I'm hoping Thanksgiving. They know I want you in town this year before the snow flies again. You're going to have to make a decision pretty soon, Mom."

"I know."

"I'm thinking we should just plan on November," Joe continued apprehensively. "If you don't have a spot by then, you can stay with us until it becomes available. It's time for this old place to be a summer cabin again." He patted the wall affectionately. "I promise I'll bring you out, Mom. It's not like you'll never be here again."

Addie's attempt to sound comforted failed miserably. Joe helped her finish packing before he set about to make sure the house was locked. Rufus rubbed questioningly against Addie's legs when she entered the kitchen.

"I'll be back tomorrow evening, old boy," Addie reassured him with a stroke of his long, sleek body. He thanked her by turning on his automatic purr.

"You'll be fine, you silly cat!" Joe bellowed entering the kitchen with Addie's bag flopping over his shoulder. Rufus scurried beneath the table where he watched, uncertain of this fact.

When they were in the car and headed toward town, Addie again summoned up her courage to ask her son, "What about him?"

"Who?" Joe was tuning the radio, which lost his favorite signal each time he drove into the mountains.

"Rufus! What will happen to Rufus *if* I decide to move to Gateway?"

"You make this sound so negative, Mom!" Joe countered. "Some people would give anything to live there. It's top of the line—the best there is."

"I know that, Joe. But do they allow cats?"

Joe fiddled with the knob, then sighed heavily and turned the radio off. "No, they don't allow cats. They have a specially trained dog that they keep in a kennel at night, but he's free to roam during the day. Most of the residents like that. It sort of takes the place of pets they may have had to leave behind."

"You're suggesting I leave Rufus behind?" asked Addie

"Judy told me not to bring this up until the time came," Joe said apologetically.

"Maybe the time has come," said Addie. "I need to know these things. November isn't far away."

"All right then. Remember, you asked me, okay?"

"Go on," murmured Addie.

"You remember Beth, Michael's girlfriend?" Joe asked.

"Of course, she's a lovely girl."

"There you are, Mom," Joe forced a laugh. "You and I finally agree on something that has to do with Michael! Anyway, Beth and three other girls are renting a house a few blocks from the campus; her home is in Cheyenne. She's offered to take Rufus. He'll get plenty of attention with all those kids around, and she's very responsible. You'll still get to see him from time to time. Michael will take you over to visit him whenever you want."

When Addie did not respond he added, "Beth likes you, Mom. She thinks you're—what did she say—cute?"

"She's cute, too," Addie mumbled. "But I wouldn't want to live with her. Rufus and I are both too old for that sort of nonsense. They should get a kitten if they want a pet. You don't understand, Joe. Rufus is set in his ways."

"Like someone else we know!" He teased.

"He's too old to go to college!" As soon as she said it Addie realized how foolish she sounded, and Joe's light mood quickly evaporated.

"For God's sake, Mom," he moaned. "He's only a cat—an old, stray cat. And it's not like you'll never see him again."

The rest of the ride was silent. When they reached the flats, Joe retrieved his radio station and music filled the awkward hush in the car. Only a cat. Addie could think of no response for that. He could never understand the bond between her and that "old stray," as he put it. Numbly, she rode without conversation, her arms crossed heavily upon her chest.

The ride in the car the following day was a sharp contrast to the previous journey with Joe. Michael was filled with excitement about his project and seemed eager to have a special day with his grandmother. Practically before they were out of town, he told her all about the history class and the professor who was encouraging him to analyze what war means to Americans who have lived through it.

As he drove, Addie agreed to Michael's request to tape record notes from their conversation to use in his paper later. She explained to him that she regularly recorded ideas on a micro-cassette player she always kept with her now that she could no longer see to jot down something she wanted to remember.

They slipped into a philosophical discussion of patriotism and the value of laying down one's life for one's country. As they turned east into the morning sun, Addie found herself telling Michael of her first husband's death with surprising ease.

"He was by all counts an American hero," she said as Michael listened intently to the story George had told her years ago about Jacob's death. "If your paper is about patriotism and a love for one's country, that's who Jacob McNeil was. I can tell you all about that."

"Doesn't it make you angry, Grandma? I mean doesn't it bother you to think he had to be the one to give his life for our country?"

"Not any more," Addie answered truthfully. "At first, yes. I was young and in love. I had a new baby to think about. Yes, I was angry that the war took Jacob away from me. But after awhile, I accepted what happened. I believe in my heart that Jacob did what was right. That doesn't mean I haven't missed him every day of my life. If anything, it makes me love my country more, because he's a part of the freedoms I enjoy each day. He made it possible by his own contribution, which sadly, was his life."

"Wow," Michael breathed. "Okay if I put that in my paper?"

"You may quote me, as long as I get recognition when you're a famous writer, okay?"

"Done deal!" he laughed. They drove on in relaxed companionship, the morning sun exaggerating the bright mood of their day.

"You loved him a lot, didn't you Grandma?" asked Michael.

"Yes, I did," said Addie. "He was a wonderful man, Mike. He was, after all, my first love. That's a very special thing."

"Yes," Michael said softly. "I think that Beth is mine."

Addie reached over and patted his knee.

"Is that how you felt about Jacob, Grandma?" Without waiting for a response he hurried on. "When I'm with Beth, I lose track of everything but her. I feel so aware of her, the way she moves and laughs and even the perfume she's wearing." He laughed. "I mean, she really smells good, like a flower, only better. Oh, Gram, I must sound nuts to you! Is that what it was like, though, for you?"

"Yes, Michael. Exactly. You don't sound nuts to me. You sound like you're in love!"

"I am."

"I'll tell you something," said Addie.

"What?"

"The first time I saw you and Beth together—the Fourth of July at the lake—I almost cried. The two of you reminded me of Jacob and me. It's nothing I can explain, just something I felt."

"That's so cool, Gram," said Michael. "How could you stand losing him? If something happened to Beth, I don't know what I'd do."

"It was hard, Michael. Very, very hard," said Addie. "In a lot of ways I've never been able to stand it. But you go on; you have to. That's just something I learned with time."

Michael thought about this before asking her, "What about my Grandpa? You met him when he came to see you after Jacob's death?"

"Yes."

"Did he make up for it? I guess you were able to fall in love again."

"Of course," Addie sighed. "I suppose George Marsh was the one man I could love, because he knew and loved Jacob, too."

"You talked about him then?" asked Michael.

"Often," replied Addie. "We wanted to keep Jacob's memory alive for my son, Jake. We both thought that was important."

"That's neat," said Michael. "A lot of people wouldn't have handled it that way. I mean, even if I put myself in Grandpa's shoes, I might be jealous. Does that sound crazy, to be jealous of a dead man?"

"Not at all," said Addie. "In some ways your Grandpa was jealous of Jacob and the way I felt about him." Addie's mind drifted back in time as melancholy memories reached for her. Michael slowed the car as they passed through a small town.

"Need a pit stop? A cup of coffee maybe?" he asked her.

"I'm all right. Stop if you need to."

"I'm all right, too." He accelerated again to a comfortable cruise as they returned to the open highway.

"Can I tell you something?" asked Addie. "I've never discussed this with anyone before."

"Sure, Gram," he answered. "You can tell me anything, and it won't go any further. I think it's great that you and I can talk like this, don't you?"

"I do," she smiled reaching over to pat him once again.

"Tell me."

"It was hard for George," she said thoughtfully. "He never felt he was the man that Jacob was. He always felt in some way that he had to compete, and yet his competitor had been one of his dearest friends, the man who saved his life. When he was feeling low, he would tell me that if I had loved him enough, he wouldn't have had to share me with Jacob all our lives."

"Did he have to share you, Grandma?"

"I suppose," replied Addie. "It was never intentional—but yes, I think he did."

"It was your first love, Gram," Michael sighed. "I don't imagine that feeling ever really goes away completely, does it?"

"I don't think so, at least not for me," said Addie. "Now I sound terrible, don't I?"

"You sound real," the boy answered softly. "And I like that quality in a Grandma!"

"You are something!" laughed Addie.

"I don't remember much about Grandpa," Michael went on. "How old was I when he died, about five?"

"Yes, remember? It was the fall you started kindergarten. He'd been so sick, and I felt like he held on just to see you start school," recalled Addie. "I drove him into town that morning, so he could eat breakfast with you and watch you leave for your first day in the big world."

"I remember that," Michael laughed. "Dad looked out and saw you two coming up the walk that morning and said 'Now what?' And Grandpa was wearing that old fishing cap he always had on. Mom says every year she bought him a new hat for his birthday, and he always thanked her and made a big deal out of it. Then before she knew it, he was wearing that old hat."

Addie joined his laughter. "That was your grandfather,

195

all right. He was good, Michael. He had a big heart, a heart of gold. Maybe it broke a little too easily, but he was a good man."

"Whatever happened to that hat?" asked Michael.

"It's at the house," answered Addie. "I ran across it not long ago when Sybil was helping me to sort through things. Why?"

"I'd like to have it," said Michael, "to remember him."

"Of course you can," said Addie. "He'd like that."

"You know, Gram," Michael sighed, "I have another question for you. If you don't want to talk about this, it's okay. It's probably none of my business anyway."

"Go ahead."

"Well," he hesitated, "Dad says Grandpa drank too much. I don't remember that. Dad called him something like a closet drinker—he said he was always finding half-empty bottles hidden around the house, but Grandpa didn't drink in front of people. I think it bothered Dad. I don't feel like they were very close to each other. Sometimes I think that's why he and I aren't close at times, you know, because he didn't feel good about his own dad."

Addie took a deep breath. "Oh, Michael," she sighed. "Maybe you should become a psychologist. You're a thinker, aren't you?"

"I guess I am," he acknowledged. "So, what I've said is true?"

"Yes, it's true; although I don't like remembering all of that. I've only tried to remember the good times in life. I guess I push a lot of things I'd like to forget to the back of my mind and leave them there."

"That's the difference between your generation and mine," said Michael. "People my age talk about everything. We're into our feelings and what makes people act the way

196

they do. I think your generation is more quietly accepting of things. You didn't question as much—just took the good with the bad. Maybe it's better that way, I don't know. It's probably more realistic."

"And what about your parents' generation?" asked Addie.

"They're the worst," Michael moaned. "Baby Boomers! They're caught between wanting to be open to their feelings, while pushing them down at the same time. One day my dad is so tuned in it's scary, and the next day he won't open up at all. My mom's that way, too. Don't get me wrong, they're great! The older I get, the more I understand and appreciate them. I know Dad loves me, and I know he means well. But I think he really struggles with some things, don't you?"

"I think you *should* become a psychologist!" Addie laughed. Then in a more serious tone she added, "What your dad said about George is true. Your Grandpa did turn to alcohol to hide his pain. As he got older, it happened more. He was never a sloppy drunk or belligerent. He just had to have it to function. I suggested to him many times that maybe he was an alcoholic; maybe he needed help. But, he wouldn't think of it. I guess that's why he kept it hidden, or at least, he thought it was hidden. We knew, and it was an embarrassment to the boys when they'd run across his 'containers.' Maybe if he'd been more like you, more able to open up . . ."

"Why was he like that? Do you think it was from his war wounds?"

"Yes, but not the wounds you're thinking of. He was probably a victim of what was called shell shock back in those days. After World War II, society didn't do much to help the vets like they do now with post-traumatic stress syndrome. He had to deal with it on his own, and I guess the drinking helped him to cope. He was tormented by memories of the war. The older he got, the less he talked about it. He tried to manage his pain, that's all he thought he could do."

"It's too bad," Michael sympathized, "I mean that he couldn't deal with it or get any help."

"A lot of men his age were like that," said Addie. "It was a sign of weakness to ask for help or share their troubles. I think it's better now that the world acknowledges that people do have feelings and need to manage them constructively."

"Why isn't Grandpa buried out here?" asked Michael almost as an afterthought. "He was a veteran, he's entitled to be here, isn't he?"

"Oh, yes, he could be, but that wasn't his choice," explained Addie. "Your Grandpa is in the Pinecliffe cemetery because he wanted to rest near Bear Lake where he was the happiest. He was so badly haunted by the war that he didn't want to be buried among its other casualties."

"What about you, Gram? Where will you go—I mean when the time comes?"

"To heaven, I hope," she quipped. "No, dear, I know what you mean. I'll lie beside George. One way or another, I plan to stay close to my home!"

"Did you ever think about how weird that is, Grandma?" Michael speculated. "I mean, you've had two husbands and you loved them both. If it's true that we all end up together in heaven, which one will you be with?"

Addie laughed. "Well, I hope we'll all end up together again. After all, we were all friends in a sense. I suspect your Grandpa and Jacob are already together."

"But which one will *you* be with, Grandma?" Michael laughed.

"I think that we'll just leave all of that up to God," said Addie. "He gave them to me, and he took them from me. He'll know how it all should end!"

They rode in comfortable silence. After a time, Michael said thoughtfully, "You've had a hard life, Gram."

"I've had a great life!" Addie countered. "I've loved two good men; I had two fine sons; I have you and your mother in my life; and I've had Bear Lake to call my home."

"I think there's something to be said for your approach to life. Maybe your generation is on a more solid track than mine in many ways." Michael took his foot off the accelerator and flipped on his right blinker. "We're there," he said softly.

"Already?" Addie tried to envision their approach to the veteran's cemetery and nearby hospital. It amazed her how this tree-lined mirage suddenly sprung up out of the dry, desolate plains. In contrast to the surrounding fields of yellow wheat, the cool, green grass and trees provided an unexpected and gentle refuge.

As Michael slowed the car to the posted limit for government property, Addie said, "Maybe you should include your Grandpa Marsh in your paper about the effects of war, too. There's a sort of tragic valor in his story as well."

"I plan to," was his sober response.

Michael pulled the car to the curb and turned toward his grandmother. "I have an appointment with an officer at the hospital in about fifteen minutes. It shouldn't take too long. I have a list of questions for him, and I know he's a busy guy. Do you want to go with me, or would you rather wait in the cemetery? It's a nice day."

"I'll wait outdoors," said Addie. Michael pulled away again and turned down the thin tree-lined drive to the graveyard that led away from the old brick buildings. The black, wrought-iron gates were open, and they found they were the only visitors this fall morning.

"It's in the northwest corner, Michael," Addie pointed as he drove in that direction then came to a stop where she instructed. Addie took Michael's arm, and together they crossed the grass past rows of identical rounded tombstones, each bearing a name, rank, and dates of birth and death. Some also noted the name of the war in which they'd served. Above the identifying information on each stone was engraved a small white cross.

"Here they are," said Michael softly. "Jacob McNeil. Two of them."

The boy and his grandmother stood together silently. The melancholy drone of a tractor passing down a dirt road adjacent to the cemetery briefly interrupted their communion. The tranquil cooing of a dove in a nearby tree was the only other sound. Michael took Addie's hand and both stared without seeing that which cannot be viewed, but is felt, beyond the concrete marker of the grave.

"Are you okay, Grandma?"

"Yes, dear, I'm fine."

"I need to leave for my appointment. Will you be all right here by yourself?"

"Yes," she replied, "You go ahead."

"Have you got your cane?"

"Right here," she patted the deep pocket of her jacket exposing the folded, white metal shaft.

"There's a gazebo just across the roadway, and I noticed a bench inside. If you get tired, you can go over there and wait for me in the shade, okay?"

"I will," Addie assured him. "Now go on, don't be late for your meeting."

Unexpectedly, he kissed the top of her head before

darting away, and she heard the rumble of his motor starting. When finally she knew she was alone, Addie knelt and ran her hands across the recently cut grass which covered the resting place of her loved ones. Then she moved her hands up to the rough, cold stones at the head of each grave. Her fingers lingered on the engraved letters which told their names. For a long time, she remained on the ground lost in her thoughts and prayers. Then she rose, extending the cane to make her way across the road to the small pavilion.

It was a peaceful place, and as Addie settled comfortably upon the bench inside, she realized she was in no hurry for Michael to return. All of the turmoil of her life seemed to disappear in this tiny enclosure. A breeze drifting from a nearby farm filled the autumn air with a musty fragrance. Addie breathed deeply, saturating herself in memories of another farm years and miles away.

She heard the flutter of the dove and his soft familiar greeting. From the corner of her eye, where sight still slipped past the blind circle, she saw his soft white form settle into the eaves above her, watching her, and perhaps wondering, too, at the love which brought an old woman to this lonely place.

Addie, he seemed to call to her from his perch above. *Addie, Addie.*

Then she found she was no longer alone but sitting with a soldier in uniform at her side. High above the gazebo the red, white and blue flag of the United States of America danced on the morning breeze. For a long time before Michael returned from his research to pick up his grandmother, the couple sat, hand in hand, on the wooden bench. They talked quietly and laughed softly, so as not to disturb the slumber of those about them. And they promised, before the boy arrived, to be together again soon.

201

Chapter 11

Fall. This is truly my favorite of all the seasons, thought Addie, sitting comfortably at her kitchen table, the door open in anticipation of Sybil's arrival. Her fingers ran across the Braille book before her, but her mind did not detect the meaning of the tiny arrangement of dots. She was more keenly aware of the quiet—the intense, sometimes melancholy quiet that returned each year with the exodus of the summer people. Addie realized that this fall the changing colors, which brought carloads of "leaf lookers" to the area each weekend, were no longer as brilliant as before. In fact, they were dull and blurred. But she could smell the pungent dry leaves in a way she had never before noticed. She could hear the anxious calling of flocks of geese flying overhead, although their V-shaped battalions were not visible to her as they had once been. Most of all she heard the absence of human sounds replaced by the acute, vibrant declaration of nature.

She missed the children the most. Their laughter provided entertainment throughout the summer months, and they were often company for her as well. They knew that they were always welcome at Addie's cabin, where they would be greeted with not only friendship and an interested listener, but also lemonade and fresh-baked cookies. The summer children loved and admired Addie with her long white cane, lovable yellow cat, and endless repertoire of stories. If there was anything to fear in the mountains, Addie knew it was not the children.

"Why did I keep the boys away?" she thought, remembering the many times she had warned her sons not to "bother" their older neighbors who came to the lake to relax each summer. What a mistake that had been. For it was the children who could brighten the golden days of retirement from the sometimes boring effects of too much "relaxation." Laughing, she supposed that Joe had ignored her advice anyway, and all of the neighbors had known him well!

She was aware of Sybil before she either heard her footsteps or saw her obscure outline walking up the path. For several weeks, there had been a heaviness about Sybil that seemed to precede her like a dark, storm cloud. The familiar, awkward Sybil of the year past had changed into a dismal, solemn person, engulfed in a sadness from which Addie could not retrieve her.

"Good morning, dear!" Addie called out in response to the timid tapping at the hooked screen door. "Isn't it another beautiful day? I'm airing the house out with fall. I've got the windows open and just the screen on the doors. Sybil?"

"Good morning," the answer was dull and faraway.

"How are you today?" Addie retained her brightness in hope that it might somehow be contagious.

"I'm okay."

Sybil methodically set about straightening an already-tidy kitchen. Addie put away her study books for another time, then suggested that they resume the task that both of them knew awaited them in the spare bedroom. Its walls were now lined with cardboard boxes with varying labels upon them. In one corner were objects which would be donated to Goodwill and another held the items which Judy and Joe wanted. Addie rarely entered the room these days unless it was with Sybil, to continue their rummaging and organizing. On her own, it was a forlorn place, forcing Addie to face the decision that was soon to be made.

"We need to go through the roll top today," said Addie gesturing toward an old oak desk which had sat in her uncle's study when she was a girl. It had seemed much larger then and had held so much knowledge when the Judge sat behind it. Now, it was old and tired, Addie guessed, like everything else in the home. It would go to Michael when she moved, and she hoped he would recognize its eminence and refrain from covering it with a new coat of paint.

"We're nearly finished then, aren't we?" asked Addie.

"I guess," responded Sybil. "What about the kitchen?"

"There's really nothing to do in there. Even if I do move to town, I'll need my kitchen when we come out to visit."

"You still haven't made up your mind?" asked Sybil.

"No," said Addie. "A part of me knows that Joe is right. There are many advantages for me living in the city. But another part just isn't ready to leave this old place."

"Listen to that part," advised Sybil. "I can't bear to think of you moving away."

"I don't think I can, either," whispered Addie.

Quietly, Sybil pulled a stack of papers from a drawer and sat on the end of the bed to look through them. After a few moments the girl set the papers beside her and stared out the small bedroom window. "It doesn't matter," she said almost to herself. "I probably won't be here, anyway."

"What do you mean?" Addie moved to sit on the other side of her.

"I'm thinking about going back to California."

"Alone or with Stoney?" When the girl didn't respond Addie continued. "Are you planning to leave soon? Before winter?"

"I don't know," Sybil answered miserably. "I'll probably

go alone. Maybe Stoney will go. We're talking about it."

"I'm worried about you, Sybil," said Addie. "You've been so down lately, you aren't yourself anymore. Do you want to talk about it?"

"No, Addie, it's okay. Don't worry about me. You have enough to think about."

"Did you ever see a doctor?" Addie probed gently. "Are you feeling well?"

"I feel all right," Sybil said. Preoccupied, she picked up and replaced two more stacks of papers before turning back toward Addie. "In a way, I'm glad you're thinking about going to Gateway, Addie. It isn't safe here for you anymore. You trust people too much, and you're going to end up getting hurt."

Addie felt a chill run up her back, but maintained her composure. "Nonsense!" she retorted. "I'm perfectly safe here. What makes you say that?"

"You said yourself you've been robbed," argued Sybil. "And I didn't tell you before, because I didn't want to worry you, but we have, too."

"You've been robbed?" asked Addie incredulously.

"Yes. All kinds of little things are missing. I had some money hidden in an envelope, even Stoney didn't know about it. It was from my mom—she gave it to me to keep for her one night when she was drunk, and then I think she just forgot I had it. She'd given me her old high school ring a few years ago, and it's gone. There was a nice vase and an old chime clock and some other odds and ends that belonged to Stoney's grandparents over there—it all disappeared, too."

"The Roberts's things?" Addie whispered.

Sybil was talking more to herself than Addie. "At first Stoney tried to blame me, but now I think he knows I didn't do it. I mean, how could I? I don't even have a car or any-place to hide anything!"

"What about Stoney?" Addie ventured. "You don't think he . . ."

Angrily, Sybil replied, "No! It's that hermit!" she accused.

"Hermit?"

"The guy across the lake," said Sybil. "The one that's fixing up the logging camp. Have you seen that place, Addie?" she asked. "When we first moved here we hiked over there. It was just a dump. Now, it's really something. You told me yourself he was a retired soldier. Where do you think he got the money to do all that work? He's stealing from everyone, that's where!"

Stunned, Addie did not reply. Since the day Paul had come by to apologize, they had become good friends. He was interested in Braille and her training with Laura, even more so, it seemed, than her own son. They both loved books and had spent hours discussing classical literature, what they were currently reading, and recommending novels to each other. Now that he finally had a phone, he would call her when he was going to town to see if she needed anything or to tell her about a program on television that he thought she might enjoy.

"No, Sybil, I'm sorry," Addie finally said. "It's not Paul Curtis. I've gotten to know him, and I can assure you he's an honest man."

"That's just what I was saying, Addie. You trust people too much," she argued. "Why do you think he's over here all the time? To check things out, that's why. He acts like he's your friend to get into your house."

"That is nonsense! I respect your opinion, Sybil, but you are wrong about Paul."

"He tried to kill Stoney." This Sybil coldly revealed, sending more shivers up and down Addie's back.

"What on earth . . .?"

"I'm not kidding!" cried Sybil. "Stoney went over there to look around for our missing stuff. He thought the guy was gone, but he showed up from behind the house and started shoving Stoney and telling him to get off of his property. Stoney said if he hadn't high-tailed it out of there he knows the guy would have killed him. He said he had this look on his face that wasn't even human. I'm real scared of him, Addie. You should be, too!"

"Did you call the sheriff?" asked Addie.

"No," Sybil murmured. "I told Stoney to, but he didn't."

"But, why? Sheriff Johnson needs to know things like that!"

"Oh, you know Stoney," defended Sybil. "He doesn't want people getting involved in our lives, especially not the sheriff. He just told me to stay indoors when I'm alone and keep away from that guy. And you should, too. He gives me the creeps. I think he's crazy!"

Addie sat quietly, trying to collect her thoughts. When she didn't speak Sybil retrieved the pile of papers at her side and began to go through them, one by one. "There's an old book here about how to work your television set."

"Toss it," said Addie. She rose and went to the stack of boxes beneath the window and leaned against them.

"Something about taxes—dated 1989, I think . . ."

"Put it in the pile for Joe to look at."

"And this looks like—" Sybil paused holding something up to the light. "Okay, this is something about car insurance."

"No more car. Toss it."

"This is for Joe's stack." When Addie said nothing, Sybil explained, "More tax stuff."

Sybil grabbed another stack from the drawer. Abruptly Addie turned toward her, changing the subject from the girl's curiosity about an old valentine signed "Love, Sarah (your sis!!!)."

"Sybil, do you really think that Paul is dangerous?"

"Yes, I do." The girl came and stood beside Addie, putting an arm protectively around her shoulder. "You know I wouldn't try to scare you or tell you these things if they weren't true. I can't believe I'm saying this, but your son is right about going to that place. As much as I don't want you to leave, it isn't good for you to be out here all by yourself. I can see that now. I'm afraid that Army guy has been waiting for all the tourists to leave, and he's going to pull something. I don't feel safe at all when Stoney's gone. I lock the doors, and you don't know how bad I wish we had a phone."

"You need one, all right. Couldn't Stoney put one in?"

Ignoring this Sybil continued, "I'm glad we've almost got you packed up and ready to go, Addie. If you were called today and told there was a room ready for you at Gateway, you really should take it."

"Oh, Sybil . . ."

"I mean it! The sooner the better. I wish I could go, too!" She forced a light-hearted laugh.

"I wish you could, too," Addie smiled. "But I can't go this week." She tried to keep the light mood between them. Addie was troubled by Sybil's revelations and wanted to push them from the forefront of her mind, at least for now. "I have my support group meeting and you know I can't miss that."

"Oh, no, of course not," teased Sybil sounding more like

her old self. "You've got to see your boyfriend."

"Good heaven's, Sybil!" Addie laughed as the girl returned to her papers.

As quickly as their levity had come upon them, it was dashed as Sybil became quiet, her body rigid as she stared at the document before her. Addie seemed not to notice as she busied herself placing the papers for Joe in a shoebox reserved for that purpose.

"Oh, God, Addie . . . No!" Sybil gasped. "Two of them." She looked up at her friend with questioning eyes. "Oh, God!" she repeated.

"What . . . ?" Addie began.

"It's a telegram from Vietnam," the girl whispered. "We regret—oh, Addie, you lost them both at war!"

The look on Addie's face, the look of a person who is busy concentrating upon a task, froze in place as she reached blindly for the document and gently removed it from Sybil's grasp. It seemed as if the room was closing in upon them and without a word, Addie, still clinging to the yellowed paper, wandered into her living room, and then out the back door to the refuge of the big porch George had built for her with so much love.

"Mom!" Jake rushed into the kitchen of the house in the shadow of the mill. He still held his schoolbooks under one arm and had not taken off his blue letterman's jacket with the big white "R" above the pocket. His face was beaming as he spilled his news. "I got the appointment! I was called into the guidance office today. I made it, Mom!"

He dropped his books and stuck both arms out sideways, then ran about the room diving like a human airplane in a manner uncharacteristic for this usually serious young man. When he reached his mother he pulled her into his arms, laughing and shouting at once. "I'm going to be a pilot! In two months they're going to shave this mop." He was still laughing as he pulled at his soft brown hair. "I'm going to be a cadet at the Air Force Academy! Me, Mom! Your own son, Jacob McNeil! Can you believe it?"

"Oh, Jake!" Addie joined his joy. "That's wonderful news! Today? You just found out today? Oh, Jake! I knew you'd make it! I'm so proud! Your dad will be, too. Shall we call him at work? Oh, Jake . . ."

"My real dad would be proud, too, don't you think so, Mom?" His eyes glistened as they met his mother's.

"Yes," she whispered in return. "Very, very proud."

Addie knew it had been his lifelong dream to fly and to serve in the U.S. Air Force. One month after receiving the appointment, he gave the valedictory address for the Richmond High School graduating class of 1960, and spoke of soaring to new heights. A few months later as Addie watched the solemn moment from the stands when he was accepted into the ranks of the Academy following a grueling period of training that summer, Addie knew this had been Jake's fate from the moment she had held him in her arms and fed him at her breast. Tears filled her eyes with the instant, naked discernment of her son standing on the field before her that afternoon. He was a boy in an airman's uniform, schoolbooks in his hand. He was a soldier in a letterman's jacket, missiles at his command. He *was* Jacob McNeil.

Four years later he threw his white hat into the bright blue summer sky following his commencement from the United States Air Force Academy along with the other cadets. His mother, watching from the stands, knew once again that this was meant to be.

But in 1966, when he called her from the Pacific air base where he had been stationed for two years in pilot's training, to solemnly report that he had been given a promotion and received orders to fly over Vietnam, she objected. Addie Marsh, who had given her life to the whims and antics of fate since seeing her parents die when she was but a little girl, refused.

She had moved without question from her home in Chicago to the stately residence of a respected judge in Denver. She had gone on with her life in the face of the untimely death of her husband, when she was barely an adult herself. She had worked hard and held her head high in the years that followed as she struggled to maintain her home and be a good wife and mother. But this new direction so proudly pronounced by the boy whose heart beat closest to her own—this she would not allow.

"You can't go, Jake," she told him as if forbidding the privilege of an afternoon at the movies.

"Mom, I have to go!" he replied, and then, "I want to go."

George Marsh had never before or since thrown himself into anything so grand. When he learned that Jake would have a short leave before being sent overseas, he rented the union hall and had a dinner catered. He invited all of their friends and all of the young people and teachers Jake had known in school. The neighbors came, clothed in outdated suits and homemade dresses.

Halfway through the party, the elaborate entry of Jake's aunt and uncle from Denver almost brought the gathering to a nervous halt. Jake rose smoothly to greet the family and reunite with his cousins, the two oldest girls holding babies of their own, escorted by young husbands Addie had never met.

Her younger son kept eyes which never stopped glowing

on Jake all night long. Joe Marsh was the center of attention among his own female classmates, who seemed almost to wait in line to meet the quiet, handsome older brother for whom a local six-piece band played in the corner throughout the evening.

"Going to Nam, huh?" Joe asked him almost too casually as they sat side by side eating piles of fried chicken and spaghetti.

"Yeah, I'm going."

"Think it'll be tough?" the younger boy asked.

"Naw, it'll be all right." Jake exchanged a few pleasantries with friends who stopped behind him, their plates heaped with food as they searched for a place to sit close to the guest of honor. The local boy made good, they were all thinking; one of our own—leaving this old mill town for a greater purpose. They were proud. Even Jake's classmates whose hair had grown long, who wore beards unlike the pilot's clean-shaven face, and one wearing a metal peace symbol about his neck—even they were proud and didn't challenge his impending plans. He was Jake McNeil, and you didn't ask questions.

"You stay in school, all right?" Jake focused his attention back to Joe.

"I have to. I've got another year after this before I graduate," Joe sighed. "I wish I could sign up right now and go with you. I really do!"

"You're a good kid," Jake punched his brother's arm gently. "But you're not going to do that. And I don't just mean high school, Joe. You finish up and go on to college. Maybe by the time you get your education under your belt this war will be over."

"I could never get into the Academy like you did!" Joe objected.

"Nobody said you should!" Jake laughed. "You're you and I'm me, Joe. We're two different people. There's something waiting out there just for you, and I know you'll find it. Remember—you'll always be my kid brother. Make me proud, okay?"

Somewhere in the time after the party and before he left, Jake found one solitary moment when he pulled his beloved mother into his arms and held her with a strength she had not felt since his father had held her years before on the farm.

"I'll be all right, Mom," he told her.

But he was wrong.

Addie welcomed that summer when they packed their belongings and headed for the lake. She found peace in the mountains, and more than ever she needed to retreat from the newspaper headlines and endless television stories of the war in Southeast Asia. She knew she would still rush to meet George when he came from the city each evening to see if his habitual mail check had produced any word from her son. But it would be easier at Bear Lake. In the shelter of the trees and sprawling sky, it was hard to think of a war raging somewhere else. It was all a bad dream, one that evaporated into the mist over the lake with the dawn of each new day.

Joe had not wanted to go to the lake that summer. Instead he had hoped to stay in the city with his friends and get a job at the mill with his father to save money to buy a car. At the last minute, he had been offered a job as a children's activity counselor at an exclusive resort not far from Bear Lake. Some of his friends were going to be employed there as well, and Addie was surprised when George encouraged him to take it over the more lucrative job at the mill.

"There's plenty of time to sweat in that old place," George had told him. "But working at the camp—well, that's something you'll always remember. It'll be fun, but still a lot of responsibility. I think you should do it."

It became the summer of young love for Joe, in contrast to the next year, which Addie would remember as the summer of the boat. After only two days at the resort, Joe came home one evening with a group of boys and girls who worked with him. Already, they needed a respite from the throngs of wealthy travelers and their youngsters who came from the cities to experience the wonders of nature first hand.

Addie welcomed them with her usual open arms and an abundance of snacks. After that, the Marsh cabin became a sort of "hang out" not only for the camp employees, but also for the "locals"—the kids who lived in Pinecliffe and took advantage of the summer to intermingle with new faces from the city. Evenings often found them wandering about the acreage in small groups, sometimes laughing and teasing, while at other times sitting seriously on the rock fortress deep in muted conversation.

One evening, Addie and George sat on the porch discussing the day behind them. Joe came from the side of the house holding hands with a young girl Addie remembered seeing among the group of teenagers sipping cokes on the porch only a day or two before.

"We're going to take a walk down by the lake," Joe said awkwardly. "Just kind of hang out, you know."

"Aren't you going to introduce us?" George asked as Joe's face turned crimson.

"Oh, yeah, sorry." He fidgeted uncomfortably and the girl with him, wearing rolled up cut-off jeans and an over-sized tee shirt, appeared equally shy almost hiding behind him. Still their hands remained tightly intermingled causing Joe's arm to twist backwards so as not to lose her.

"This is Terry, and this is my mom and dad," Joe said, nodding at his parents.

"Nice to meet you, Terry!" George boomed again. "Would you like to join us and—"

"You were here yesterday, weren't you?" Addie interrupted.

"Yes, ma'am," the girl replied.

"We're just going to walk down by the lake," Joe repeated.

"Well, be careful!" Addie immediately regretted this bit of advice, as if given to a child rather than the young man Joe was quickly becoming.

After George had gone to bed, Addie slipped back out into the darkness of the porch and sat unnoticed by the young couple who had spread a blanket under a tree, barely visible from the house. The mother felt her own face turn crimson when the less likely of her two sons was suddenly wrapped in an impassioned embrace with Terry. Embarrassed, she hurried into the cabin.

Terry did not last long. Within a few days, Joe comfortably draped his arm around Nancy. The following weekend he and his best friend double dated to the drive-in movie near Richmond with two Pinecliffe girls named Mary Lou and Colleen. After that, Addie lost track. It was a startling revelation to observe Joe's newfound popularity with girls following her older, more handsome son who had always had a date for school dances and plenty of female admirers, but who seemed disinclined toward more serious romantic involvements.

The late August day when George came home from the city—a hint of beer on his breath, with red, swollen eyes and a rumpled telegram in his fist—Addie wasn't even sure where Joe was. She vaguely remembered that he'd run in from work to take a quick bath and said something about hamburgers, and he wouldn't be eating with them, and he might be late. As the sun set over Bear Lake, Addie didn't know where either of her sons were. She did know that only one of them would be coming home again, and that he'd never be the same after that night.

The pork chops she had baked for supper were never eaten. As the news spread, summer neighbors filled the small house, spilling out onto the porch in their grief for the family they held in high regard. Their voices were serious and muffled, although Addie spoke levelly to each of them, returning hugs and condolences with a reserved warmth of her own. Within an hour the more familiar faces of city friends began to arrive, sobbing with the fresh memory of the going away party none of them had ever guessed would be a final farewell to the young man they all loved.

"He was a fine boy, George. They just don't make them any better than that!"

"A hero!" Addie choked each time this too-familiar word was used.

"When will they send him home to you? What about funeral plans?"

"Damn! It's just a damn war, that's all I can say!"

"Addie!" Sarah's voice sobbed through the telephone. "I just found out. Oh, Addie, come to Denver for awhile. I'm here for you, Sis, you know that, don't you? Is Joey all right? Oh, Addie, he was such a good boy. Oh, Addie, you don't deserve this!"

It was after nine o'clock when young Joe Marsh came through the door alone. His face was pale and he left in his shadow a group of somber youngsters who milled about the impromptu parking lot, which hours before had been the front yard of the Marsh summer cabin. Addie later learned that Henry Roberts had driven into Pinecliffe searching for the boy, after dropping Elsa off to comfort the family in the cabin above their own. Now, the middle-aged man leaned heavily against the wall just inside the doorway, sorry to have to deliver his likeable young neighbor to this fate.

Addie took hold of Joe's arm and quickly led him into his small bedroom, closing the door behind them. George did not follow.

"It's bullshit!" the boy sobbed. He fell into his mother's arms as his weight lowered both of them onto the metal twin bed. "Why'd you let him go? You could have stopped him!"

Addie clung to her son, her arms about him as he sobbed into her chest. "What's the big deal about going off to war?" he stammered, hoarse and gasping for breath.

Still she clung to him. His body heaved and twisted, yet her small arms contained him in a protective cocoon.

"Big . . . deal . . ." He moaned. ". . . Damn air force . . . God . . . damn . . . pilot . . . Mama, Mama!" He sobbed unyielding to the horrible reality which consumed him. And Addie never let go.

A different sun was rising over Bear Lake. Having spent the night sitting on the porch, Addie knew that sunrise would never again be the same. She wasn't sure why, but she knew it never would be; and it never was, which troubled her. The evening before was a blur to her now. Somewhere late in the night, the mourners had left the cabin, alone or in pairs. All of them had offered to help. This, too, bothered Addie. What could they do now? What help could ever take away the hard, cold orb forming deep inside of her? Which one of them could bring Jake back to her?

She had helped George into bed after seeing him crumpled in the corner, long, silent tears flowing down his cheeks. A few remaining, embarrassed friends had looked away as Addie and Henry Roberts led him to the bedroom. As she pulled a quilt under his chin, he stared at her in silence through the frightened eyes of his own disbelief and haunted memories.

"Try to sleep," she had told him, and sat on the edge of the bed until he closed his eyes.

Joe had eventually gone outside to rejoin his friends, who somehow offered the right words of comfort his mother couldn't find. They were the last to leave as Joe slipped back into his room, avoiding an answer or to make eye contact when she asked, "Are you okay, son?"

She promised Henry and Elsa she'd call if they needed anything. "We all just need some sleep," she assured them.

But sleep wouldn't come, and she was equally bereft of tears or words. Nothing came, but an emptiness that seemed to devour her as dark as the night which swallowed the trees and the lake below. Alone, she retreated to the porch wrapped in a blanket, a small embryo within the rocking chair Joe had presented to her on Mother's Day with a card signed: "To the best mom on earth! Love, Jake and Joe."

She concluded, as the sun barely emerged from the clouds of night, that she could not live another day. Like her son, she would die. When a man appeared at the end of the porch and walked slowly toward her, his eyes intent upon her face, she was not frightened or startled. She felt that she *had* died and looked eagerly about for a second familiar face.

Addie? His voice was strong and kind, a salve for her

gaping, wounded heart. *Are you okay, Addie?*

The first trace of a tear found its way down her cheek.

Let me sit with you awhile.

He was beside her then, and more tears gradually followed as he took her into his arms. *Cry, girl. It's okay. I'm with you now. Cry.*

She sobbed endlessly, her face buried in the strong familiar warmth of long ago. Finally, she lifted her eyes and looked into the face of her consolation. *Jacob?* she whispered.

Yes, love. It's all right now. I'm with you.

But where is Jake? Where's our son? she demanded.

He's not here, but I'll take care of him. He's okay, Addie. You've got to believe that, he reassured her.

But why? Why did he have to die? Why him? Addie began to sob again and he held her close. *I can't bear it! Not this. Not my boy!*

Dear, Addie, Jacob sighed. *I can tell you anything but why. That is the one question I can't answer. But let me tell you this.* He pulled her upright to look at him holding her face in his palms, speaking gently as if to a small, frightened child. *You raised Jake into a fine young man. You did everything right, Addie, and I'm proud of you for that. You were all alone, and it wasn't easy when he was small. But you did it! Now it's my turn. I'm his father. You don't need to worry about Jake anymore, okay?*

I want to go with you, Jacob! She pulled his hands from her face and clung to him. *Take me with you! I can't stay here. I can't go back into that house, knowing he'll never be there again. Please!* she begged. *Please, please, Jacob! Take me with you!*

Again, he pulled her into his arms and let her cry until the tears stopped and her breath shook in the aftermath. He whispered, *You've got to stay here, Addie. I can't take you with me.*

But why? Why, Jacob?

Because you're needed here. He nodded toward the house. *There are two men beyond that door who need you badly. You're their hope, Addie. You can save them. I know you don't feel like you can, but you will. Your love will sustain all of you. It has to. There's no one else but you who can do it.*

The sun was now fully exposed, and the sweet morning sounds of birds awakening from their slumber began to fill the air. A new day was beginning, and she would be a necessary part of that day.

I need you, Jacob, she said in quiet resignation. *I can't do it without you.*

He did not respond but stared across the lake to the distant horizon, his eyes filled in peaceful contemplation. He tightened his arm about her shoulder and gently kissed her cheek.

I'll be here for you, Adeline, he whispered. *I promise.*

It was a promise he would keep.

Chapter 12

After introductions, announcements, and recognizing October birthdays, Laura said, "Let's spend some time today catching up. What's going on with everyone? Any problems? Good news is welcome, too. With this crazy weather we're having, it's a good day to just relax and visit."

"Agreed," said Cecil. "Mama almost didn't bring me for the rain."

"Now, Cecil, you were the one," Maggie Parks began, but was interrupted by Leo who was anxious to be the first with his news.

"I'm going to college!" he announced, and before the others could react, he continued. "My Grandma takes me to Richmond two days a week. I'm learning to use a computer. You guys wouldn't believe it—they have computers that talk! You don't have to be able to see the screen to use it. It tells me what's up there. I know we've talked about this before at our meetings, but I couldn't imagine it until I got in this class. I'm learning fast; it's not as hard as I thought it would be. Do you know I could get a job working with a computer someday?"

"Leo, slow down, you're making my head spin!" Tom was laughing as he nudged the young man at his side. "When I taught school we didn't even have computers. That's incredible! How does it talk?"

"There's a little man inside," Leo teased. "And if you're a nice guy like me, he talks to you!"

"I knew you'd do something like that, Leo." Walter chimed in. "That is great. You'll have to keep us informed.

Maybe some of us old folks will learn something from you."

"Anybody can use a computer, Walter. There's nothing to it." Leo's growing confidence crept through his voice, and Addie beamed with pride for him. "When I get it down pat I'll teach you guys everything I know."

"Leo's worked hard for the last few weeks. Very hard," said Laura. "He has a lot more work ahead of him, but I'm with you, Walter. He's going to make something out of himself." Everyone spoke at once encouraging their youngest member. "He's going to need our support," Laura added.

"He's got it." Cecil reached past Maggie and patted Leo on the back. "Way to go, buddy!"

As the comments faded, Alice Mumford was the next to share information. "Most of you knew Maude Ellis. I saw her last week at Gateway when my daughter and I went to call on a member of our church. Maude just celebrated her ninetieth birthday, and she's doing better than ever. She loves it there, and asked me to tell everyone in the village 'hello.' She says they keep her very busy—it's a beautiful place, you know? I was surprised."

Addie knew despite the battle inside of her that this was her chance to speak. "Since you mentioned Gateway," she began, "I do have some news. Whether it is good or bad news, we shall have to wait and see."

Someone cleared his throat and a chair scraped the floor, but without further encouragement, Addie began, "My son, Joe, called me last night to tell me that he'd been notified by Gateway that they have a room available for me now. My name has been on a waiting list for some time, and Joe had been hoping I'd settle in before the first snow. As Alice said, it's a very nice place."

Addie forced a smile. For once she was grateful that her

friends could not see what a miserable charade that smile was.

"You're leaving?" Harriet broke the stunned silence of the group. "I know you've talked about it, but I just can't believe it."

"To tell the truth, I haven't really decided. I agreed to look into it when Joe suggested that I move closer to him and his family. Quite frankly, there are many advantages. It probably isn't safe for me to live all alone out by the lake. In Richmond, I'd be close to other people if I needed help. I'd have access to transportation and shopping. And it would be much easier on Joe."

As her friends digested what she was saying, Addie explained, "When Joe took me on a tour almost a year ago, he suggested that I put my name on a waiting list. There are few vacancies, and I knew I'd have plenty of time to think it through. Believe me, I *have* thought hard about it. Now we're down to the wire." She forced an uneasy laugh. "I have to commit by Monday, or I'll lose my spot. And Joe—he's already planning to help me move this weekend."

"Addie," said Walter, his voice barely audible, "I didn't know. I hope you'll be happy if that's what you choose to do. We'll truly miss you."

"There wasn't time," she mumbled. "He called just last night." She knew she should have prepared Walter for this, but something had stopped her each time she'd tried. When he'd made his regular morning call to check in with her, she had found it easier to discuss the weather than tell him the news.

"You can't go, Miss Addie!" Leo called abruptly from across the table. "You're the only one who helps me with my Braille when Laura's not around. I know I can call Walter, but he's too hard on me!"

Walter laughed a shallow, good-natured response.

"We'd really miss you if you move, Addie. We all admire you and think so much of you." Maggie was genuine in her remarks and Addie thanked her.

"I'd still come to the meetings from time to time. Joe told me he'd bring me out when he could. I know I want to continue to see all of you. Let's not even think of saying . . ." her voice again cracked causing a flood of red to cover her face as tears filled her eyes, "good-bye."

An uncomfortable silence followed until Laura said, "Addie, you know you're always welcome here. It goes without saying how much you'll be missed. But I want you to know there are a few different groups for people who are blind or visually impaired meeting in Richmond. I'll get you information about them, and we'll see that you are involved if you move. I know there's another lady at Gateway who attends one of them, and maybe you can go with her."

"Thank you," Addie replied.

As the thirsty ground soaked up the gently falling rain, so the group seemed saturated by Addie's announcement. When no one else spoke Laura prompted, "Anyone else? What's new with the rest of you?"

"I have good news," Susanna finally volunteered.

"Great, what is it?" Laura found herself struggling to facilitate the support group, which had abruptly lost its enthusiasm following Addie's announcement. She could count on Susanna to bolster the group at these times.

"I had an examination at the Colorado University Medical Center in Denver. Everything checks out great! My diabetes is under control, my heart and kidneys are doing well, and I haven't felt this healthy in a long time."

Spontaneously, the group broke into applause and words of congratulations as Susanna added, "It's a major accomplishment for me with teenagers in the house and all of their junk food and crazy schedules."

As the last pattering of applause faded away, David's more serious tone pervaded the gathering. "Can we go back to Addie for a moment? I'm sorry, Susanna, were you finished?"

"Sure, go ahead."

"I'm confused, Addie." He turned to face the woman between him and Walter. Gordon poked his nose between the two of them and David patted the dog's head as he continued. "Everything I've heard you say about Gateway is what *Joe* has planned and what *Joe* wants. But beyond that, I don't understand. Why are *you* thinking about going to Gateway?"

"Well, I . . ." Addie stammered. "As I said, there are many advantages. I probably should go because it's what is best for me. I'll be taken care of—you know, they fix all of the meals and take care of the rooms and laundry. And being closer to Joe is important. He can't help me as easily living out here, and he worries about me being all alone at the lake. I know it's the best thing."

"Those aren't reasons, Addie!" Disgust filled the man's voice and Gordon quickly retreated to lie at Walter's feet. "Is there something you aren't telling us? Look, I'm sorry. Maybe I'm prying, and if you don't want to answer me, don't. But when I'm faced with the possibility of losing someone dear to me, I want to know why." Then with genuine concern he added, "Are you sick, Addie? Is it your health?"

"My health is as good as ever," Addie replied sincerely. "I just had a physical with John—Dr. Siegfried. It's kind of like when you go to church camp, they require a physical before they let you in." A trickle of tense laughter momentarily filled the air. "Anyway, he told me I'm in great shape. Oh, I had a scare a few years ago with my heart, but that's all it was. He says I've got the body of a twenty-year-old."

More nervous laughter arose, but David remained steadfast. "Then why, Addie?" he demanded. "Do you *want* to go? If you do, then that's a good reason, and I'll wish you well. But I haven't heard you say that!"

The room fell silent. Addie wished she could get up and run out the door into the cool, wet afternoon. But she owed these people more than that. These were her friends. These were the people who had been there for her when she was lost and confused. His questions were fair; they deserved an answer.

Unfortunately, Addie didn't know the answer. Taking a deep breath she said, "No, David, I don't want to go to Gateway."

"That's what I thought," he muttered.

"I guess," she hesitated, "it's mostly for Joe. And my eyes," she added, "I'm getting older and I don't know what the future has in store for me."

"I'm old, too," Marie quipped bringing a surprised response from the group, who seldom heard her speak out. "You couldn't drag me out of Pinecliffe. It's the best place in the world to be when you're old. When I leave here it will be in a pine box, and my kids know it!"

"Good for you, dear." May Evans patted Marie's arm.

"That leaves your eyes," interjected Leo. "Now, Miss Addie, you know we can't buy that here. What do you think this is all about, refreshments? All of these meetings and Laura teaching you how to cook again and use a cane and read Braille? C'mon! Your eyes? That's a cop out and you know it!"

In spite of themselves, the members again broke into

clumsy applause as Walter leaned over and whispered, "He's got you there, girl!"

"It is a nice place for the right person, but I'm afraid *you* would be awfully bored at Gateway, Addie!" Alice Mumford's robust reflection rose above the noise. "And all of your hard work for nothing! What are you going to do when somebody else is doing everything for you?"

"Hold on a minute," Cecil interrupted. "We're meddling in someone else's business here. Addie, you know we all agree with your son in one respect. We want what's best for you. If you go, we'll miss you. No doubt about it. Think a little more before you decide for sure, okay?"

"Cecil's right," said Laura. "We've worked Addie over pretty good today. It needs to be her choice, not ours."

"And not Joe's . . ." said David under his breath.

Addie sat thoughtfully for a few moments then whispered, "I love you all."

Carol arrived early to take her band of riders home from the meeting. One by one she escorted them to the waiting van, holding a bright red umbrella over their heads. The rain showed no sign of relenting. It had intensified since the Old Mobile had arrived at the lake two hours before. Addie giggled in spite of herself as she clung to Carol's arm, and they danced their way around the puddles.

As the driver expertly maneuvered her vehicle, she explained that she had come early because she feared the roads would be getting slick and muddy, making travel dangerous. "I hope you don't mind."

Addie did not mind at all. It was a relief to have an escape from the scrutiny of the group, especially Walter. He had remained cordial as the meeting drew to an end, but the hurt in his voice was evident. Addie knew it had not been the right way to tell him.

Carol grew quiet after dropping off the last passenger in Pinecliffe and heading toward the lake road. The rhythmic swish-swish of the windshield wipers almost lulled Addie to sleep, as her trusted driver studied the way and proceeded slowly.

"Hello, Mom?" She remembered Joe's call the night before and the almost too formal sound of his voice. "I have two things to tell you. First, I realized I haven't winterized the boat yet. You remember Judy and I were gone over Labor Day, and I plain forgot about it. The weather's been so nice, it doesn't even seem like summer's over."

"I forgot all about it, too, son," replied Addie. "I just heard on the news a prediction of heavy rain tomorrow."

"We need it, everything's so dry. Listen, I'll come out this weekend and take care of the boat and a few other odds and ends I've put off. I'm sure it'll be all right until then."

"What's the other thing?" she asked.

"What?"

"That you called to tell me."

"Oh, yeah." Joe took a deep, deliberate breath. Addie guessed he was rehearsing a speech in his mind that he'd already practiced a dozen times before calling. "I hope you'll consider this good news, Mom. You should. I got a call from Kelly today. You remember her, the social worker at Gateway?"

"Yes, I remember."

"Well, she told me they have a room available. It faces east which will be good for daylight and looks over the park," he rambled. "It's available right now, clean and prepared for you. I'm going by tomorrow to check it out, and, if you're ready, we can start moving anytime, maybe this weekend after I take care of things out there. Looks like we're going to beat the snow after all!"

"Joe . . ." Addie was surprised at her voice, how level, how calm it came across. "I don't know if I'm ready for a move like this. I'm getting along so much better now, and I . . ."

"Mom," Joe said, "I can't believe we're still having this discussion after all this time. I guess I thought you'd made up your mind."

"Well, I haven't," she responded. "Yes, I've thought about it. Yes, I know it would be good for me. But, Joe, I love this place."

"And you can visit often, Mom. You know that," impatience crept into his voice. "Look, I don't want to go through this again. I've done what I thought was right for you. Now we've reached a point where you have a real opportunity that may not come up again. All I can say is, you must decide. If we don't go in Monday and sign a contract, your name will be removed and the room offered to the next person on the list."

"I know, Joe. I promise to have a decision when you come out this weekend," she sighed. "I do appreciate you and everything you've done for me. I'm sure I'll make the right choice."

"That's great, Mom. Hey, thanks for not yelling at me!"

"Oh, Joe," she sighed again, this time in resignation.

George carried the small glass canning jar to the shore of the lake and filled it with water. On his way back up the hill he picked tiny purple wild flowers which covered the rocky ground. When he reached the cabin he sneaked onto the porch and placed them in the center of a log picnic table, which his wife had already covered with a blue checkered cloth.

"Addie, come out here!"

Her face beamed as she walked through the doorway. "They're beautiful, George! How I love those little flowers. Thank you, dear." She kissed his cheek and held his gift up to examine it more closely.

"Joe should be along soon," George said. "I thought we could eat dinner out here, you know, sort of break it in."

"I'm planning on it." Addie gave him a gentle hug and turned toward the house to check her meal. "Tonight and many, many more nights. I think we'll start eating on the porch all the time when the weather's nice, don't you, George?"

Since the death of their oldest son, George had thrown himself into projects. He had overhauled an old car that he'd bought for Joe, but given to Addie, after the boy had earned enough during the previous summer at the resort to purchase something more to his liking. He had painted the interior of their house in town. At Addie's urging he had done volunteer work hanging Christmas decorations for the Richmond Chamber of Commerce and made several hand-carved ornaments to adorn the tree at home. These Addie had painted at the kitchen table as Joe watched with detached interest.

George was good with his hands. His latest project, a picnic table for their summer cabin, renewed his sense of accomplishment and helped to fill the chronic ache inside of him which time seemed unable to erase. When Joe arrived, the family of three gathered on the porch to admire the father's work. They settled into easy conversation as Addie brought a pot roast with mashed potatoes and gravy from the kitchen.

"You're great with wood, Dad," Joe said sincerely as his father smiled sheepishly. The recent high school graduate had not joined his parents at their summer retreat for the first time since they had brought him there as a child. Instead he had signed on at the mill, turning down an offer to return to the resort for a second summer. He had chosen not to commute back and forth with his father but to remain at home in the city. Still, to his mother's surprise, he had arrived every Friday evening to spend the weekend at Bear Lake, returning to town at the crack of dawn on Monday.

Occasionally, Joe's weekends included the friends he'd made the summer before. Often he drove up to the camp where his former employers buoyed his spirits by begging him to come back to work. Sometimes he'd make a date with Mary Lou, who had one year of high school left in Pinecliffe. But more often, he spent his weekends hiking alone or fishing quietly on the shores of Bear Lake. He was a different young man from the pubescent lad of one year before.

"What's your next project going to be?" Joe asked his father as Addie began to clear the dishes from the table.

"I thought you'd never ask!" George teased. "I'm going to build a boat, Joe, and I need your help."

"A boat?" Joe's eyes widened as Addie came up behind and placed her hands on her son's shoulders, equally inquisitive.

"A boat," George repeated. "Think about it, Joe. You and I have been fishing from the shores of this lake all these years. Now don't you think the fish are getting smart? They're all out in the center or hiding in the coves where we can't reach them!"

"A fishing boat." Joe digested the idea while his father continued.

"Motorized boats are prohibited on Bear Lake, for which

I'm grateful," George explained. "I'm talking about a little wooden boat, a few cross benches, a couple of good, sturdy oars . . . and look out rainbow trout!"

"From the looks of this table, Dad, you don't need *my* help," Joe commented.

"But I do!" George insisted. "A boat is a more complicated undertaking. For one thing, it has to float."

"Good point," Joe remarked.

"I'd really like some help," George ventured, studying the continually rigid, sober contour of his son's face.

Joe picked up the Mason jar vase as Addie had done earlier and turned it around absentmindedly in his hands. A few drops of water spilled over onto the tablecloth, and the boy blankly rubbed them into the fabric. Finally, he spoke, "Sure, I'll help you, Dad, when I'm out here."

"Good! We can start tomorrow. I've got some good pine and drew up a few plans. You can look them over—see what you like the best."

"Mom can help out, too," Joe added as he rose to leave the table.

"Oh, no, you don't!" said Addie. "I've got two unfinished novels to read and a dozen pieces for a quilt waiting on me. You guys are on your own with this one."

The next morning Addie watched as the father and son headed toward a large shed, where George had created a makeshift shop. As the morning progressed, Addie often peered anxiously toward the building where the most constant sound was the blare of Joe's radio producing the brazen, steady beat of late-sixties rock 'n roll. She wondered at George's tolerance, and saw it unravel from time to time when their voices rose above the music in apparent disagreement.

When they came in for lunch both were dirty and quiet.

Addie feared the boat had already met an untimely end, but she was wrong. As soon as the meal was finished, they rose in false tranquility and headed back to the shop, equally stubborn in their determination not to be the one to quit.

At sunset, they headed toward the cabin together, walking a little closer, Addie thought. After dinner they sat on the porch and reviewed their plans for making the boat just right. Eventually they sought the light of the kitchen table where together they mulled over papers, changing the original draft over and over again. Thus began the summer of the boat.

In the close-knit summer community of Bear Lake, it did not take long before the construction of a boat was known and discussed by everyone. When Elsa came to visit her neighbor, the two women laughed uncontrollably as they imagined what went on beyond the log walls of the shop. "I never thought I'd like the sound of a buzz-saw," Elsa teased, "but I have to tell you when it starts up, at least I know they're working the boat over instead of each other!"

"Yesterday, I surprised them with brownies and milk," began Addie, wiping her eyes. "When I showed up at the door you'd have thought I'd invaded their clubhouse. They both escorted me out and made it clear that they're working on a top-secret project. No girls allowed! Nobody sees the boat before it's finished. What I got a glimpse of looked awfully big."

Elsa again burst into laughter. "What if they make it so big they can't get it out of the workshop?" she mused. "I plan to set up my lawn chair back in the trees and watch on that day."

One Sunday afternoon, Addie heard the escalation of voices, then Joe stormed through the door. "That man is absolutely impossible!" He threw himself into a kitchen chair and began drumming his fingers on the table as his mother watched in surprised silence.

A moment later George flew through the door and collapsed into a second aluminum chair. His eyes momentarily met Joe's before each quickly turned away.

"Drink anyone?" Addie's timid question broke the silence.

"You don't know everything, Dad!" Joe exploded. His mother took a cautious step backward.

"I know I don't!" George's voice rose above his son's.

"But you think you do! You act like you do!" Joe managed a decibel higher as he glared at the man across from him.

"I know I do!" George bellowed.

"I don't know it all, either!" screamed Joe.

"I know you don't!"

To the surprise of both of them, Addie jumped upon one of the remaining kitchen chairs, waving her hands back and forth in the air. "Now wait just a minute!" The two men stared at her in startled silence, their mouths gaping open. "You're arguing the same points. You're agreeing with each other. That's not an argument. Listen to yourselves!"

"Mom, you wanna get down off that chair?" Joe asked solemnly as with deadpan charity he reached a hand up to help her. Then the three of them burst into laughter. In no time, the carpenters headed cordially back to their labor, deep in conversation as they walked side by side. This was how the summer of the boat would be.

It was the rage that troubled Addie. Anger she could recognize and deal with, but the sharp, raw edge of rage was something she hadn't seen before in her child. It had been strange, almost ethereal, the first time it happened.

Unfortunately, Joe had inherited his mother's small,

234

agile frame instead of the broad, muscular build of his father. As a result, any athletic efforts beyond the neighborhood street games were met with failure. This had never
seemed to particularly trouble Joe, who enjoyed acting in
plays and taking part on the debate squad, where his talent
for arguing was an asset. The boy never seemed jealous of
his older brother's accomplishments on the football field
and basketball court. In fact, Joe was one of Jake's most ar-
dent fans. He'd never missed a game.

Still it surprised Addie when, in his senior year, Joe announced that he had tried out for the wrestling team and
been awarded a spot.

"Wrestling?" Addie asked in surprise. "I never knew you
liked to wrestle. You've never done anything like that before."

Joe shrugged in response. With George and Addie sitting
nervously in the bleachers for their son's first meet, Joe
nonchalantly joked with his teammates and ambled to the
mat when his match was called. But the moment he stepped
from the wooden floor of the gymnasium to the gray pad
where his contender awaited him, a conversion occurred.

Addie saw it first in the cold, black liquid of his eyes. His
jaw set and his nostrils flared. As the two young bodies
joined, a terror seemed to grab hold of Joe, and he savagely
tore into his opponent. As if sensing her move, George
reached an arm across Addie to hold her back, their eyes
meeting quizzically. The match ended quickly, as Joe expertly pinned the surprised competitor, then ambled leisurely to the sidelines where his teammates hugged him in a
roar of pride. He resumed joking with them as though the
intermittent activity had been but an interruption.

The high school coach marveled at this unexpected new
talent. "Why didn't you try out for wrestling sooner?" he

questioned the boy. "Do you know where you'd be now if you'd have started as a freshman?"

But Addie knew it wasn't about wrestling. It wasn't about earning the blue letter jacket that had eluded Joe Marsh throughout his high school career. It wasn't even about winning. It was about rage—cold, bitter rage, which consumed the young man in a way no amount of training or coaching could instill. How many times, Addie wondered, did Joe attack the Viet Cong or an official of the United States pentagon when he stepped onto the mat? Did he see the plane flying over, losing power as the explosion took out its mid-section, while he, on the ground, passionately sought to destroy the enemy?

Addie attended every match, her body tense, her heart pounding and palms wet, as she and George watched the tragedy of their son that the fans interpreted as triumph. His fury took him into the state finals, where he was defeated by an unbeaten senior from northern Colorado, who had prepared for that moment since he was seven years old. As Joe left the mat that afternoon, a humbled, knowing smile crossed his face.

"Joe, I can get you onto a junior college team," his coach prattled as he walked alongside him toward the dressing room. "It won't be a big school, but you're good. You're damn good! You could have had that guy—one more year in the program—you'd have brought the trophy home!"

But in spite of his coach's objections, Joe wasn't interested. He left the gymnasium and went with his friends to eat pizza and check out all the girls at the state tournament. And he never wrestled again. But then, it had never been about wrestling.

One morning, with the boat project well underway, Addie was surprised to see Joe and his father heading for the lake carrying lumber between them with a metal tool box in tow. She soon realized they were fortifying the little pier at the bottom of the hill, which was used for fishing or as a diving platform when the boys went swimming. Now it would have the greater purpose of harboring the boat and reinforcement was needed.

When George entered the house a few hours later, dripping wet from head to toe, Addie could not help herself as she doubled over on the sofa with laughter.

"Now don't you start!" George left big, wet tracks through the living room into the bedroom where he changed and headed back out.

"Maybe you should try a swimming suit?" his wife asked with feigned innocence.

"Addie . . ."

The morning of its launching, the newly varnished boat shone in the summer sun, having just made it through the door of the improvised shop. A small group of neighbors milled about as Addie produced coffee and donuts for the well-wishers. A few of the men helped George and Joe carry their craft to the lake amid cheers and applause from the onlookers.

Henry Roberts ceremoniously produced a bottle of champagne, which he handed to George. "For her christening before the maiden voyage!" he droned with tones of Ireland in his accent. "What do you name her, Good Captain?"

"Aye," George played along. "I am but the mate. Here is our Captain." He deferred to a slightly embarrassed Joe who took the bottle good-naturedly.

We christen thee—" he began, looking about the group. "We christen thee, *The Boat*."

"The boat?" George asked as the bottle splintered

against the edge and the foamy, liquid bubbles ran down its wooden side.

"You said I was the Captain," Joe reminded his father as everyone broke into hearty laughter.

"*The Boat*," George mumbled in fun as he climbed aboard. When the two were settled, he looked at Addie, still standing on the shore. "You coming?" he asked her.

"No, sir, the honor of the first trip goes to the creators. It isn't my place. Another time."

"She's just afraid it will sink," Joe whispered loudly to his neighbors, causing Henry to suggest they take bets on it.

"If you don't help with the fishing, you're stuck with the cooking," George teased. "You'd better get some cornbread and home fries going, Mother!"

"Aye, aye, sir!" Addie saluted, and with one hard shove off the pier from Joe, the boat, now dwarfed by the tall stately pines on the lake's edge, glided across the glassy surface. The neighbors cheered as George and Joe held up their fishing poles in a symbol of victory.

It was late afternoon when Addie saw them walking up the hill. Joe carried poles and tackle boxes, while George held a wire, laden with fish. Halfway up, they stopped and looked back upon their boat, talking in hushed, serious tones. Their burdens still in their hands, Addie watched as, awkwardly, they wrapped their arms about each other in a quick, tumultuous hug. As they turned to finish their trek to the cabin, George placed his free hand on his son's back, and for one wonderful moment, they threw their heads back in unified laughter.

That evening as they lay together in bed, Addie wrapped an arm comfortably over George. "That was a beautiful thing you did," she whispered.

"What do you mean?" he asked turning to face her in the dark.

"The boat," Addie answered. "That whole project was just plain, good psychology. You reached him, George. After all this last year, you finally found our son again."

He studied her moonlit face for a while before he told her, "That wasn't psychology, Addie. I was just being a father."

Years later, when Addie visited the cemetery overlooking Pinecliffe, that was how she most liked to remember George Marsh.

Addie had experienced her own moment in the sun a week later when Joe, unexpectedly, took a day off and showed up at the cabin after George had left for work.

"C'mon, Mom!" He pulled out the wicker picnic basket and gestured toward the refrigerator. "You're going to learn how to handle the boat today."

"You mean drive it? Me?" Addie automatically began opening the bread wrapper to make sandwiches. "It doesn't even have a steering wheel!" she objected.

"It's going to be a long day," Joe sighed.

Once on the water, Joe lectured her about wearing a life vest and not standing in the boat. She listened obediently, like a child heeding its parent. Gently, he wrapped his arms about her, as he taught her the smooth, steady motion that would force the oars to propel the boat through the water. It was a day Addie would always remember. They laughed and talked in a way that was new to the two of them.

As the hours passed, they covered the entire lake, and Addie saw its beauty from a new perspective. They stopped in an overgrown cove to eat lunch, as the boat rocked in time to their endless conversation. When an afternoon rain cloud forced them back to the dock, Addie realized she felt alive for the first time in so long.

"Did you have a good day, Mom?" Joe asked lazily as they strolled toward the cabin.

"One of the best days of my life. You're fun to be with, Joe. And, you're a good teacher!"

"Aw, shucks," he feigned embarrassment. "You know, Mom, that's your boat, too. And if I must admit it, you handled it well out there today. You should take it out sometimes. It's peaceful on the lake. You and your friends could go out during the day—you know—take a picnic like we did today. I'll bet Elsa would enjoy it."

"That would be fun." Addie had never thought of doing something like that on her own, but the idea, as well as Joe's confidence in her, was intriguing.

"Maybe we'd better not mention it to Dad, though, until you get really good at it."

"Why not?" asked Addie.

"You know Dad. He thinks it's guy stuff. He wouldn't understand."

"Okay, Joe. We'll keep it a secret until I'm in my first regatta."

"That's for sailboats, Mom," Joe mussed up her hair, then charged ahead of her. "I think I'll run up to the camp for a visit," he called over his shoulder and disappeared into the house.

Addie looked back to where the little boat could barely be seen beneath the sharp slope to the shoreline. "Maybe I'll just do that," she mused.

George's last project that summer was the normal end-of-the-season maintenance, which the cabin always required before closing it up after Labor Day. One evening, after putting his tools away, he sat with Addie on the porch sipping a hot cup of tea. They never tired of sitting and watching the lake. Addie's words pulled her husband back from a peaceful fantasy with surprise.

"I'm thinking of staying on a little longer this year, George."

Struggling to grasp the meaning of her words he asked, "Here?"

"Yes, it's too beautiful to leave, and besides, I'm getting involved in projects in Pinecliffe. There's actually more to keep me occupied out here than in the city. There isn't a reason to return to Richmond now that Joe's moving out with his friends." She turned to face her husband whose eyes affirmed what she was feeling. "I can't imagine being in that house day in and day out without my boys."

A few days before, Joe had nonchalantly informed his parents that he had registered to attend the fall term at the small, but growing, college in the city. "A couple of guys I wrestled with have a basement apartment in a house that's walking distance to the campus. They've asked me to go in on it, and I've decided to do that." Seeing his mother's startled look he'd added, "I need to learn to do for myself more. It'll be good for me, and I can afford it. I'm staying on a weekend crew at the mill while I go to school."

"So you're really going to college after all?" George asked sounding half-pleased.

"Sure," Joe acknowledged. "If I've learned one thing in the mill this summer, it's that I don't want to spend the rest of my life there." Then realizing what he'd said he quickly added, "No offense to you, Dad."

"Hey, I understand." George waved his hand in acknowledgment. "If I had it to do over again, I wouldn't spend a lifetime there, either. That's not to say it hasn't been good to me, but I know what you're saying. It's hard, back-breaking work."

"I'm not afraid of hard work." The too-familiar challenge entered Joe's voice.

"We know you're not," Addie soothed. "We're glad you've decided to go to school. But you're moving out, too?"

This time he looked at her squarely. Their eyes met, leaving no question to his intent. "Yeah, Mom, I'm moving out the first of September."

He then told them he'd planned to meet some friends at Scottie's that evening and light-heartedly bent down to kiss his mother goodnight. In the next instant, as he headed for the door, he stopped abruptly; the sober Joe was once again among them. "I filled out my student deferment papers with the draft board today, too," he scowled. "But if I had my way, I'd be shipping out for Vietnam right now!"

"Then why aren't you going?" George responded sharply to meet Joe's tone.

"George!" Addie cried.

"Because I made someone a promise, and I'm good for my word." With that he disappeared out the door into the night.

George reluctantly agreed to stay a little longer at the lake. Addie did not realize then that they wouldn't be going back at all to the little house they'd shared near the mill for all their married life. Until he retired, George often stayed there alone when the weather kept him from making the trip home to Bear Lake at night. After his first year in college, Joe moved back in to take care of the empty place and to have more privacy than the basement apartment allowed him. But Addie never returned, except as a visitor.

Years later, when their son married and George spent his days fishing instead of shoveling coal, the little house was sold. By then the Marshes were recognized as permanent residents of the Pinecliffe area. In time, Addie Marsh became a familiar sight rowing across Bear Lake in her wooden boat—sometimes alone, sometimes with a friend, but always with a wave and a smile.

The rain continued to fall on Bear Lake the evening after the group meeting. It was a steady, unyielding rain which gave Addie no consolation as she sorted through the events of the day. She was amazed, but also relieved, when no one called her that night to help her make a decision about moving to Gateway. Even Joe seemed willing to give her some time, and the solitary evening passed with only the purring of Rufus and the cadence of the storm for company.

She knew there were chores awaiting her beyond the closed door of the extra bedroom, but she could not bring herself to confront them. Instead, she spent a restless night. Moving from television to radio to talking books, nothing captured her attention from thought that this little home, which had held and comforted her through so many seasons, could soon become just another closed-up summer cabin on Bear Lake.

After listening to a weather report that predicted heavy rainfall throughout the night, but a return to Indian Summer by tomorrow, Addie gave up and went to bed. Maybe it was the rain that had her feeling so blue inside. Rain had never bothered her before, but she'd heard that it could cause depression in people. Maybe in tomorrow's sunlight, the prospect of moving to Gateway wouldn't seem so dreadful. As she lay in bed, she thought again of the changing seasons on Bear Lake, and the joy each transformation had given her as the years passed. She thought of all the creatures of the forest surrounding her home, whose presence seemed to say, "We're out here. You're not alone." She buried her head in her pillow and cried softly until Rufus pushed his cold nose under her chin in dismay.

When finally she had drifted to sleep, a man entered the room and sat comfortably on the bed beside her. He reached for her warm hand beneath the quilt and squeezed it gently.

I'm with you, love, he whispered into the night. *You've got to be careful, Addie!* He was more stern and serious than usual. But the emotions of the day and the solitude of the evening had taken their toll, and Addie fell into fitful slumber. She never heard his warning.

Chapter 13

As if in a dance, Rufus soared through the air in unison to the sudden, cymbal-like crash. He flew across the room to shelter beneath a corner table. Addie was up and to the doorway of her bedroom before her eyes opened. In her confusion she could not comprehend the horrible, banging sound. Could it be thunder?

With bare feet, she stumbled through the dark toward the kitchen, aware that the noise she heard was not from the storm, but a closer, deafening clamor which awakened the usual, deep stillness of the mountains. The blast that had shattered her slumber had come from a gun. The kitchen was black. There was no moon to spill light on the cold linoleum floor.

As quickly as the sound reached Addie's ears, silence returned. Then the momentary calm was replaced with a repetitive, dull thud. Addie grasped for the light switch, but pulled her hand back as a shrill, piercing scream filled the air. Once, twice, in terror, the sound rushed through the trees like a sudden gust of wind. Stunned, disbelieving, Addie stood in the doorway, small and frightened.

"No!" a voice cried out, near enough to touch. "Oh, God! Stoney . . . No, no, stop, please!"

It was Sybil—pitiful, terrified—hurt. Now fearing the light, Addie rushed through the darkness to the phone. Her ear was met with silence. There was no welcoming tone, in spite of the woman's persistent pushing on the small, plastic buttons. Addie realized the phone was dead, as another wail filled the night.

"Help me! Somebody . . . please! No! Stoney! No!" An-other terrible scream rose, then fell into the shadows. "Addie! Hide!" was the last, furtive warning. Then the only sound was the steady falling of rain on the roof.

Addie let the useless receiver fall from her hands. She yanked her jacket from the peg where it hung by the door and pulled it on over her nightgown. She shoved her feet into the rubber boots she'd left drying on an old newspaper earlier that evening after she'd ventured out to check the mailbox. As she placed her hand on the doorknob, she heard footsteps approaching from the other side. Addie raced back across the room toward the rear of the house, aware that someone was unlocking her door—not breaking in as she expected—but walking in, as casually as she her-self might do.

Quietly, slowly, she opened the door to the porch, and slipped out into the night. As the rain pounded her, she pulled up the hood of her jacket, tying it under her chin, for what little protection it could offer against the storm. Then she waited, hoping that the intruder was Joe, and the lights would click on. He'd call her name and laugh when he saw her standing outside in her nightgown and rubber boots. But there were no lights. There had been no car to an-nounce the arrival of her son, the only person other than herself who had a key.

The moment before she disappeared down the steps and stumbled toward a protecting thicket of trees, Addie heard the unmistakable voice of Stoney from within her home. "Bitch!"

Once hidden in the trees, Addie stopped to catch her breath and think of what she must do. From the deep pocket of her jacket, she retrieved her cane, and in an in-stant opened it, turning her back to the house for fear the white reflective tape would be seen. If she tried to sneak down her driveway to the road, he would surely spot her. There was no way to get to Sybil without being seen.

Addie knew she must get help, but where? She knew she could not make it to the village in the storm, even if she could somehow get past the Roberts's house and find her way down the road leading to Pinecliffe. She stood in the shelter of the trees until her body began to shake with cold and fear.

Her only hope was the other resident of Bear Lake, Paul Curtis. If she could somehow make it to the logging camp, surely he would help. She began to move through the brush in the only direction that offered safety—the lake. Carefully, she used her cane to avoid tripping or running into obstacles.

When she reached the shore, still hidden by the trees, Addie again stopped to think her situation through. She was acutely alert and aware of her predicament. She must move quickly. Sybil was hurt, and Stoney was in her house, presumably looking for her. She also realized she faced exposure if she did not get out of the storm soon. In the dark of the moonless night, her peripheral sight was useless. Addie was blind and would have to rely upon her memory and her cane to walk around the lake to her neighbor's isolated home.

She felt for the water's edge but after a few steps stopped again. It would take hours to walk to the opposite side of the lake following the shoreline. How many times, when the boys were young, had they walked the full circle, taking a good part of the day to make the excursion? There were places on the shore where rocks made it impassible, forcing them to climb up and around. With two boys and a bright summer sun, this had been fun. But that was years ago, and it could not be done alone on a cold, dark, rainy night.

Turning back, Addie's only other alternative became clear to her. *The Boat.* She could hear it above the rain, softly rocking into the pier. She had not taken the boat out by herself for the last two summers, but relied upon Joe or Michael for an occasional ride. Now, it beckoned her to navigate the waters of Bear Lake alone. Creeping onto the pier, she carefully laid her cane inside the hard cavity of the wooden craft. Then, taking the heavy wet knot in her hands, she fumbled to untie it.

"C'mon!" she whispered under her breath, her hands cold and wet as she followed the rope's contour. At last, it came loose, and Addie scrambled into the boat, pushing herself away from the dock with both hands. She heard a faint "meow" from the pier and called out in a soft but commanding voice, "You can't go, Rufus. Run to the trees. Hide!"

The little boat rocked uncertainly on the unsettled waters, causing Addie to grab both sides in panic. For what seemed several minutes, she clung in terror, awaiting her almost certain fate of drowning. The boat continued to rock, and water splashed threateningly against its sides. Addie couldn't tell if her nightgown was soaked from the falling rain or the lake crawling into her wooden sanctuary.

Addie! She could see nothing, even an outline, in the darkness, but she recognized the voice. *Addie, pay attention! You can do it! Think . . . you've got to think!*

Jacob? She whispered. A distant flash of lightning startled Addie. Half-standing, she rocked the boat even more causing an oar to slide along the bottom.

Addie!

Yes, yes, of course! Obediently, she sat down and reached beneath the seats until she recovered a life vest and the two oars, which she held between her feet while she fastened the wet jacket around her. Oars in position, she closed her eyes tightly and pulled with all her power. Slowly and awkwardly, the resistive vessel righted and began to move across the fighting waves.

She considered the direction she must row and realized her best chance was to stay as close to the shoreline as possible without hitting its shallow, rocky edge.

Listen! The evasive voice called to her. Addie suddenly realized that she could hear the tide lapping against the rim where the water met its boundary. If she followed the sound, carefully compensating with her oars, she would not drift out into the center of Bear Lake. Eventually, she would be in front of Paul's house, which sat closer to the shore than her cabin. How she would recognize it in the black night, how she would get from the boat to land, she did not know. For now, she must listen, concentrate, pull, steady, steady . . .

Slowly the little boat found its way along the bank. The rain continued, persistent and cold, as Addie clung to the oars, her eyes tightly shut, biting her lower lip, every move an interminable threat of peril. When her body began to shake uncontrollably, it occurred to Addie that she did not know if she was laughing or crying or freezing. Her face was soaked with tears and rain. She could no longer discriminate cold from fright. Her body felt numb to sensation, giving instead every ounce of its attention to the task of maneuvering the boat safely.

I'm laughing! She concluded in dismay. *I'm laughing because Addie Marsh is on the lake in the middle of the night, and I shall be the talk of Pinecliffe forever! But no, no! I can't be laughing. Sybil could be dying! This is really happening. Help! I have to get help!*

She continued to shake, biting her lip harder and pulling firmly on the right oar, trying to generate speed while keeping parallel to the sound of the shore. She thought of one day when she and Laura had been walking on a mobility lesson. Laura had told her to concentrate as she passed a building to "feel" its presence. Then when they had passed an open field, Laura had encouraged her to "feel" the difference.

"I never noticed that before in my life!" Addie had marveled, and Laura had gently reminded her, "You never had to."

Now she realized she could sense the trees along the bank, and if she drifted too far out, she could feel the open space of the lake. She concentrated so hard it hurt. Once an oar nearly dropped from her tired hand, and she willed her entire body over to the fight.

You can do it! You've rowed around this lake many times before; you must think! Remember what it looks like. Jacob called to her. Somehow she kept going, fighting the incessant storm.

As the unremitting struggle continued, she felt her mind drifting like it does just before one falls asleep. She was tired now, so tired. She wanted to sleep, to forget this night, to wake up later . . . where? In a hospital bed with Joe and Dr. John arguing in the dimly lit room? With Michael sobbing in the corner?

"They found you bobbing on Bear Lake. If it hadn't been for that life jacket, you'd have drowned!"

"Mom, I told you the boat would be okay until the weekend. I told you, Mom. You don't listen to me!"

Cecil and Leo were standing on the dock with fishing poles. The Group was there. Gordon was drinking from the lake's edge and was it Walter? Yes, Walter was echoing

Tom. "Blind people are portrayed as super human or as very pathetic creatures."

"Which are you, Miss Addie?" Leo was laughing and May scowled at him. "Are you just plain crazy?"

She shook her head. *Pay attention! Yes, Jacob, I'm sorry. I'm paying attention now. Oh Sybil . . . are we almost there?*

It was one of Addie's favorite things that solved the dilemma of finding Paul's house. The familiar smell of a burning fireplace welcomed her. Addie knew that it could only have come from his home because the rain would make a late autumn campfire impossible. She pulled her left oar to steer closer to the shore and was immediately startled by a bump as the boat came to a stop. She was against something—a rock? Carefully laying down the oars, she stood and leaned over to feel the object.

The flat surface of a wooden pier jutting into the water was even more welcome than the smoke-filled air. Addie pulled the boat along its side until her hands found a smooth, metal cleat protruding near the end of the dock. Clumsily, she tied the boat and scrambled onto the platform, half crawling, half walking—a phoenix rising from the misty sphere of the lake.

With the tip of her cane bouncing, Addie found her way from the dock to a path that ended at the base of a flight of stairs. Several steps above, she pounded fiercely on Paul Curtis's heavy, wooden door.

"What the . . . ? My God, Addie!" The man reached for her and pulled her in. She stood before him, a small creature in a bright orange vest, a hood with dark wet strands of hair protruding, and soft folds of an old drenched flannel nightgown gathering above the knee-high ridge of green rubber boots.

Words rushed through her mind but all that was uttered

was the sound of her teeth chattering against the crackling backdrop of a blazing fire. Paul grabbed her arm and pulled her closer to the fireplace.

"You're freezing. Here!" He drew a heavy blanket from a nearby couch causing an open book to fall to the floor. As he wrapped it about her tiny frame he muttered, "I couldn't sleep. I was reading. I . . ." He adjusted the blanket from falling off her wet shoulders. "Addie, what the hell is going on here? Are you all right?"

"Sybil!" she finally uttered. "She's hurt. Stoney . . . He . . . he's . . . trying to kill us. He's in my house. Call for help, Paul . . . I think she's hurt bad!"

Paul rushed to his phone, pushing impatiently on the buttons as Addie had done earlier. Finally, he slammed the receiver back into its cradle. "It's dead!"

"Mine is, too. It . . . it's the storm," Addie stuttered. "That's why I came. I couldn't call for help."

"You walked?" Paul asked in disbelief.

"No. The boat." Her teeth chattered again defeating her effort to speak. Addie tightened the blanket and realized for the first time since leaving the pier below her cabin that she was very, very cold.

"Dear God!" Paul ran a hand through his hair then without explanation he grabbed Addie and steered her down a dark hallway into another room. There he rummaged about for a moment, then pushed a bundle into her hands. "Put these on!" he commanded. "They're some old clothes my son left here."

"Your son?"

"They'll fit you better than anything of mine. You need to get out of those wet clothes or you'll catch pneumonia! I have a new cell phone in my truck. I'll run out and call the sheriff while you change."

Addie quickly exchanged her gown for the comforting warmth of blue jeans and a sweatshirt with an enormous caricature printed on the front. Only when she pulled on a pair of bulky tube socks, did she realize her feet had been bare inside the boots. She found her way back into the living room, just as Paul returned.

"We're in trouble, Addie. My cell phone is dead. I haven't used it before, and I guess I forgot to charge the battery. We're going to have to drive to town for help."

"Oh, dear." Addie could hear her voice although it sounded distant and hollow. "I'm sure I heard gunfire. Will we be safe going down the lake road past Stoney's house? Who knows where he is by now? If he's near the road or sees us go by, I'm afraid he'll shoot."

"We could take the old logging road," Paul suggested. "It intersects the highway east of town. If, by chance, he's around here, that old car of his wouldn't be able to follow us. C'mon, let's get moving!"

"You can't go over that road!" exclaimed Addie, her thoughts clearing. "You'd never make it, especially after all the rain we've had!"

"I'll make it. I've got four-wheel drive. Let's go."

"But . . ."

"Addie, that kid is on a rampage if he's got a gun. He may have plans to kill all of us tonight. I don't think our phones are out because of the storm. When that happens, the line crackles, but my line is dead. He may have cut the wires at the main unit. I don't think that Stoney wants anyone calling for help. You said he's hurt the girl, and he was in your house. It could be just a matter of time before he heads over here. We've got to get out of here."

"I guess you're right. We aren't safe here, and we're no good to Sybil without a phone."

"Put this on." Paul shoved an old army fatigue jacket into her hands. It hung heavily over her shoulders and fell below her knees, but at least it was dry. "If you aren't a sight!" Paul sighed.

As he took Addie's arm and moved toward the door, he called over his shoulder, "Blaze! Come!"

Inside the truck, Paul commanded the black dog to lie down in the back seat of the extended cab. He angrily pushed the useless cell phone to the floor, his hands shaking as he searched for the ignition in the dark. "It's cold in here. I've got a window that won't wind up all the way. I should have . . ." he muttered. When the motor turned over on the first try, he whispered, "Thank God." A click on the side of his door locked them in as he pulled slowly down his driveway without turning on the headlights. Then he turned right, away from the beckoning civilization of Pinecliffe, into the forest.

"Are you warm enough?" Paul had turned the heater and the fan on high, but cold air and drops of rain still found their way into the cab through the open window.

"I'm fine."

They drove with concentrated silence in darkness for several minutes before Paul turned on his headlights. Still, Addie could see nothing of the old road. It was worse than she imagined. The truck bounced and growled as it pulled along, causing Addie to ricochet with it, while trying desperately to stay on the seat. At last, Paul stopped and fumbled in the dark for the seatbelt, which he fastened securely around her.

"That should help," he said as he started driving again. "This road is awfully bad. Don't worry, though. We'll make it." He reached over and gently touched her shoulder. "How on earth did you get to my place in that boat?"

"Determination," Addie answered. "And perhaps a little foolishness." Suddenly, the ground seemed to slide out from under them, and Paul gripped furiously at the steering wheel to stay in the road.

Addie grabbed the door handle and hung on tightly as she'd earlier clung to the sides of the boat. They rode together silently, bumping and turning in the darkness. When the road smoothed out a bit, Addie surprised even herself with her first words, "I didn't know you had children."

"One son. He's ten years old—about your size!"

Addie laughed in spite of herself. "His clothes fit well, though they're not my style!"

"Not a Batman fan, huh?" Paul chuckled. "My son was with me for a week this summer. I hope to see him more as he gets older. He lives with his mother in North Carolina, and she makes a big deal out of letting him visit me. But things went well this year, and he really liked the lake. He wants to come back and help me with all of my projects."

"You're divorced?" she asked him.

"Yes," Paul answered softly. "We were divorced when Jimmy was two years old. His mother hated army life, all the moving and me being away for months at a time. Eventually she remarried, and now they have a couple of kids besides my son."

"I see," Addie said.

The truck gave another jerk causing Addie to gasp in spite of her efforts to remain calm. "Sorry," she whispered.

"This is quite a road," Paul sympathized. "When did the county quit maintaining it?"

"The logging industry in Pinecliffe was actually developed by the Works Progress Administration during the depression to help stimulate the economy. It was a good business for awhile, but started to decline after the war. By the time we bought our place, early in the fifties, the camp was deserted."

"Was it the logging industry that brought people to settle in Pinecliffe?"

"Oh, no," explained Addie. "Long before that, Pinecliffe was established as a summer retreat for wealthy investors. When coal was discovered in the mines south of Richmond and the mill was built, many speculators moved here from the larger mills in Chicago and other mid-western cities. They were successful and turned to the mountains for their enjoyment."

"Really?" Paul slowed momentarily to study the road, then veered cautiously to the left.

"Yes," Addie continued, relieved to have a topic away from their dilemma. "There were a few farms and ranches out here before that, but mostly near Fremont. In its beginnings Pinecliffe was a summer community, a very festive place I'm told. Then gradually people started to live in the village year-round. A school was built, a few businesses sprang up, and pretty soon it was a thriving little community. As transportation improved people didn't mind commuting to the city to work in exchange for a simpler way of life."

The truck came to a stop. "We've reached the highway," Paul explained as he turned onto the pavement. "We'll be in town soon."

"Already?" She exhaled a weary, jagged sigh. "What time is it?"

"A little past two a.m. We will probably have to wake Bill up. We might as well just go to his house." Paul's familiarity with the sheriff surprised Addie, but she said nothing as they turned down the hill that led to Main Street. Paul hesitated, trying to decide whether to stop at the first establishment or continue on to the sheriff's home.

"Well, I'll be," he muttered pulling to the curb. "He's in his office. I can see him through the window."

Quickly, Paul helped Addie down from the pick-up. "Blaze, stay." The dog whined and obediently flopped down on the seat. Relief filled Addie as they hurried into the small brick building, and Bill Johnson's voice echoed his surprise at seeing this unlikely pair enter his office in the middle of the night. "Addie, are you all right? Paul, what is this?"

"There's trouble at the lake," Paul explained. "That kid, Stoney—he apparently worked over his girlfriend, and broke into Addie's place."

"I heard Sybil screaming," Addie interrupted, "and then Stoney came into my house. He had a key."

"Did he hurt you?" Bill demanded. "What did he want?"

"I ran out the back door. I don't believe he saw me."

"Our phones are out. I think he cut the main line," Paul interjected.

"I managed to get down the hill and to the lake. Then I took our little rowboat across to get Paul's," Addie explained.

"*You* took the rowboat?"

"It was the only way. Then Paul and I drove across the logging road so he wouldn't see us. He may have a gun. I heard a couple of shots fired. I'm worried about Sybil, Bill. I hope she isn't . . ." Addie's voice trailed away, exhausted.

"The logging road, a gun . . ." Bill reached for a small microphone which cackled as he spoke into it. "I need backup at Bear Lake. I've got an armed kid terrorizing out here. Better send an ambulance, too!"

The sheriff rose and grabbed for his jacket. Addie found a chair beside his desk, and giving in to the fatigue which consumed her, she fell into it. "I'll go with you, Bill," Paul offered. "That kid's dangerous!"

"Thanks, Paul, but I'll feel better if you stay here with Addie. If by any chance Stoney is headed for Pinecliffe, she might not be safe alone, and there isn't time to take her anywhere else. There was a bad accident tonight out on the highway. That's why I'm here instead of at home. I was just finishing up my reports. There were still some county deputies on the scene when I left, so I'll have backup out there pretty fast tonight."

"We'll just stay put then and wait for you to come back," Paul agreed.

"Good! I'll want to talk to both of you before you leave. If I need help I'll holler for you over that radio," Bill nodded as he headed into the night. "There's a fresh pot of coffee there—help yourselves!"

The red lights of Bill's cruiser filled the room, as the siren blasted its farewell to the twosome. The radio spurted unclearly—numbers, instructions. Addie again felt numb, foreign to the world around her. For the first time that night she was hot and removed the heavy jacket.

"Batman suits you!" Paul teased. Then more gently he asked, "Coffee?"

"Please."

He handed her a warm mug and dragged a chair across the floor to sit down beside her. "You're safe here, Addie. What could be safer than the sheriff's office?"

"Yes," Addie sipped the coffee savoring its warmth. "I feel better now. I can't believe . . ."

"It's been a crazy night," Paul sympathized.

Addie shook her head. "I should have called Bill when things started disappearing from my house."

"You've had things stolen, too?" he asked in surprise.

"And you didn't tell anyone?"

"Well, no, I . . ." Addie paused. "I discussed it with Sybil. As a matter of fact, she'd had things missing, too. She even tried to convince me it was you who was the thief."

"It's that kid, Addie. And her. I can see that now."

When Addie didn't respond he asked, "You didn't honestly suspect me, did you?"

"No, Paul, I never believed that. But," Addie sighed heavily. "You have to understand that people were a little put off by you at first. You weren't the most friendly guy in town. Even Bill mentioned it to me when we were discussing Bear Lake one day. Now he acts like you're old friends. Of course, that's been awhile . . ." her voice trailed off as she tried to sort it out.

"I guess you're right. I made a reputation for myself early on as the local hermit," Paul said "Will you hear me out, Addie?"

"Of course."

The radio interrupted their conversation and they listened to a deputy nearing the lake. Sheriff Johnson responded with his location, then all was still again.

"When I first came to Bear Lake," Paul began, "maybe I did create some suspicion. I was an unknown who'd paid a God-awful price for a piece of property nobody wanted to be sold. Instead of explaining myself, I more or less hibernated. I'm sure people got the impression I was up to something. Actually, I was just taking some time, licking my wounds if you will."

"Licking your wounds?" Addie asked.

"Literally," Paul responded. "You know, Addie, there's a certain blessing attached to your vision problem. I think that's why I liked you from the start."

"I don't understand."

"You can't see my face," he explained gently. "Before I took my retirement—my early retirement—from the service, I was in an explosion in the Persian Gulf. I'm lucky I didn't lose my sight, like you, or sustain any permanent damage. It just horribly scarred my face and arms. I'm not the hand-some devil I used to be."

"Oh, Paul, I'm sorry!" Tears filled Addie's eyes.

"But you, Addie," his voice trembled, "you couldn't see my face. You saw me for who I am. No one else could do that in the beginning. My appearance stopped them before they got to know me. And the chip on my shoulder didn't help much, either." He forced a laugh and Addie heard him sniff.

"You're a beautiful human being," she countered.

"Thank you." Paul squeezed her hand. "When items started ending up missing around my place, I called Bill. We didn't find the burglar, obviously, but we got ac-quainted, and I let him know about my plans for the logging camp. He became interested and gradually some other people opened up to me. I think if you asked him now, he'd tell you I'm not such a bad person."

"Oh, Paul," Addie moaned. "I've always known you're a good man, but what a terrible mistake for Sybil to make. She is a simple girl in many ways. She was so sure that you were the thief, and she warned me to beware of you. She couldn't figure out where you got the money to buy that place, and she even told me you tried to beat up Stoney."

"I should have!" he exclaimed. "That little scoundrel! I caught him snooping around one day. I guess I should have realized . . . And the money. Addie, let me explain."

"No!" Addie replied. "I've said too much already. It's none of my business."

"But I want to tell you," he laughed. "While I was recuperating, I wrote a book. I needed something to distract my mind from the pain. It's a little dime store western based on stories my Grandpa told me when I was a kid. It somehow was published and did fair—not great—so I wrote another one. It generated a little more cash, and here I am."

"You're a writer!" Addie marveled.

"Not a very good one," he laughed. "But I'm having them put on tape for you. It was supposed to be a surprise."

"Paul—" Addie reached over and patted his arm, as the radio again interrupted them.

"I need that ambulance out here right now!" Bill Johnson shouted. "We have a seriously injured female here!"

Addie shuddered. "I'm sorry," Paul whispered to her.

She shook her head. "Do you think she was involved? In the stealing, I mean?"

"I don't know, Addie. I stayed away from those kids, never got to know them after that time with Stoney."

"I don't think she was!" Addie defended Sybil stoutly. "She's a mixed-up girl but not corrupt. I would have sensed that, I think."

"It's possible she didn't know what Stoney was up to," Paul comforted.

"And that's what I must believe." Their conversation was again hushed by the radio, a mixture of comments that didn't reveal much more. "Tell me about your plans," said Addie when the silence returned. "Help me think of something else."

"My plans for Bear Lake? They include you."

Addie did not respond. Her thoughts were on Sybil, the tiny creature who had for the last year been her friend, her ally. Now she lay at Bear Lake, waiting with a group of strange men for an ambulance to save her.

"I'm going to turn the old logging camp into a natural reserve," Paul began. "The idea is to maintain the environment. No more development. No more houses. I want to keep it, you know, pristine. My dream is a nice, clean place where families can come and enjoy the lake and learn about it. That's where you come in."

"Me?" Addie asked in surprise, her mind relinquishing Sybil momentarily.

"Yes, you. We're forming a committee to direct the development of the park. I want you to serve on it."

"I'm honored, Paul, but I can't."

"Why not?" he asked.

"Well, I can't see to read the agenda, the minutes. I'd just be a nuisance!"

"Addie," Paul was very serious. "We have eleven other people on the board who can see to read our minutes. But you're the only one who knows that lake. You are the last walking historian who can tell us what we need to know to create authenticity. We need you, Addie. Not your eyes, just you."

"Why didn't you tell me about all of this before?" Addie asked. "And your writing?"

"I don't know," he said. "I did want to surprise you with the books. And the rest of it? I enjoyed our conversations about your activities and the things we've read. I guess I never got around to it. I respect your love for the lake. Maybe I didn't want to seem like I was taking over."

Addie smiled, but when she did not answer Paul rose to refill their coffee. The police radio provided occasional bits of news, and the rain outside continued to fall. Together, the two neighbors waited.

★ ★ ★ ★ ★

When the ringing of the telephone interrupted Joe's sleep, it was with that sickening fear a parent has when his grown child isn't home yet. He glanced at the bedside clock and realized it was past Michael's curfew, and he hadn't heard him enter the house in that half-sleep state in which Joe always remained until all members of the family were accounted for.

"Joe? Sorry to wake you. It's Dave Adams."

Joe's hand tightened on the receiver. Dave was an old friend who had early-on achieved his childhood dream of becoming a policeman. "What is it, Dave?" His heart pounded as Judy sat up beside him.

"Look, I don't want to startle you, but I thought I should call. I heard on the scanner tonight that there's trouble at Bear Lake. Does your mom still live out there?"

"Bear Lake?" Joe's mind raced to change gears from Michael to his mother. "Yeah, Dave, she's out there. What's going on?"

"I can't really tell too much. A kid terrorizing with a gun and they've sent for an ambulance. A female's been seriously injured."

"No," Joe murmured under his breath.

"What is it, Joe? What is it?" Judy whispered from behind him.

"I'll head out there, Dave. I appreciate your call."

"No problem!" his friend responded. "Take it easy on the highway. We had a bad one out there tonight because of the rain. There's probably still a clean-up crew on the road."

"Do you want me to go with you?" Judy asked as Joe hurriedly dressed. She had tried to call his mother and found the line was not in service.

"No, you stay here. I'll call you as soon as I know something." On his way out of the house, he paused at Michael's closed bedroom door and slowly opened it. His son was in bed, asleep.

Dr. John Siegfried had also had his sleep interrupted when the local sheriff called with a "favor to ask."

"Addie Marsh is down at the station, and I'm on my way to Bear Lake, John. I'm not sure what's going on out there, but she spent some time in the rain tonight. Can you go down and check her out?"

As the only doctor in a rural community, John was no stranger to middle of the night calls. He'd learned over the years not to ask too many questions; the story always came out in the course of time. Still, Addie Marsh at the sheriff's office at two in the morning?

The doctor had listened to her heart and accomplished enough other tests to determine she was unharmed, when Addie's son flew through the door. His hands were shaking as he knelt beside her chair.

"Mother, are you all right? What is it, John?" He turned briefly to face the doctor, then back to his mother. "Did someone hurt you? Who's he?" he nodded toward Paul who started to speak but was cut off when Joe turned back to his mother. "Why are you dressed like that?"

Before anyone could offer an explanation, they heard Bill's cruiser pull up alongside the building and he joined them, water dripping from the brim of his hat.

"Someone tell me what's going on here!" Joe demanded. Addie rose and passed her son, reaching for Bill Johnson's hand. "Is she all right, Bill? Is she alive?" Her voice quivered, and Paul took her by the arm and gently helped her back to her chair.

"Who are you?" Joe raged.

"I'm your mother's neighbor," he answered softly, extending his hand, "Paul Curtis. There was some trouble at the lake tonight. Your mom might very well have saved my life."

"You saved mine," Addie corrected.

"Is everything okay, John?" the sheriff's tired voice interrupted.

"Addie's fine. Just fine." The doctor's eyes met Joe's briefly, reminiscent of another night not so long ago.

"All right then." Bill's raised voice brought them all to a halt. "Joe, it seems your mother's neighbor—that young kid who's been staying out at the Roberts's place—went a little haywire tonight. Shot that little gal and beat her up pretty bad." Bill turned to Addie and softened his voice. "She's alive, Addie, but it's serious. She's on her way to Richmond in the ambulance. She was unconscious when I got there, and hadn't come around before they left."

"Sybil?" Joe whispered.

"We've got the boy in custody. The deputies are taking him to the county jail. We ran a check on him and he's been up to no good for a long time. He's wanted in California, Arizona, Nevada . . . he's a damn troubled kid!" The sheriff shook his head sadly.

"Where did you find him?" Paul asked.

The sheriff looked from Joe to Addie before responding. "He was sitting on Addie's porch in her rocking chair—sobbing."

Paul placed a hand on Addie's shoulder as tears streamed. No one spoke as the radio announced: "Let's proceed with flight for life. We're stabilizing. We'll meet you at the helicopter pad."

Bill Johnson leaned heavily against his desk and sighed. "Let's call it a night here. I've got a pretty clear picture of what went on out there tonight. If I need more from either of you two," he nodded toward Addie and Paul, "I'll talk to you tomorrow. It's safe out there now. You can go home."

"I'll stay with Mom tonight," Joe said. When no one spoke or moved toward leaving he continued, his voice still shaking. "How did you get away, Mom? Did Paul help you?"

"Yes," responded Addie wiping her eyes with a tissue.

"She was the hero, not me," ventured Paul.

Dr. Siegfried turned his back and gazed out the window as the sheriff rested his chin anxiously against his hand, peering up at Joe.

Paul explained, "When your mother discovered her phone was dead, she rowed across the lake to me. Then we realized my phone was . . ."

"She what?" Joe's hollow voice echoed through the office.

"She rowed to my place—in the boat. She's incredible! Then we . . ."

"You took the boat across the lake? Tonight? In the dark? In the rain?" Joe was nearly screaming by the time he finished.

"Yes."

"What were you thinking? You could have been killed!" he cried.

"I could have been killed if I hadn't gone," stated Addie with control. "I did the only thing I could do, Joe. And I guess I'm lucky. It worked out right."

"He was after you? Chasing you? What happened?"

"Joe," Bill began. "Why don't you take your mom home? It's late. I'll talk with you in the morning, and we'll sort this out."

"What I don't understand," said Addie speaking to no one in particular, "is how he had a key. He didn't break in. He unlocked my door. In all the time she helped me, I never gave Sybil a key. There was never a reason . . ."

"I did," Joe said softly.

"You?" the sheriff asked. "Why?"

"When you were in the hospital last spring," he told his mother. "When she took care of Rufus. I gave her a key and asked her to keep an eye on the place."

"Then they probably made a copy off of that," Bill ventured.

"They didn't have to," Joe groaned, his face flushed. "I forgot to get it back. I was so busy—I forgot all about it."

"Well, it's over now," Bill stated. "I don't expect any more trouble at the lake. And I'm as much to blame as anyone. I should have been on top of that situation. Those kids minded their own business and I didn't think . . ."

"It doesn't matter," Joe's voice was stern now as he faced all of them. "Mom's moving to the city tomorrow. I've got her a room at Gateway. And I'll stay with her tonight."

A dazed hush fell over the group in the little office at this new revelation. It was Addie who finally spoke. "I'm not going," she said simply.

"You *are* going!" Joe retorted. "This is exactly why you're going! It isn't safe out there!"

"It is now," replied Addie.

"Mom, we've talked about this. Why are you changing your mind now, especially after what just happened?"

"I need a reason to go to Gateway, Joe. And I don't have one. Anyway, I have too much to do," she went on. "I'm going to be on the board for the new park and . . ."

"I'll look after her," Paul began.

267

"And my health is good, isn't it John?"

"You stay out of this!" Glaring at the three men, Joe reached beneath his mother's elbow and gently helped her from the chair. "I know you all mean well. But this is a family matter. It's between my mother and me. Bill's right. Let's call it a night."

The rain had nearly stopped when they arrived at the cabin above Bear Lake. After a call to Judy from a pay phone, the ride from Pinecliffe had been quiet with neither mother nor son having enough energy to continue their discussion.

As Joe helped Addie into the house he broke the silence. "You never answered my question, Mom. When did you start wearing Batman?"

Chapter 14

"Hello? No, she's still sleeping. Can I take a message? Yes, yes, she's all right. She just . . ." Joe's deep voice, which he was straining to keep quiet, slowly pulled Addie from slumber. Or was it the constant ringing of the telephone? Addie pulled her blankets up under her chin and turned over, away from the sounds of the cabin and the aroma of coffee brewing.

If it was the phone she'd heard, then maybe it had all been a bad dream. The phone had been dead in her nightmare. Addie closed her eyes and tried to go back to sleep. She was in no hurry to leave the comfort of her bed, this room, all that was home to her. But the phone continued to ring, and a return to sleep eluded her.

The conversation was repeated again and again. Joe patiently, without emotion in his voice, reported that his mother was well, and he appreciated the concern. "Yes, I'll tell her you called."

Reluctantly, Addie arose and pulled on her robe before going into the kitchen.

"You're up!" Joe exclaimed when he saw her. "Did you get any sleep?"

"I slept like a baby." Addie hugged her son and accepted a cup of coffee from him. "Did I hear the phone?"

"It's been ringing off the hook," Joe laughed. "I don't know how you slept through it. Well-wishers. I didn't think there were that many people in Pinecliffe. You'll never guess who else called."

When Addie didn't respond, Joe exclaimed, "Aunt Sarah!"

"Oh, dear!" moaned Addie. "How does she always know when I've gotten myself into trouble?"

"Must be genetic," laughed Joe.

"Is she all right?"

Joe shrugged. "How could she not be? Servants waiting on her hand and foot. Every possible comfort at her beck and call."

"And she still has her husband," said Addie wistfully.

"For whatever that's worth," laughed Joe. "Good old Uncle Dan!"

Addie couldn't help but laugh with him. Through the years her sister and brother-in-law had evolved into an eccentric, lovable, old couple who provided plenty of material for family stories. Their constant efforts to "help" Addie were always met with a polite no-thank-you.

"She said she was calling to chat, and I didn't tell her about your little escapade," Joe shared. "I told her you'd call her back later."

"But the phone line was cut last night, wasn't it?"

"Yes, the repairman came out first thing this morning and fixed it." Joe joined his mother at the kitchen table. "I have a feeling Bill put him up to it. I think he's embarrassed about this whole incident."

"Why should he be?" asked Addie. "It certainly wasn't his fault."

"That's what I love about small towns," Joe mused. "The sheriff feels personally responsible when anything bad happens. The private telephone company works on Saturdays. And everybody cares about the little lady who lives out by the lake."

Tears filled Addie's eyes as she reached across the table, found her son's hand, and gently squeezed it. "I'm sorry about last night, Joe. I gave you quite a scare."

"Never mind," was his hasty response. "We have a full day ahead of us, Mom."

"How well I know."

"You hurry and get dressed and we'll go down to Scottie's for breakfast, okay?"

Addie was surprised by her son's unexpected proposal. "Don't we have too much to do?"

"Yeah, but I think we'd better go to Scottie's first." Joe tried to sound serious but a hint of teasing crept into his voice. "That's where all the talk will be this morning. I'm sure the rumors are flying. That's the other thing I love about small towns. We'd better go down there and introduce some facts! You realize there are people in this town who think you drowned last night?"

Addie could not join his fun. Her heart ached for her young neighbor. "Have you heard any more about Sybil?" she asked.

"No, but Bill called this morning. He suggested we meet him in the village later, and he'll update us. He's still working on reports."

"Poor Bill," Addie sympathized. "I'll get dressed, but I have to tell you, I'm a little embarrassed to go into Pinecliffe. The last time I had an encounter with the lake, the stories were bad enough. I don't think I feel up to being around people just now."

"You'll feel better when you get there," Joe reassured her. "And we won't stay long. Like you said, we have a lot to do." When Addie didn't respond Joe ventured. "When we get back from breakfast, I'll help you organize that bedroom. Then I'll get the boat from Paul's and cover it for the winter."

"You'll help me what?"

"Get that room straightened," said Joe gently. "I guess you're going to be here awhile, and you don't need a spare room full of boxes." He rose and put an arm around his mother.

"Joe," she whispered, overcome once again with tears.

"Anyway," he forced a wavering voice, "we're going to turn it back into a bedroom. Judy and I will need a place to stay when we come out—which I plan to do more often."

"Joe," she repeated.

"Paul wants me to see his place and get involved in this park project he's developing. He called this morning, too. He seems like a nice enough fellow."

Addie couldn't agree enough with this assessment. A short time later when she'd changed and exuberantly returned to the kitchen, she told her son, "I can get help with organizing the bedroom. You have enough to do rounding up the boat."

"I can help you," he began but she interrupted.

"I'll take care of it. Carol Wilmont's older sister, Joan, just moved back to the area. She and her husband are retiring here. She wants to take on a few odd jobs helping people like me. Carol asked if I'd be interested, and now that Sybil's gone," she sighed. "It will be a good way to break her in, you know, get acquainted."

"Miss self-sufficient," Joe laughed. "You've got all the bases covered, haven't you?"

Addie laughed with him, bursting inside with a new-found sense of life. The forecast had been right. Steam rose from the wet ground responding to the call of a bright autumn day. It felt good on her face, in her lungs, in her mind. Addie knew she could even endure the crowd (and there would be a crowd!) at Scottie's.

"What about the boat?" she asked Joe.

"Well, first I have to find it. Then I'm going to cover it too tight for even your nimble little hands. And I'm hiding the oars in the top rafter of the shed where a certain lady can't reach them!"

"Now, Joe, I promise. If you'll row me out on the lake from time to time, I won't try it by myself!"

"Let's put that one in writing!" Joe teased.

Scottie's was overflowing with activity and noise when the Marshes walked in together. A momentary hush fell across the restaurant but was quickly replaced by everyone speaking at once.

"Addie! You're all right!"

"Look, she's here!"

"There's Joe with her. Addie, Addie, over here!"

Joe led his mother to a table in the back of the room where they were swamped with friends, neighbors, and a thousand questions. With uncommon patience, Joe assessed their inquiries and reassured everyone that his mother was well, and finally that they'd enjoy just having some breakfast. For once, Addie remained silent, proud to be with the young man who kindly shielded her from the disconcerting attention.

A high school girl, who worked in the café on the weekends, squeezed her way through the crowd and was able to take their order for eggs and pancakes. Soon, Paul joined them giving Addie a quick hug and falling into relaxed conversation with Joe. He, too, had been bombarded with questions and concern throughout the morning.

"We're practically celebrities," he teased. "Maybe we should kick off our fund-raising for the park today while everyone is so glad to see us."

"I'll take that spot on your committee if you still want me," Addie beamed. "I'm not moving away just yet."

"So I heard." Paul ribbed his elbow into Joe with a smile. "Yeah, I still want you!"

"Addie! Addie, are you all right? It's Maggie and Cecil."

Addie turned to face yet another set of friends. "Good

morning! Yes, I'm fine. Everything's fine."

"Been fishing?" teased Cecil.

"I knew you'd say something like that," Addie laughed. "Wait until Leo gets a hold of me."

"Are you leaving today?" Maggie's voice was serious now.

"No, ma'am. I'm not leaving. Not today, tomorrow, or hopefully for a long time. You see, I don't have a reason. And there are many, many reasons to stay."

"Oh, Addie!" Maggie's arms were around her and Cecil's big, gentle hand was patting her back as he turned away from the group at the table.

"What's this? Not leaving?" A warm familiar voice called from behind Cecil as Walter was led by his dog to a spot near Addie.

"Walter! Join us, will you? I want you to meet my son."

The conversation in the little country diner was endless that bright October morning. There was talk of the excitement the night before. The gossip spread that the matriarch of Bear Lake was not leaving after all. The more somber conversation of a young girl and her troubled male companion was heard in softer, understanding tones.

As they finished their meal and were enjoying a second cup of coffee, a hush again fell across the tightly packed restaurant as the local sheriff entered. He put everyone at ease and held up his hand to stop a torrent of questions. Making his way to the back table, he hung his hat on a booth and took the remaining seat near Addie.

"How are you this morning?"

"I'm fine, Bill. Did you get any rest at all?"

"As a matter of fact, I did." Bill signaled the young waitress for coffee and a menu before assuming a more serious posture.

"Let me tell you what I know now about last night. To

begin with, Sybil is in Denver in a special trauma unit. She's still alive this morning and they think she'll pull through. Her recovery will take a long time and may not be complete."

"I must go see her!" Addie cried.

"Mom . . ." Joe began, but the sheriff interrupted him.

"You know, Addie, I've been in law enforcement a long time. There isn't always a happy ending. Sometimes just a suitable ending is enough. I think this is one of those times." He studied the old woman thoughtfully.

"I don't understand what you're saying, Bill," she said after a moment.

"I know Sybil meant a lot to you, and I believe she's a good person," Bill continued as everyone at the table listened intently. "If it helps at all, there won't be any charges filed against her. She wasn't involved in her boyfriend's extra-curricular activities. Stoney told us last night she's not guilty of anything but being stupid. Those were his exact words."

Addie sighed in disgust. "All she wanted was to be loved. Does that make her stupid?"

"You know, Addie, that little gal is only fifteen years old." Addie covered her mouth as a cry escaped.

Bill nodded his understanding. "I couldn't believe it, either. She was a tiny thing but her eyes looked liked they'd seen more years than that. We should have gotten Social Services involved—I didn't realize. Sometimes we're too comfortable out here."

"I should have said something," Addie sighed remembering the many times her inner voice had called upon her to do so.

"We're all a little guilty," Bill agreed. "I should have followed up with you after Paul reported missing property. As a matter of fact, I'd planned to, but didn't get it done. But 'should-haves' won't do any good now."

"What will happen to her?" asked Addie. "Maybe when she's better she could stay with me."

"Mom . . ."

The sheriff interrupted. "You're a good lady, you know that, Addie? But sometimes, you have to let go. I was told this morning that they located an aunt from Wisconsin or somewhere. She is flying out to stay with Sybil, and she'll be given custody when she's released from the hospital. What happens after that we'll probably never know. I do know that little girl has many problems, and they won't go away overnight. Unfortunately, there's nothing in the world you or I can do to change that."

"I didn't even get to say 'good-bye,' " Addie murmured.

For a time the sheriff turned his mug thoughtfully in his hands, the depth of Addie's loss sinking into all of them. Then he said, "If she pulls through, maybe she'll remember that a nice lady in the mountains of Colorado taught her what it means to be a decent person. You gave her that, Addie. You did more for her than any of us. You've already done everything you can for Sybil. The rest is up to her and her family."

"She was lucky to know you," claimed Walter.

"Agreed," whispered Joe.

"You two will need to come by the station," explained Bill gesturing to Addie and Paul. "We've recovered a number of items from a shed that Stoney was supposedly repairing for someone. I found a little cross that I think belongs to you, Addie. I've seen you wear it in the past."

"My cross!" exclaimed Addie. "It's the one your father brought back from the war," she told Joe. "After, well . . . after the battle."

In groups of two and four, the residents of Pinecliffe drifted out of Scottie's into the bright, fall morning. The sheriff and Paul did not leave before vehemently reassuring

Joe that they would keep a close watch on Addie and the little cabin at Bear Lake. Joe sincerely thanked them before he and his mother started up the dirt road together.

"What else can I do for you today, Mom?" Joe asked. "I know I need to get the boat, but beyond that I'm not feeling very useful."

"I need what we just did," Addie responded.

"I don't follow you."

"Joe," Addie said softly. "I'm your mother, but I'm not your responsibility. It isn't up to you to take care of me. When that time comes, then I need you to help me into Gateway or someplace like it. But for now, I need to have you at my side in Scottie's. I need to sit beside you feeling proud that you're my son and everyone knows it. That's what you can do for me."

He thought for awhile before speaking, a grin slowly crossing his face. "I'll still be obnoxious, Mom. I can't quit worrying about you. You know me better than that."

"That's what I love about you," she answered. "You've kept my life interesting and unpredictable since the day you were born."

"Hmmm," Joe pondered. "Wonder where I inherited that trait?"

Addie laughed, comfortable to be riding up the familiar road to home; comfortable with the knowledge that she was going there to stay.

"Do you still know how to cook meat loaf?" Joe asked.

"Of course!"

"Maybe Judy and I will drive out for dinner next weekend."

"I'd like that," said Addie softly. "Thanks, Joe."

She had finally decided. Autumn *was* her favorite season

of all. It smelled the best, and it offered the most color for her dimming eyes to see. There were the geese and mallards, their honking and splashing on the lake a noisy going away party before the first winter storms. She sat as she had many evenings before in the still consolation of her rocker. Rufus lay curled in a tight ball upon her lap, oblivious to everything but the security, which always awaited his return from his adventures in the surrounding hills.

Addie pulled her shawl around her shoulders. Soon she would go indoors and build a fire. It would be a cool enough night for that. But she was expecting a visitor, and they loved to sit together on the porch. She would wait a little longer.

Rufus stretched a long arm up to her cheek and, without claws, softly patted her face. "Do you need attention, sir?" Addie stroked him gently. "Well, old boy, you don't know how close you came to going to college. We almost landed in the city, you and I." He purred his grateful acknowledgement, his eyes glued to her face as she spoke. "I'll make a vow to you, Rufus, but it will have to be our secret. When you and I leave this place, ours will be a short journey—to the hill overlooking Pinecliffe."

You're doing it again, Addie. The kind, familiar voice she'd been waiting to hear called from the side of the cabin. The man strode across the wooden porch and sat down beside her, his dark eyes dancing above his straight and courteous face. As he sat, he removed his hat and placed it formally upon his knee, as any officer might do.

Jacob, you finally came! Tell me, what am I doing again?

Changing your story! His gentle laugh filled her. *You told Joe you'd go to Gateway when the time comes. But this conspiracy you're developing with that cat sounds like a different tale altogether.*

You caught me! Addie blushed. *That is how I hope the story will end, God willing.*

It probably will, Jacob conceded. *You have a knack for getting your way.*

Poor Joe. It seems I'm always plotting against him.

Of all your soldiers, said Jacob, *the one who never enlisted is the one most deserving a medal.*

I'm afraid you're right, she agreed.

What will you do now to stir things up, my love?

I have reformed, Jacob. No more trouble from me! She pledged. *I do have an idea, though. I've thought about inviting Walter out to dinner some evening. I'd like to meet his family and I think his nephew would bring him. We've become friends, you know. We enjoy each other's company.*

Jacob nodded, his eyes shining.

What do you think of that, Jacob?

I think it's a fine idea, he answered. *I like Walter. He's a nice man. You're good for each other. Both of you are vibrant and intelligent—and maybe just a little bullheaded!*

She smiled. *Sit with me awhile, Jacob. Listen to the ducks.*

The sun set brilliantly over Bear Lake. Its wonder flooded the mountainside and encompassed the two sitting hand-in-hand in its shadow.

After a time the soldier sighed, *My dear Addie.*

What is it, Jacob?

I love you, he whispered, *but I must go. The ducks have flown away. Go indoors, build a fire, and rest. You have work to do, busy days ahead, people counting on you.*

He rose and walked slowly to the edge of the porch. *Good-bye, Love,* he said softly.

Good-bye, she whispered to the dusk.

The last thing Addie heard Jacob say as he disappeared toward Bear Lake was . . . *I'll see you on the other side.*

Pam Rice is a Rehabilitation Teacher employed by the State of Colorado, Division of Vocational Rehabilitation. She teaches adults who are blind and visually impaired throughout the southeastern part of the state and facilitates three vision support groups. Pam is a graduate of the University of Southern Colorado. She lives in Pueblo with her husband, Brad, and has two children and two grandchildren. In addition to a love of writing, Pam enjoys skiing, golfing, and spending time in the mountains of Beulah, Colorado. This is her first novel.